Patsy of Paradise Place

Rosie Harris was born in Cardiff and grew up there and in the West Country. After her marriage she resided for some years on Merseyside before moving to Buckinghamshire where she still lives. She has three grown-up children, and six grand-children, and writes full time.

Also by Rosie Harris

Turn of the Tide
Troubled Waters
One Step Forward
Looking for Love
Pins & Needles
Winnie of the Waterfront
At Sixes & Sevens
The Cobbler's Kids
Sunshine and Showers

Patsy of Paradise Place

ROSIE HARRIS

arrow books

Reissued by Arrow Books in 2005

5 7 9 10 8 6 4

First published in the United Kingdom in 2002 by William Heinemann
First published in Arrow Books in 2003

Arrow Books
The Random House Group Limited
20 Vauxhall Bridge Road, London, SW1V 2SA

Random House Australia (Pty) Limited
20 Alfred Street, Milsons Point, Sydney,
New South Wales 2061, Australia

Random House New Zealand Limited
18 Poland Road, Glenfield
Auckland 10, New Zealand

Random House South Africa (Pty) Limited
Isle of Houghton, Corner Boundary Road & Carse O'Gowrie,
Houghton 2198, South Africa

Random House Group Limited Reg. No. 954009

www.randomhouse.co.uk

A CIP catalogue record for this book is available from the British Library

Papers used by Random House are natural, recyclable products made
from wood grown in sustainable forests. The manufacturing processes
conform to the environmental regulations of the country of origin

ISBN 0 09 943624 8

Typeset in Palatino by Palimpsest Book Production Limited,
Polmont, Stirlingshire
Printed in Great Britain by Cox & Wyman Ltd, Reading, Berkshire

For my grandchildren:
Susie Harris, Kathryn Sak, Michele Harris,
Nicola Sak, Hayley Harris and Robert Harris

Acknowledgements

My sincere thanks to Rhona Caretti for specialised information, and to my Agent, Caroline Sheldon, for her help and advice.

Also to Kate Parkin, Kirsty Fowkes, Georgina Hawtrey-Woore, Lynne Drew, Joanna Craig, Anna Dalton-Knott, Beth Humphries, and everyone else in the Heinemann/Arrow team who have all played such a supportive role.

Chapter One

'Dad . . . Dad? Is it really you?' The skinny tousle-headed child, swinging from a rope tied to one of the lampposts in Paradise Place, scraped her clumpy boots along the pavement to slow herself down.

She peered through the murky gloom of a mid-December night in disbelief as a tall, muscular man carrying a heavy canvas kitbag on his shoulder came striding down the road towards her.

The next moment, Patsy's exclamation of surprise and astonishment ended in a wild scream as the man dropped the kitbag and she found herself being swung high in the air by a pair of strong arms.

'What do you think you are doing out here on your own at this time of night?' he asked in a voice laced with concern.

'Waiting to see if anyone else was coming out to play.'

'At this time of night?'

Patsy giggled. 'Sometimes Janie Grant or Maureen Murphy pretend to go to bed early and then they sneak out so that we can play chasers in the dark or creep up the jowlers and spy on some of the older boys and catch them smoking ciggies.'

'Does your mam know about this?'

Patsy shrugged, but ignored his question. 'Anyway, I don't care if they come out now or not. You've come instead and that's even better,' she said fervently as she hugged him.

'I'm not going to let you go away ever again!' she vowed, locking her hands behind his neck and smothering him with kisses.

'So if I stay at home will you promise not to sneak out in the dark to play?' he asked, lowering her back on to the ground.

Feet placed wide apart, hands on hips, Patsy Callaghan tipped back her head and stared up at the giant of a man who towered over her, her green eyes wide with astonishment.

'Do you really mean that?' she asked in disbelief. 'You really mean that you're never going back to sea again?'

Patsy thought she must be dreaming. The last time her dad had come ashore he had been at home for three weeks and he'd taken her and her mam out for a day that she would remember as long as she lived.

He'd bought her a new green dress, some white shoes and a bow of green ribbon to tie in her hair and when she was all dressed up in her new clothes he'd taken them on the train all the way to Chester. They'd walked along the city walls and they'd sat by the river with a bag of buns and a bottle of pop and had a picnic.

John Callaghan stretched out a hand and ruffled her mop of unruly red curls. 'It's like I say, me darlin' girl, I'm not going away any more. From

2

now on I'll be living at home with you and your mam.'

'For ever?' she gasped.

'For ever and a day,' he told her gravely.

Patsy drew in a deep breath. Father O'Brian must be right after all and your prayers did get answered if you prayed long enough and hard enough. 'Does me mam know?' she asked cautiously.

John Callaghan laughed, a loud jovial sound. 'Not yet, so why don't you run along indoors and tell her?'

Patsy hesitated, then slid her tiny hand into her father's massive one. 'Why don't we do it together,' she said and her face split into a wide grin.

'Whatever you say.' John Callaghan swung his kitbag up on to his shoulder and let his young daughter lead him by the hand towards the back door of the terraced house that was their home.

Patsy paused in the scullery and looking up at her father held a finger up to her lips. 'Hush, don't make a sound!' she whispered. 'Let's surprise her. You wait here a minute.'

John Callaghan nodded. Carefully he lowered his kitbag to the flagstone floor leaning it against one wall.

As Patsy moved towards the door that led into the living room, walking in an exaggerated fashion on the tips of the toes of her laced-up boots so as not to make a noise, John Callaghan looked round him in distaste.

He sighed. Maeve had never been house-proud,

which was something he couldn't understand because she was so finicky and meticulous about her own appearance.

Her fastidiousness seemed to end there. It never seemed to trouble her in the slightest what Patsy looked like. Even when she was a tiny baby she could be filthy dirty and dressed in grubby rags and Maeve hardly seemed to be aware of the fact. Today he'd noticed that Patsy's frock was soiled, and the hem hanging down, her pinafore was torn and the toes of her boots were badly scuffed.

He looked around him and even in the dim light filtering through from the main living room he could see that everywhere was utterly filthy. Dirty dishes and saucepans were piled up high in the stained sink, leftover food lay around uncovered and a distinctly unpleasant smell hung in the air.

Patsy had left the door slightly ajar and he could see his wife standing in the living room, leaning over the fireguard that was draped with clothes that she'd washed out and hung there to air, peering into the mirror above the fireplace.

A pretty woman with shoulder-length strawberry-blonde hair, she was attractively slim yet enticingly curvaceous. She was wearing the very latest silk jumper blouse in leaf green over a matching pleated skirt. The lower edge of the blouse had an elaborate crochet border that emphasised her shape and the cap sleeves were trimmed in the same way.

Her face was heavily made up and she was concentrating on outlining her mouth with a

4

bright pink lipstick as Patsy entered the room.

'Mam, there's someone to see you,' Patsy told her.

Maeve ignored the intrusion until she had finished applying her lipstick then turned briefly. 'If it's your Uncle Peter then tell him to go on to the pub and I'll see him there like we arranged. I'll be another five minutes at least.'

'No, it's not him. I bet you'll never be able to guess who it is . . .'

'Not now, Patsy, I'm trying to get ready to go out and I haven't time for your silly games,' Maeve told her peevishly. Then, as she looked back into the mirror and caught sight of the figure standing in the doorway gasped in disbelief.

'John?' She swung round to face her husband. 'This is a surprise! You nearly frightened the life out of me! What are you doing here?'

'Hey, what sort of greeting is that for a man who has been at sea for almost a year?' He grabbed hold of his wife, pulling her into his arms and kissing her hungrily.

Breathlessly, Maeve wriggled free. 'Hold on, John, do be careful, you're ruining my make-up!' she complained, raising her carefully pencilled brows as she peered over his shoulder into the mirror.

'You've got me mam's lipstick all over your face,' Patsy giggled as he released his hold on her mother and stepped back.

John Callaghan wiped his mouth with the back of his hand and then stared down at the vivid pink stain.

'Why do you put that bloody muck on your face,' he muttered.

Maeve gave him a withering look. 'It's what women do to make themselves look more attractive when they're going out,' she said sarcastically.

His gaze darkened as his eyes swept over her, taking in the low neck of her dress, the shining beads, dangling earrings, the pale silk stockings and the high-heeled shoes laced with coloured cords in the same shade of green as her dress.

'Going somewhere special, were you?'

'I certainly was,' she told him as she turned back to the mirror and began repairing the damage he had done to her make-up.

'And what about young Patsy, then? he asked in a steely voice.

Maeve gave him a puzzled look. 'Patsy. What about her?'

'If you were going out then what was Patsy going to do? Judging by the state of her and the way she is dressed you weren't exactly planning to take her along with you.'

Maeve's mouth twisted as she looked across at Patsy in her grubby cotton dress, torn pinafore and cumbersome boots. 'You know bloody well that I wasn't taking her with me!' She laughed. 'Patsy is a big girl now, in case you hadn't noticed, aren't you, luv? You don't mind staying on your own if I go out for an hour or so, do you, pet?'

'An hour or so? You mean for the entire evening and half the night, don't you?' John commented.

Maeve shrugged. 'An hour or two or the entire evening, what difference does it make?' she said lightly. 'Once Patsy's tucked up in bed and I've kissed her good-night she's soon fast asleep so she doesn't know whether I'm here or not.'

'If she is asleep. More likely she'll be lying there fretting and worrying, too scared to go to sleep,' he argued. 'A nine-year-old shouldn't be left in the house on her own.'

'Well, she won't be on her own tonight, will she?' Maeve smiled smugly. 'She'll have her dad here to keep her company.'

'And for every night in the future.'

Maeve paused with her lipstick in the air, her mouth agape. 'Yer wha'?'

'I've decided that I'm not going back to sea any more.'

Maeve remained silent as she completed the task of outlining her mouth in brilliant pink but her brain was working overtime. What was he saying? Not going back to sea again? She couldn't even begin to think of what that was going to mean. If John was to be at home all the time from now on then it would turn her life completely topsy-turvy. She felt annoyed. She hadn't expected him home for another few weeks and this meant the end of her freedom for the near future.

As things stood, apart from the few weeks two or three times a year when he came home on shore leave she was free to do as she pleased. While John was away she didn't bother to do any cooking and cleaning unless she felt like it, or if she was entertaining one of her many men friends.

If the place was a tip most of the time it didn't

matter, because there was only Patsy there to notice it. Maeve's lips tightened: she'd soon cured Patsy of complaining about the state the place was in by making her help with the cleaning and clearing up.

If John was at home all the time though, that was another kettle of fish completely. He was a stickler for order and he'd expect the place to be clean and tidy all the time. He'd expect her to wash his clothes, iron his shirts and put food on the table at regular times. What was even more to the point, he wouldn't approve of her gadding off out on her own three or four nights a week. In fact, he'd probably try and put a stop to it.

Now was probably not the time to let him know how much she resented his decision, she decided. As she turned from the mirror there was a feigned look of delight on her pretty face.

'John, this is wonderful news,' she cooed as she twined her arms around his neck and her glistening pink lips curved into a tantalising smile. 'You're really going to be home for good from now on? I can't believe what I'm hearing!'

Patsy had been holding her breath as she waited for her mother's reaction to the news. Now she let it out in a cautious sigh of relief.

From now on things would be so different, she thought happily. They'd be a proper family. She wouldn't have to fend for herself when she came home from school, or spend long evenings sitting at the window staring out into the dark street, wondering when her mother would be coming home.

She was so afraid of being in the house on her own that she could never sleep. As soon as her mother had kissed her good-night and she heard her go downstairs and the front door slam and she knew she was on her own there were all sorts of strange noises and shadows that she never noticed when her mother was there. The rustling, scuttling noises as mice and cockroaches scurried about, and even the house seemed to creak and groan as if it was alive.

She'd once tried to tell her mother about her fears. Maeve had simply given her a hug and told her not to be so fanciful and then packed her off to bed early, telling her to get to sleep before she went out.

She had lain there with her eyes tight shut trying desperately to fall asleep, but it hadn't worked. She was still awake when her mam came up to kiss her good-night and the moment she heard the front door slam she'd been out of bed and huddled by the window as usual, watching and waiting until she saw her mother coming home again.

When she saw her approaching, if she was on her own, then Patsy would scuttle back into bed and pretend to be asleep in case she came upstairs to check up on her.

With her dad at home all the time that would stop, she told herself gleefully. There would be no more lonely nights.

She couldn't have had a more wonderful father, Patsy thought as she studied him. With his lean tanned face, shock of dark brown hair and gentle blue eyes he was the most handsome man she'd ever known. Her heart felt as if it was bursting with love and pride and she looked forward to boasting about the fact that he was home for good when she went to school next day.

She'd make him promise to come and meet her after school ended and that would stop all the teasing she had to put up with because he was so often away from home.

He was so tall and broad shouldered that he made her mother look slim and dainty as they stood there embracing. She had her arms locked round his muscular neck and she was gazing up at him with her wide-set green eyes as if she adored him.

Patsy sighed again. She knew only too well that those limpid green eyes could become emerald hard and the soft curving lips tighten into an unforgiving line. And the dainty fingers that were at this moment stroking the blue stubble on John Callaghan's cheeks could inflict a stinging slap, or curl into a fist that left bruises on her arms and chest when things didn't go the way Maeve wanted them to do.

There were times, Patsy reflected, when she wished her mother was fat and blowsy like some of the other women in Paradise Place. They seemed to be content with their lot and stayed home at nights, and were always around for their kids when they came home from school. They were there waiting to give them a hug if they were unhappy because they'd been bullied, or console them if they'd been told off at school.

Nevertheless, she took a pride in the fact that her mother looked so lovely. She wished her own red hair shone like gold and that she was as neat and dainty as her mother instead of being so clumsy. She always boasted that her mother was as beautiful as a princess. If, sometimes, their house was so filthy that she was ashamed for anyone to see it, she always managed to dream up some excuse or the other as to why she couldn't bring her friends indoors.

Now things would be different. Her dad liked things spotlessly clean and everything neat and tidy. 'Ship-shape and Bristol fashion' he called it, and he was always telling her that was how things had to be on board ship because there was so little space that everyone had to be tidy.

'A place for everything and everything in its place,' he would scold whenever he found their living room or scullery in a shambles.

Her mam couldn't be tidy if she tried and she would laugh when he started ranting on about it. Then she would light up a cigarette, perch on the arm of a chair or the edge of the table, and watch as he picked things up and put them away.

With her dad at home they'd have to stop piling up the dirty dishes in the sink and simply rinsing off a cup or plate when they needed it. They'd have to wash up after each meal and dry the dishes they'd used and put them away on the dresser or in the cupboard.

There'd be no more running off to the chippy for a fish supper or foraging around to see what scraps she could find in the larder when she was hungry and her mam was out at the pub. Instead, they'd sit down at the table to eat their meal every night and on Sunday there'd be a roast dinner and she'd be so full up afterwards that she would hardly be able to move.

Yes, she thought happily, life was going to be very different. If her dad was at home all the time her mam wouldn't need to go out at nights because she was fed up and lonely. And she wouldn't be bringing any of her strange friends home either.

Patsy shuddered as she thought about some of the uncles who came to the house. Most of them had unpleasant beery breath and she hated it when they tried to kiss her. She hated it even more when they tried to cuddle her because they usually had hot sweaty hands that seemed to roam all over her body. Or else they made her sit on their lap and then they held her so tightly that she could hardly breathe.

Most of the time though they didn't seem to want her around. Some of them gave her a few coppers and told her to take herself off and get lost for an hour or two. If she came back too early she found the front door and the back door locked and no matter how hard she knocked, her mam took no notice. Once one of the uncles had given her a shiny silver tanner and she'd been able to buy a bag of toffees and a big bottle of pop to share with Janie and Maureen. And there'd still been enough left over for her to buy them all an ice-cream.

All that sort of thing would be in the past, she

thought pragmatically. At long last they'd be all together like a proper loving family.

When the summer came they would be able to have days out together. There would be trips to the park to feed the ducks, or in the summer they might even go across on the ferryboat to New Brighton. She loved it there because there was so much to see and do, so many exciting things going on.

Her dad liked to walk along the shore for miles and miles and watch the huge liners and massive cargo boats coming down the Mersey and being guided into dock in Liverpool by fussy little tugboats. He seemed to know where each one had come from and how long they had been at sea. She liked visiting the fairground where there was music, and brightly coloured swings and slides and roundabouts to ride on.

Sometimes there was a circus in the grounds of New Brighton Tower, with ferocious wild animals in huge iron cages and her dad would tell her about the foreign places they all came from, where they roamed wild.

She liked the elephants best even though they were so huge and cumbersome that she was afraid they might crush her with one of their enormous feet if she stood too close to them. Some of them did tricks, like picking things up with their long grey trunks, and sometimes they let people have rides sitting up on their backs in special basket chairs.

Patsy sighed happily as she snuggled down in bed that night. There were going to be so many wonderful times ahead now that her dad had promised not to go back to sea ever again. It really was as if all her dreams, as well as her prayers, were coming true at once.

Chapter Two

John Callaghan had suspected that adapting from being a seafarer to becoming a landlubber was bound to present problems. Even in his most uncertain moments, though, he hadn't envisaged anything like those he experienced during the first two months of his change of lifestyle.

His return home in mid-December was so near to Christmas that he decided to leave looking for work until the New Year. He deserved a holiday, he told himself, and he needed time to adjust to being a family man.

Patsy was overjoyed.

'Can I stay home from school so that we can go out together every day?' she asked. Her sharp green eyes shone with enthusiasm. 'We can go looking at all the lovely shop windows in Lord Street and Church Street. They've been specially decorated up for Christmas! And can we make paper chains to hang up in the house and make our own Christmas pudding?' she asked him excitedly.

'You can't stay home from school just for that,' he told her gravely. 'I'll still be here when you break up from school for your Christmas holidays so we can do all those things then if you want to.'

'Of course I want to! I want to do them with

you, though, Dad. Me mam isn't interested, except in going round the shops and then she only wants to buy things for herself.'

'Patsy!' John Callaghan frowned disapprovingly.

She pulled a face. 'Well, it's true. You ask her yourself if you don't believe me.'

John Callaghan didn't say anything more on the subject. He suspected that what Patsy had said was probably right even if he didn't approve of her saying such things.

Unlike Patsy, right from the start Maeve seemed to resent his continuous presence in the house. She acted like a caged bird, beating her wings because she had to adjust to his needs and ways, sulking when she didn't want to fall in with his plans.

It wasn't easy for either of them. When he tried to establish some sort of order and routine Maeve accused him of being a fusspot. Sometimes, or so it seemed to him, she deliberately opposed his efforts by leaving her clothes strewn all over the place in the bedroom and dirty dishes piled up in the sink.

As a result of years of strict routine on board ship, John Callaghan was used to rising early each morning. Maeve refused to comply.

On his first morning at home he was up before seven and down in the kitchen making a pot of tea. When he took a cup up to Maeve who was still in bed she struggled up on one elbow, rubbing the sleep from her eyes like a small child. Pushing back her tangle of strawberry-blonde hair from her forehead she stared at him, bewildered. 'What the hell do you think you're playing at waking me up in the middle of the night?'

'It's not the middle of the night,' he told her. 'I know we sat up late last night talking, but it's time we were up or Patsy won't have time to eat her breakfast before she has to go off to school.'

'Breakfast? Have you woken me up at this ungodly hour to talk about Patsy and her breakfast?' Maeve asked sulkily. 'If Patsy wants something to eat she knows where the bread's kept and she's quite capable of putting some margarine on it. Half the time she doesn't bother to eat any breakfast, anyway.'

She pushed the cup of tea away and wriggled back down in bed, pulling the covers over her head.

'Stay where you are then if you're all that tired,' John told her. 'I'll see to Patsy this morning.'

Maeve didn't answer so he went back downstairs. He'd already stirred the dying embers in the firegrate back to life so that he could boil the kettle so now he might as well cook a pan of porridge and cut some bread ready to make Patsy some toast, he decided.

Patsy looked astonished when she came downstairs and found that the dirty dishes from the night before had been cleared from the table and that it was now laid for breakfast for the two of them.

'Is this a special treat because it's your first day home or are we going to have breakfast like this every morning?' she asked in surprise.

'From now on you'll be having breakfast like

17

this every morning,' he told her crisply.

She grinned gleefully as she sat down at the table and tucked into the food he set in front of her.

'Now go and get ready and I'll walk as far as the school with you,' he said when she had scraped her bowl clean and eaten a slice of dripping toast.

'I am ready,' she told him.

He studied her for a moment in silence. 'You're going to school dressed like that?' he frowned.

'Yeah! What's wrong with me?' She ran the back of her hand across her mouth. 'I've had a wash!' She looked at him sideways to see if he believed her. 'Well, I wiped me face over with a wet flannel before I had my breakfast.'

He shook his head disapprovingly, then decided not to make an issue of it. 'Your dress looks grubby. Hadn't you better go and change it?'

She rubbed ineffectually at the greasy stain down the bodice of the drab blue serge dress. 'I haven't got another one,' she said slowly.

He felt irritated by her prevarication. 'Don't talk silly! You must have more than one dress.'

'Not winter ones. Me mam said she would get me a new one for Christmas.'

'Christmas is weeks away. Are you going to wear that same dress every day until then?'

'I wears one of my summer ones with a jumper over it on Saturdays and then I wash this one and it's clean for me to wear to Mass on Sunday and to school all the next week,' she explained.

John Callaghan opened his mouth to speak then shut it again, his lips tight together holding back the exasperation. He wasn't sure if Patsy was telling the truth or whether she was being cheeky. Maeve had the cupboard in their bedroom packed full of clothes so surely Patsy must have more than just one warm dress.

He looked at Patsy again and shook his head sadly as he noticed the grubby socks with a great cobbled darn in the leg of one of them.

'Well it's Friday so as it's only for today I suppose it won't matter too much. Go and get your coat on or we'll be late.'

'No we won't, because I'm ready now.' Patsy grinned. She reached down a thick red-and-black striped scarf that was hanging behind the kitchen door and began winding it round her neck.

'Your coat,' he repeated patiently.

'I haven't got one so I wear this,' she told him.

'And what about when it rains?' he queried.

'I pulls it up over my head and I run as fast as I can to try and dodge the raindrops,' she grinned.

'Come on, Dad,' she grabbed at his hand. 'I don't want to be late. I want all me mates to see you. Some of them don't believe I have a dad. And some of the others say you run away from home because . . .' Her voice faded away and she bit down on her lower lip and gave him a nervous sideways look.

John Callaghan felt his insides churn. He was pretty sure he knew what she was going to say and he was glad that she hadn't.

'Come on then, let's be going.' He ruffled her

untidy red curls with his free hand. 'Do you want to nip upstairs to say goodbye to your mam?'

'No fear!' Patsy's eyes widened dramatically as she pulled a face. 'She'd skelp me if I woke her this early in the morning,' she giggled.

Maeve was still in bed when John returned from taking Patsy to school.

'You know I'm not a morning person,' she yawned when he went upstairs to waken her. She gave him a provocative smile. 'Why don't you come back to bed and we can have a cuddle and another sleep.'

'No, I'm wide awake and want to get on with things,' he told her. 'I'll go downstairs and start cleaning up. Give me a shout when you decide to get up and I'll cook some breakfast for you.'

She pulled the bedclothes back up over her ears. 'Oh, don't bother,' she snapped. 'I never eat breakfast anyway,' she added with a noisy yawn.

It seemed to set the pattern for the days that followed. No matter what he said or did, Maeve was rarely out of bed before ten o'clock in the morning. Then she would spend ages putting on her make-up and combing her hair. After that she would potter round the house for the next hour or so in her flimsy blue silk dressing gown and pale blue mules with white swansdown trimming looking like a stand-in for Clara Bow. This irritated him even more than the fact that she was a late riser.

If anyone came to the door he would rush to answer it, afraid of what they might think or say if they saw Maeve in that state. Not that she didn't look lovely, seductive even, but that was not the point. He couldn't think of another woman in Paradise Place who was ever seen in a dressing gown. Probably none of them had one, and certainly not a silk one. If there was a middle-of-the-night emergency then they either pulled a skirt or dress on over their nightgown, wrapped a blanket round their shoulders, or put on their outdoor coat.

He wondered what the other women thought about the fact that Maeve was always dressed up to the nines and yet young Patsy's clothes were little better than rags.

The first weekend he was at home he took Patsy out on a shopping spree. He bought her two winter skirts, one navy and one brown, two thick wool jumpers, one blue and one green, and a heavy navy-blue gabardine coat that would also keep the rain out. He also bought her sensible leather shoes to replace the boots she'd been wearing and several pairs of knee-high woollen socks.

Patsy was like a dog with two tails as she displayed all her new clothes for her mother to see, but Maeve was not impressed.

'Complete waste of money,' she said dismissively. 'Have you any idea what she is like with her clothes? When she's swung from a few lamp-posts and climbed a few walls, or been in a fight with some of the other kids, those things will be in tatters, you'll see.'

'She's only a tomboy because you let her run wild,' John protested. 'From now on she's going to behave like a little lady, aren't you, kiddo?' he murmured, ruffling Patsy's curls.

'Until she gets herself into a scrap with some of the other kids round about and they start fighting and tearing the clothes from her back.'

'Why does she get into those sort of scrapes?' John asked, his eyes narrowing speculatively, as Patsy walked out of the room.

Maeve shrugged. 'How the hell should I know? When she comes home with a black eye or a bloody nose she never tells me how it happened.'

'Have you ever taken the trouble to find out why she won't tell you?'

'Got better things to do with me time,' Maeve grinned. 'If she wants to be secretive about things then that's up to her, luv, now isn't it?'

'She gets into fights because she's defending you,' John told her quietly.

'Defending *me*? Worra she got to defend me about, I'd like to know?' she demanded hotly.

'I think you do know,' John said firmly. 'She doesn't like it when the kids start teasing her, calling her names and saying she doesn't know who her father is.'

'Bloody load of rot!' Maeve snapped. 'Course she knows who her father is.'

'Not when I'm away at sea and you're bringing home a different man every night of the week,' he said bitterly.

'Who youse been gossiping with then?' Maeve asked defiantly. 'Been down the boozer listening to all the local scandal from those beery bastards, have you?'

He nodded. 'It didn't take long before some of your so-called friends were putting me wise to the way you carry on when I'm not here.'

Maeve shrugged, but her cheeks were now bright red and her eyes shooting sparks of venom. 'You shouldn't have buggered off to sea and left me on my own for months at a stretch then, should you,' she spat.

John sighed. 'No, I shouldn't have done, but I did it so that I could earn the money to give you and Patsy a good life,' he said flatly.

'Money's not everything,' Maeve told him, her luscious pink mouth curling sardonically. 'I need a man about the place for company and if you preferred to bugger off on your own for months at a time then I had to find someone else to fill your shoes . . . and your bed!'

He flinched as if she had struck him. How could a woman who looked so angelic talk and act like that? he asked himself, struggling to hold his anger in check.

'You didn't have to neglect Patsy,' he said lamely.

'What lies has she been telling now?' Maeve asked, taking a cigarette from the packet lying on the table and lighting it. She puffed out a cloud of blue smoke. 'You don't want to let her wind you up, you know. She's a contrary little madam, likes to go her own way so I let her. She'll tame down in time.'

'If she doesn't land in trouble first! Dressed like an urchin and playing out in the streets at all hours of the night and day she could very easily end up in bad company.'

23

'She's on the ball, that one,' Maeve told him scathingly. 'She's well able to take care of herself.' She stubbed out her cigarette angrily. 'What's brought all this on anyway? You got a guilty conscience about leaving us for months at a time or something?'

John's steady blue gaze levelled with her face. 'Maybe I have,' he said thoughtfully. 'I never dreamed that Patsy was leading the sort of life she is. Or that she was being taunted and teased.'

'Kids' stuff, that,' Maeve told him. 'The little buggers are always picking on each other. One minute they're fighting and the next they've got their arms round each other's necks and you can't tear them apart.'

'I always thought mothers looked out for their daughters and that they cherished them and taught them how to behave and dressed them in pretty clothes. I made you a generous allowance all the time I was at sea so I knew you were all right for money, and I thought you'd be enjoying each other's company.'

'Doing what? She's a kid, she wants to play with other kids of her own age not sit around with me watching me paint my nails!'

'I imagined you'd be taking her to the pictures, or on trips to the shops or even over to New Brighton and places like that. If I'd known for one minute that she was being left on her own at nights while you went gadding off out with other blokes I'd have been home like a shot.'

'And are you telling me that you never went out on a drinking binge with the other fellas on

24

the ship when you put into port?' Maeve jibed.

'Out drinking, no! I looked round the different places we docked in and took in the sights, but I didn't squander my money boozing. You must know that from the amount I was sending home to you.'

Maeve's mood suddenly seemed to change. Her face softened and her sneering was replaced by soft wheedling tones. Her eyes became limpid green pools as she looked up into her husband's face 'What are we quarrelling about, luv? You're home now so why don't we make the most of it?' She reached up, slipped her arms around his neck and gave him a seductive smile. 'I know of far better things we could be doing,' she breathed coquettishly, the tip of her tongue teasing the lobe of his ear.

Chapter Three

For Patsy Callaghan, Christmas 1922 was a mixture of sheer delight that her dad would be at home for Christmas for the first time since she could remember, wonderment that one of her most cherished dreams had come true, and fear that something would go wrong and spoil everything.

She would have given almost anything not to have had to go to school in the week leading up to the Christmas holidays. She wanted to spend every magical moment she could with her dad.

In the past, huddled in the dark waiting for her mam to come home from the pub, or wherever else she had gone in the evenings, Patsy had tried desperately to remember what sort of man her dad was. She wanted him to be strong yet gentle, kind yet authoritative. She hoped he didn't have a temper or shout, but above all she wanted him to be understanding, yet firm.

It was so long, more than ten months, since he had been at home that her memory of him was rather confused. She hardly expected the real man to live up to her anticipations, but it was consoling to daydream.

To her astonishment he seemed to match up to her expectations in every way. Except for the shouting. He hadn't shouted at her yet, but then she had been trying so hard not to do anything that might upset him or make him cross with her.

He had shouted at her mother a number of times and Patsy hated it when he did that, despite the fact that she could understand why it happened. Her mam could be so difficult to live with. In a matter of minutes she could change from being girlish and giggly into being mean and snappy. She could turn the atmosphere from one that was pleasant and relaxed into one that was fraught with tension.

It had happened several times since her dad had been home. Patsy had sensed they'd been rowing before she came into the house. She could hear their raised voices out in the street and then they would stop talking the moment she walked through the door. Her dad would look grim and her mother would be sulky, or pouting, and ignore whatever was said to her.

She'd confided in her best friend, Maureen Murphy who lived only a few doors away, about her mam's moodiness.

'One minute she's all sunshine and kisses and the next minute for no reason at all she's thumping me! Is your mam like that?'

Maureen's blue eyes had widened; her plump pallid face had looked perplexed. 'Not really. Sometimes she boxes my ears if I cheek her, but that's about it. Mostly it's a tongue-bashing I gets. I can shut my ears to that so it don't bother me too much.'

Patsy pulled up the sleeve of her jumper and displayed the bruises at the top of her arms to

Maureen, who shuddered at the sight of them.

'Does your dad hit you, then?' Patsy asked

Maureen pushed her long dark hair behind her ears and shook her head emphatically. 'Me mam wouldn't let him! She's boss in our house and if me or me sister needs telling off then she's the one that does it.'

'So you never get hit, not unless you're being cheeky?'

'Our Megan sometimes slaps me one. She's a right bossy-boots, but then you know that. She tells you off too!'

Patsy shrugged. 'Words don't matter, it's the thumping that hurts. I've got bruises everywhere.'

'What, as well as on your arms?' Maureen asked.

'On me back, me chest and me bum. The new ones are blue but later on they turn a greenish yellow. They don't hurt then and I forget about them. Until the next time.'

Patsy couldn't imagine her dad ever hitting her. She wasn't too sure though whether one of these days he might lash out at her mother. Sometimes she seemed to be deliberately winding him up, teasing him, provoking him almost as if she wanted him to thump her.

Patsy wondered what would happen afterwards if he did. Would she walk out for good as she kept threatening to do when things didn't go her way?

She hoped nothing like that would happen before Christmas. She wanted it to be an absolutely perfect occasion.

Slowly the days to Christmas crept by. She breathed a deep sigh of relief on the day school ended and she knew that from now on she could spend every moment with her dad. He'd promised her he'd help her make paper chains from strips of coloured paper and all sorts of other things to decorate the house. They'd never done that before and she was a bit surprised that he'd agreed, because he liked everything to be neat and tidy. Her mam said she didn't care what they did as long as she wasn't expected to join in or clear up after them.

On Christmas Eve he suggested they go into the centre of Liverpool to look at the decorations in the big shops in Church Street, Lord Street, Ranelagh Street and Clayton Square. Maeve said she would sooner stay at home, but at the very last minute decided she would come along as well.

Maeve wanted to visit Bold Street but John Callaghan said what was the point of looking in shops where everything was so highly priced you couldn't even begin to dream of buying them?

He was far more interested in the shops like Bunney's with their bright window displays that included toys and gadgets as well as clothes and things for the home. He was as keen as Patsy on looking round the toy departments and shared her enthusiasm for wind-up action toys and the Hornby train sets.

'What an utter waste of time this is, looking at toys,' Maeve grumbled. She pulled the fur collar of her dark green coat up around her ears until it was almost touching her green cloche hat. 'Patsy is too big now for such things. She's never played with dolls anyway.'

'Only because I've never had one to play with!'

'Yes you have. For Christmas last year I brought you home a lovely china doll from Spain,' John reminded her.

'You didn't come home last Christmas.'

'Well, no, but I brought it home in February and it was meant to be your Christmas present. Anyway, it settles the point. You do have a doll.'

As Patsy opened her mouth to explain about the doll Maeve grabbed her arm, her slim fingers with their long hard nails penetrating like talons, making themselves felt even through the thick gabardine sleeve of Patsy's new raincoat. She turned quickly to face her mother and shivered as she saw the warning in the icy glare Maeve gave her.

She drew her breath in sharply, pulled her arm away from Maeve's grasp and darted to the nearest brightly decorated window and stared in with feigned interest. But she could see nothing through the mist of tears that filled her eyes.

Her mother didn't want her dad to know what had happened to his lovely present. She doesn't want me to tell him that she burned it in front of me as a punishment because she said I had been rude to one of the uncles.

The memory sent a *frisson* of revulsion through her. He had been fat and smelt of whisky, but the worst thing about him had been his moustache. It had been wet and bushy and it felt like kissing a prickly brown rat. It made her stomach churn even thinking about it.

By the time they caught up with her, Maeve was complaining that her feet were aching and they still had all the shopping for food to do.

'Why don't you cut along to T.J. Hughes or C&A and buy yourself something special for Christmas,' John suggested as he handed his wife a crisp five-pound note.

Maeve hesitated for a brief moment then her gloved fingers curled round the note and she planted a grateful kiss on his cheek.

'Ta! I'll do that and then I'll get the tram home. Me feet are killing me. You and Patsy go to the market and pick up a bird and some veggies for tomorrow. Orright?'

The day took on an even greater magic once Patsy and her dad were on their own. The market was crowded with last-minute shoppers eager to find a bargain for the Christmas dinner. There was music playing and a group singing Christmas carols and even though John and Patsy found themselves being pushed and jostled from stall to stall they enjoyed every minute of it.

By the time they set off for home they were so loaded down with shopping bags and parcels that they could hardly stagger on to the tram.

One parcel intrigued Patsy more than all the others. While they were in the market her dad had bought her a milk shake and himself a coffee and they'd had a mince pie each. He finished his first and had told her not to hurry but to sit where she was at the table as he had forgotten something.

He promised he would be back in a few minutes and told her to guard the parcels and not move from the table.

When he returned he was carrying a large parcel, but he didn't say what it was and although she was curious about it she managed to keep from asking.

To their surprise the house was in darkness when they reached Paradise Place.

'I wonder where your mam is,' John frowned. 'She can't still be in town. Perhaps she's gone upstairs to have a nap. She said her feet were hurting and that she was tired out.'

He left the shopping on the kitchen floor, all except the mystery parcel, which he took upstairs with him. Within seconds he was back down again. 'She's not there. It must be taking her longer to find something she wanted than I thought.'

Together they unpacked the foodstuff they had bought and put some of it away.

'Leave the bags of veggies and the turkey where they are,' he told her, 'and start laying the table ready for tea.'

The time ticked by. Seven o'clock . . . half-past . . . eight o'clock. Patsy began to feel really hungry. It had been a long time since the milk shake and mince pie. 'Can we have our tea, Dad?' she asked cautiously.

He frowned. 'I suppose so. I thought we would wait for your mam, but it is getting late. I can't think where she might be. I'm worried in case she's had some sort of accident. She can't still be shopping or chatting with someone she's bumped into.'

'She's probably met one of the uncles and gone off to the pub with him,' Patsy muttered.

The moment the words were out, Patsy knew she'd said something she shouldn't have done. She thought her dad was going to tell her off, he looked so angry.

'Will you be all right on your own for ten minutes?' he asked. He put a plate of bread and butter and a pot of jam on the table in front of her. 'Tuck into that while I'm gone.'

'Of course I'll be all right, but where are you going, Dad?'

'I'll be back by the time you've eaten that lot,' he told her.

'Can't I come with you?'

'No, you'd better stay here in case your mam gets back and is worried because we're not here.'

Patsy nodded and began to tuck into the food. She really was hungry and she was afraid he might change his mind and say they must wait until her mam was home.

By the time she had cleared the plate, neither of them had come home. It had been well over half an hour since her dad had gone out. She walked across to the window and peered out into the darkness debating how much longer he was going to be.

She was tempted to slip upstairs to see if she could find where her dad had hidden the mysterious parcel he'd brought home. She was sure it was something special for her for Christmas. If she squeezed it she might be able to guess what it was.

'And if I get caught then I mightn't get anything at all,' she told herself out loud.

She took her plate over to the sink and rinsed the crumbs off it, dried it and put it back on the sideboard. Then she put the jam away in the cupboard. She was wondering whether perhaps she ought to go to bed when she heard a scuffling noise outside and then the door opened and both her mother and father were there.

'Give me a hand, Patsy,' her father ordered as he pushed a pile of shopping bags into her arms and then half lifted her mother over the doorstep. 'You hold her upright while I shut the door and then we'll get her up to bed, she's not feeling too well.'

Even as he spoke Maeve heaved and the next moment Patsy found herself covered in evil-smelling vomit.

She felt like bursting into tears. Her lovely green jumper was covered with horrid smelling slime that was bound to stain it, ruin it even.

'Go and take that off and put it to soak in cold water and I'll wash it out properly later on,' John Callaghan ordered grimly. 'Don't worry, luv, it will be all right. I'll see to it as soon as I've put your mam to bed,' he added more gently.

Holding back her tears, Patsy went to do as she was told. She felt so angry inside that her head ached, for it looked as though the special Christmas she had been dreaming about was going to be ruined after all.

All she wanted to do was get into bed, pull the covers up over her head and go to sleep and hope that when she woke up it would all have been a bad dream. Instead, she did as she'd been asked. She took off the smelly jumper, then filled the tin bowl they used to wash up in with water and plunged the jumper into it.

Her stomach heaved as obnoxious yellow slime floated to the top along with particles of food. She tipped the water away and refilled the bowl and then left it for her dad to see to once he'd managed to put her mam to bed.

She knew she ought to go and see if she could help him, but she couldn't bring herself to do so because she didn't want to see her mother like that. She'd never seen her so drunk. In the past when she had been out with one of the uncles and had too much to drink she was usually laughing loudly and singing and sometimes even dancing round the room with her arms held out and her head thrown back like some film star would do. This time, though, she had been more like a rag doll, limp and droopy with her head down on her chest and her legs going all over the place as she tried to walk.

Patsy thought about all the bags of food that she and her dad had shopped for in St John's Market. Some of them were still on the kitchen floor, and tears of frustration stung her eyes. All their plans now seemed to be going wrong.

As she began to unpack them and put them away in the larder she wondered if they would be having a proper Christmas dinner after all. Her dad had splashed out and bought a turkey which he said was even nicer than chicken. She'd never tasted turkey in her life so she was looking forward to it very much.

It was to have been the highlight of their day, but now it looked as if her mother would be too ill to be interested. She wondered if she would even be well enough to get up and go to Mass with them.

Her dad's plan had been that they would prepare the turkey tonight so that they could pop it into the oven to cook the moment they got up. After breakfast, before they all went to the special sung Mass at eleven o'clock, they would prepare the vegetables. They'd put the Christmas pudding on to heat up as well so that when they came home they'd only have to wait for the vegetables to cook and their dinner would be ready.

She was to be in charge of laying the table, and her dad had bought some paper hats for them to wear while they ate their dinner.

Now there was a shadow over it all. Patsy was afraid that her dad might be so disappointed and cross about the way things were turning out that he'd decide to go back to sea again after all.

Chapter Four

To Patsy's amazement Christmas Day looked as though it was going to be every bit as wonderful as she'd dreamed.

She woke early and crept out of bed to look out. The sky was grey and leaden and Paradise Place was deserted apart from the Murphys' black cat, that was picking its way delicately across the cobbles towards home.

There wasn't a sound in the house so, shivering with the cold, she decided to creep back under the covers for a while. As she turned round to climb into bed her foot caught against something bulky. She bent down to pick it up, and saw that it was a pillowcase with several things inside it, and her excitement made her forget all about the cold.

Pulling back the curtains so that she could see what she was doing she dragged the bundle up on to her bed and began to unpack it, eager to find out what was inside.

The first thing she discovered was the bulky parcel her dad had nipped out from the market to buy. She'd suspected it was a surprise for her and was glad now that she hadn't sneaked upstairs to try and find out what it was.

She felt it all over, trying to guess what it could

be. It was something inside a cardboard box and he had wrapped it up in green paper that had holly and robins printed all over it.

Patsy was torn between desire to know what it was, and curiosity about what else was in the pillowcase. Taking a deep breath she put it to one side and began taking out the smaller items.

She spread them out on the bed beside her. An orange, some walnuts, raisins in a screw of pretty paper, a bar of chocolate, a big rosy apple, two bright new pennies that looked like gold coins they were so shiny, a comic, some coloured pencils, a drawing book and a pair of bright red slippers with white pom-poms on the front.

It was a treasure trove of all the things she liked best and she didn't know which to use first. She felt almost too excited to open the other present and even toyed with the idea of leaving it until later. Supposing it was something she didn't like? Then it would spoil everything.

She laughed out loud at the thought. She was being plain silly. How could there be anything she didn't like!

She looked at each of the many presents again, trying to stem her fascination about the one that remained. Then curiosity got the better of her and she began removing the Christmassy paper.

The lid of the cardboard box inside was even prettier than the paper around it and Patsy sat for several minutes entranced by the attractive fairground scene. When she removed the lid she could hardly believe her eyes when she saw what was inside. Very carefully she lifted it out. The colourful carousel was so pretty that she loved it on sight. Eight gaily painted horses, suspended on tiny gold poles, swung out from the brightly coloured central pivot. As she wound the metal key, not only did a tune begin to play, but the horses moved up and down one behind the other. It was a perfect replica of a roundabout she had seen at New Brighton Tower fairground and had described to her dad in detail.

She could hardly wait for him to get up so that she could thank him. The moment she heard him padding down the stairs, and knew he had gone to make a cup of tea for her mam, she followed him.

'Happy Christmas, Dad, and my present is wonderful!' she said happily as she flung her arms round his neck and hugged and kissed him.

'Like it, do you?'

'It's wonderful. Have you heard the tune it plays?'

'Not yet. They had one playing in the shop so it may be the same tune.'

Patsy shook her head firmly. 'No! This has to be a very special one,' she grinned. 'And thanks for all the other things, Dad!'

'Happy Christmas, luv. Enjoy yourself. It's going to be a very special day, you'll see. Now, why don't you run up and get dressed. I'll take your mam up a cup of tea and then as soon as we've had our breakfast you can give me a hand to prepare the vegetables.'

'How is me mam feeling this morning? Shall I go and wish her a Happy Christmas?'

He looked at her doubtfully. 'No, I should leave it for the minute, luv, she's got a bit of a headache. Wait until she's had her cuppa and is ready to get up.'

It set the pattern for the day. Maeve's headache lasted all morning. Patsy tried not to think about it as she and her father peeled potatoes and prepared parsnips and Brussels sprouts for their Christmas dinner.

'Are you coming to Mass with me?' she asked hopefully when they'd finished.

'No, I think you'd better go on your own. I'll stay here with your mam and see to the dinner.'

When she turned away and said nothing he put his arm around her shoulders and hugged her. 'Look, I'll come if it means all that much to you, luv,' he told her gently.

Her face lit up with happiness. She knew the church had been specially decorated for the Christmas Mass and Father O'Brian would be in his most splendid regalia. There would be twice as many altar boys and the choir would sing.

What was even more important, she'd be as proud as punch because her dad would be there with her standing at her side. Everybody would see him, especially all the kids who called her ugly names and said she didn't have a real dad.

'You go and get ready while I baste the turkey and top up the water in the saucepan so that the Christmas pudding doesn't boil dry,' John told her.

'What about me mam? Is she coming to Mass with us?'

Deep down, Patsy didn't want her to come, she

wanted to have her dad all to herself, but she knew her mam ought to be there. Father O'Brian would expect it on such a special occasion.

Her dad shook his head. 'I don't think she's feeling well enough to come. We'll leave her to have a nice quiet sleep and then perhaps she'll be feeling better by the time we get back.'

Maeve was still asleep when they returned from church. When the vegetables were boiling away on the fire and John had basted the turkey yet again and pronounced that it was 'done to a crisp', he went up to rouse her.

She took ages to get dressed and by the time she arrived downstairs the vegetables had been drained and were going cold and the turkey was looking very well cooked indeed.

While her dad dished up, Patsy told her mother all about the carousel and then dashed upstairs to fetch it so that she could see it for herself. When she wound it up and it began to play, Maeve clapped her hands over her ears. 'For God's sake stop that awful noise,' she snapped.

John picked up the carousel and moved it out of the way. 'Leave it for now, Patsy, your mother's head is still bothering her. It's a lovely tune and you are right it is a different tune to the one they were playing in the shop,' he told her. 'We'll listen to it again later on. Let's finish our meal now before it's spoiled.'

Patsy and John tucked into their special dinner with gusto but Maeve barely touched hers. She played around with it until it was cold and then pushed her plate to one side.

She wouldn't even taste the pudding. Patsy and her dad both had a generous helping and Patsy squealed with excitement when she found a silver threepenny bit in her piece.

'Can I keep it?' she asked, her eyes shining, her cheeks pink with happiness.

'Of course you can! Lucky, aren't you?'

'You should have tried a piece, Mam,' Patsy grinned. 'You might have been lucky as well.'

'Oh for God's sake, Patsy, stop being so childish. Your dad probably slipped it in when he was putting the pudding on your plate,' Maeve told her irritably.

'Do you have to spoil everything for the kid?' John exclaimed exasperatedly.

'What the hell are you talking about? If there's any brandy left give me a nip,' she told him. 'Bloody waste pouring it over the pudding.'

'It's traditional, and how else can you light it?'

'So that you could show off! After the amount of turkey that kid stuffed inside her she shouldn't have needed any bloody pudding.'

'Well at least she ate her meal and enjoyed it, which is more than you did,' he told her frigidly.

'Oh yeah! Going to throw that up at me for the rest of time, are you?' she snapped. 'Who the hell do you think you are?' Her angelic face was contorted with rage.

'I think it might be better if you went back upstairs to bed until you are feeling more sociable,' John told her quietly.

'More sociable? More bloody sociable! I was trying to be sociable last night when you came and dragged me away from me friends. What the hell do you think they must have thought when you marched me out of the pub as if you were my gaoler?'

'I helped you out of the pub and brought you home because you were legless and falling all over the place!'

'You mean because you didn't like to see me having a good time. It's Christmas, for God's sake, and that's what friends do at Christmas. They go out together, have a bevvy or two and enjoy themselves.'

'You weren't enjoying yourself, you were paralytic.'

'I was enjoying myself. I stood them all a drink and they were buying me one back.'

'You mean that you wasted that fiver I gave you to buy yourself a Christmas present on buying drinks for that lot?' he asked angrily.

She gave a simpering smile. 'You said buy whatever I liked and that's what I did.'

'Wasted hard-earned money, and we haven't got a lot of that at the moment.'

'Then you'd better hurry up and find yourself a job, hadn't you? If you can't find one ashore then bugger off back to sea. Life was a lot easier when you were away, I can tell you.'

'Easier for you to go gadding off out with every Tom, Dick and Harry, but not so easy for poor little Patsy left at home on her own.'

Maeve clamped her hands over her ears. 'I don't want to hear it.'

Savagely he pulled her hands away. 'You don't

want to but for once you are going to listen. I've been sending home money for you and Patsy to live in comfort all these years and what have you done with it? You've squandered most of it on drink and entertaining your no-good friends. You've not only left her to fend for herself but you've not even clothed her properly. Well, all that is going to stop. Believe me, it is.'

Patsy listened to their confrontation in growing horror. She knew what her dad said was true but she didn't like them fighting over her. She knew her mam neglected her, but she loved her just the same. There were times when her mam was lovely to her. It was the uncles who spoiled everything. She knew her mam loved her but when they came to the house her mam sent her out to play and forgot all about her.

When she was left sitting on the doorstep with a bag of crisps other children envied her. She never told them that it had been half empty when she found it, or that the reason she wouldn't share it with them was because she was so starving hungry that every morsel was precious. She hid her misery and unhappiness behind a cheeky grin and still went on loving her mam.

Patsy knew her mam only went off to the pub and got drunk because she was lonely, but she was lonely too with her dad away. She had thought everything was going to be resolved now that he was back home. She loved him so much, and if her mam felt the same way about him then she wouldn't be lonely ever again either.

She watched in dismay as Maeve tossed her

head disdainfully, her hair glinting in the gaslight. 'So who is going to change things?' she challenged.

'I am!' John Callaghan said forcefully. 'Things in this house are going to be run properly from now on. I'm not having Patsy run wild any more, do you understand?'

'You can't even find work,' she taunted. 'You've been home for weeks and you haven't managed to land a job.'

'I will do, in the New Year,' he told her confidently.

She shook her head, her lip curling. 'You aren't qualified to do any job except go away to sea. The sooner you wake up to that fact and find another ship and sign on again the better.'

'Oh, no! My days at sea are over,' John Callaghan insisted doggedly. 'I'll find myself a job ashore, don't you worry. I'm not leaving Patsy in your charge ever again.'

Chapter Five

John Callaghan staunchly refused to deviate from his resolve to find work ashore. He knew it wasn't the best of times to do so, but he persevered day after day.

He was up early every morning to make sure Patsy had a proper breakfast. He would walk as far as the school with her then head off to the Pier Head to check out if there was anything going down at the docks, before making his way back into town to the Labour Exchange.

Maeve was highly critical of the amount of dole money he received and even though he turned over the bulk of it to her for housekeeping she complained it was not enough to manage on. It certainly didn't leave anything over for the new clothes, make-up and trips to the pub two or three times a week that she'd been used to when he'd been at sea.

The atmosphere between them had settled down and most of the time she was compliant enough. He tried hard to make her life as pleasant as he could, but he knew she longed to go out more and realised that she was so gregarious that his company would never be enough for her.

Now that she couldn't afford to go to the pub every night she flirted with every man in sight.

The postman, coalman, milkman and even the men who were their neighbours in Paradise Place were all targets for her 'come-hither' smiles and flippant remarks. Some replied in the same vein, some ignored her approach, but others, emboldened by her brazen attitude, tried to take advantage of the situation. She was, after all, a very attractive woman. Her strawberry-blonde hair glinted like spun gold, her green eyes sparkled, her lips were enticing and she always dressed in a provocative manner.

Some of the men simply couldn't help themselves. They seemed to think that a stolen kiss, a surreptitious cuddle, or even a slap on her shapely rump were permissible.

Whenever John was around he made it quite clear that they were overstepping the mark. He would put his arm around her shoulders in a proprietorial way and draw Maeve close, kissing the top of her head or her cheek before leading her away from any further temptation.

When he had first done this she had been furious, but realising that she was not going to win her freedom by fighting him she pretended to be contrite and turned all her charm as well as her full attention on him.

Patsy watched this pantomime with a mixture of bewilderment and unease. Why did her mother have to play games like this? she wondered. None of the other married women in Paradise Place flirted with other men and some of them had husbands who, to her eyes, were horrible. Big paunchy fellows with stubble on their faces and lank greasy hair, or wiry little ferret-faced men with piggy eyes and mean mouths. Her dad wasn't like that at all. He was tall and broad and stood head and shoulders over most of the men he came in contact with and he was so handsome that Patsy thought he looked like a film star or one of the models used on advertising placards to sell cigarettes.

Patsy couldn't understand why her mother wasn't as happy as she was to have her dad around all the time, but it was clear from the constant bickering that went on that she much preferred it when he was away at sea.

As each day passed and John Callaghan was unable to find work ashore, Maeve's nagging became more acid.

'Nothing again today,' she would mock when he arrived home in the late afternoon looking tired out and despondent.

When his reply was that he had been tramping from one place to the next in search of work and that in each instance he was too late, or that he had waited with a long queue of other hopeful men only to be told that the position was filled, she would simply shake her head or shrug her shoulders.

'You can always go back to sea if you can't find a job ashore,' she would remind him.

'No, I'm determined to stay here in Liverpool where I can keep an eye on Patsy,' he would tell her grimly.

He meant what he said and towards the end of January he made up his mind that if he couldn't find work in the normal way then he must create work for himself. He still had a small cache of savings left from his final trip which Maeve knew nothing about and so he decided that as a last-ditch attempt he would sink this money into creating his own business. If that failed, then he would have to admit defeat and go back to sea, but he didn't intend to let it fail.

While he had been searching for work on the dockside he had got to know a number of the gaffers who handed out jobs and had studied them closely so that he knew exactly how they worked. His idea was not to apply to them for a job, but to offer them a service that they needed and which they found frustrating and time consuming to locate.

With this in mind he made enquiries about renting a stable that was at the end of the row of houses in Paradise Place. It had been empty for a long time and was in a state of disrepair, but he persuaded the landlord to let him have it at a fairly low rent if he undertook to put it to rights.

It took him another week and about a third of his precious hoard of money to carry out the necessary repairs. Once completed, the stable was warm and dry and spacious enough to house a large horse. There was room in the yard outside for a cart to be left overnight.

Buying a horse was the next step. John had been born and brought up on a farm in Ireland where all the ploughing and farm work had been done with carthorses and it was a heavyweight animal along these lines that he set his sights on.

Samson was a massive dray horse, but his previous owner assured John that he was as docile as a kitten and a steady worker.

'Goes all day as long as you feed him well and treat him right. I'll be sorry to lose him, but I'm giving up. I'm well into my sixties and too old for handling heavy loads. The wife says it's time I stopped workin' an' put me slippers on, so he's yours whacker if you want him? I might even drop the asking price if I know he's going to a good home.'

They haggled amicably, though John would have been prepared to pay the asking price in order to secure Samson if he'd had to do so. Instead he asked if the cart and tack could be included as well.

When the deal had been concluded there were tears in Samson's owner's eyes as he patted the horse goodbye.

'Hold on a minute,' he called out as John started to lead Samson away. 'Since you're having me bloody horse and me bloody cart you may as well have this,' he said, handing John a well-used piece of paper. 'It's a list of the gaffers and companies down on the docks whose goods I've been carrying for the last ten years.'

John couldn't believe his luck. In one stroke he had set himself up in business. Armed with so many contacts he couldn't possibly fail, he told himself jubilantly.

'If you ever want to see Samson, or check that we're doing a good job, you can always look me up here on the dockside. I'll be keeping an eye out for you,' John promised as they finally parted.

As he drove the horse and cart back to Paradise Place, John Callaghan felt like a millionaire. It was a long time since he'd handled a horse, but Samson seemed to be every bit as docile as his previous owner had said he was. He responded to the slightest touch of the reins and the traffic and other street noises didn't seem to bother him at all.

As he settled the horse into the newly renovated stable he couldn't wait to tell Maeve about his new venture. She'd realise now that he was serious about staying ashore and he hoped that she would stop throwing out remarks all the time about him going back to sea.

Maeve was not at home so as it was mid-afternoon John Callaghan decided to go and meet Patsy from school and take her to see Samson.

Her reaction delighted him and confirmed in his own mind that the enormous step he had taken was the right one.

For the first few minutes Patsy was nervous about standing too close to Samson. He was so huge that her mop of red curls barely reached up to his massive chest. When he emitted a noisy snort of air she jumped back in fright and when he put his huge head down and nuzzled her neck with his warm nose she held her breath in terror.

'I thought he was going to eat me,' she gasped as her dad laid a reassuring hand on her shoulder.

'No, he was trying to be friendly. He was hoping you'd have something for him to eat.'

'Like what?' she asked, looking up at her dad wide-eyed.

'I expect he's partial to a piece of carrot or an apple,' he told her. He fished an apple out of his pocket and handed it to her. 'Here, give him this.'

Patsy held the apple gingerly between two fingers and darted her hand out in front of the horse, then pulled it back just as quickly.

'No, no! Don't tease him like that or he might accidentally bite you,' her dad said quickly. 'Place the apple flat on the palm of your hand and hold it out and keep your hand perfectly steady.'

'I can't! He might bite me!'

'No he won't. He'll take it very carefully and all you will feel is his lips brushing your hand.'

Patsy shook her head doubtfully.

'Come on, I'll show you.'

He balanced the apple in the palm of Patsy's hand then, keeping his own hand underneath hers to steady it, held her arm out in front of the horse.

Patsy held her breath and screwed her eyes tight shut as the horse began to lower his head towards her outstretched hand. When, as her father had explained, Samson took the apple and all she felt was his warm lips as he did so, she opened her eyes again in wonderment.

It was the start of a tremendous bond between the huge brown-and-white horse and the diminutive red-haired girl. Patsy took an immediate liking to Samson and he responded to her voice and touch as if he accepted she was his friend.

Every night after school she would wait impatiently for her dad and Samson to return from their haulage work at the docks. The moment he crossed the cobbled yard into the stable, she had an apple or piece of carrot waiting for the horse and though she now held them out quite fearlessly she never failed to marvel at how gentle the huge animal could be. As soon as Samson's harness was removed she would help to feed and groom him. Maeve hated the horse. She declared him to be a great lumbering, smelly creature and she wanted nothing whatsoever to do with him. She complained bitterly when John and Patsy came indoors after being in the stable that they smelled of the animal and insisted they took their shoes off and left them by the back door.

Now that she knew there was no possible chance of John ever going back to sea again Maeve studiously began to replan her own life. She hated the ordered round of domesticity. She liked to dress up in her prettiest clothes, but there was no point in doing that unless there was someone to admire her and pay her compliments.

Most nights John was far too tired after his heavy day moving cargo down at the docks to want to go out. Even after he got home there was Samson to be fed and watered, the stable to be cleaned out and fresh straw spread on the floor. Even with Patsy doing her utmost to help it usually took well over an hour. Then all he wanted was a good wash, a filling meal and a quiet evening by his own fireside reading the *Echo*.

At first, Maeve contented herself with visiting the pub at midday, but most of the men whose company she enjoyed were working then. The evenings were prime time for company and after a great deal of argument and continuous nagging she managed to persuade John to take her out every Saturday night as well as at least one night during the week.

The thing John Callaghan disliked most about this arrangement was leaving Patsy at home on her own. As spring advanced and the nights became lighter and lighter it was only natural that she wanted to play out in the street after school with her friends. He had no objections to her doing this, but he was well aware that if he and Maeve were out then Patsy was in the habit of staying out until well after dark and he worried in case she ended up in some kind of trouble.

'Stop worrying your head about her,' Maeve told him crossly. 'I've told you before she's well able to look after herself. She's never got into any sort of bother up to now, has she?'

'No, but she is getting older, and prettier, and I don't want her in any trouble,' he would argue.

'Then make her stay home when we go out.'

'I don't like to think of her left here in the house on her own either.'

'Then tell her to have young Maureen Murphy in to keep her company, or Janie Grant. They're both in her class at school.'

When he mentioned this idea to Patsy she wasn't at all enthusiastic.

'Maureen won't want to stay in, she likes playing out and Janie is such a little goody-goody that she's no fun at all. I'd sooner be on my own than have her in here to keep me company.'

'So who would you like to have here with you?'

'You, of course!' she told him with an impudent grin. 'I love it when it's only the two of us and you tell me stories about all the foreign places you visited when you were at sea and about when you were a boy in Ireland. Me mam never tells me anything like that. All she talks about is clothes.'

John felt torn between the two of them. He knew what Patsy said was right, but he also knew that unless he took Maeve out she would either sulk or go to the pub on her own. She enjoyed the company of her friends who drank there, but he found them raucous. He was glad of the excuse to leave early because Patsy was at home on her own.

As he took on more and more work at the docks he felt the need for early nights rather than outings to the pub. Looking after Samson took up a lot of his time and in the end he decided he would have to find someone to help with mucking out the stable and grooming Samson. Patsy was more than willing to do it but she couldn't wield the heavy yard brush or reach up high enough to groom Samson properly.

He talked to Patsy about it and asked if she knew any likely young lad who might be interested.

'Billy Grant would jump at the chance,' she told him. 'He's always asking me about the horse. Billy loves animals. He used to take old Mr Peterson's dog, Nipper, for a walk every night after school, but then it died and Mr Peterson said he was too old to get another one.'

'You mean Janie's brother? I don't think he would be any use. He's not even as tall as you are.'

'Not her little brother, her older brother. He's nearly thirteen and ever so tall. He could reach up to groom Samson and put on his harness quite easily. And he'd be ever so good with him.'

John promised to give Billy Grant a trial. It turned out to be a tremendous success. As well as helping out after school Billy came round early in the morning to give Samson his feed. In next to no time he had learned how to harness Samson up ready for his day's work.

With help at both ends of the day, John found he was less stressed and had far more time for both Patsy and Maeve. As a routine acceptable to them all became established he congratulated himself that things were at last turning out exactly as he had hoped they would.

Chapter Six

Patsy's tousled red head was barely visible over the half-opened door, but the sturdy brown-and-white dray horse whinnied a greeting as she came inside the stable.

'Yer late, kiddo! Samson's been getting restless thinking yer weren't coming,' Billy Grant said mildly as he carried on grooming the horse.

'I know I'm late, Billy,' Patsy sighed as she fondled the warm soft nose that the horse thrust inquisitively towards her hand in search of the apple or raw carrot that was his usual treat.

'So what kept you?' he asked

Patsy shrugged. 'This and that, you know how it is.'

Billy's eyes narrowed as he cleaned out the curry-comb and studied his work on the horse's coat.

'Is yer ma playing up again, then, kiddo?' he asked casually.

'Yeah. She's got a bit of a cob on. Her head's bad and so she spent the day in bed and I had to do all the cleaning. Me dad's nipped out to the shops because I had no money to buy any food.'

Billy shook his head sadly. 'So what are you doing here?'

'Well, Mrs Murphy has just dropped in to see

me mam so I took a chance to pop out and come over to see Samson.'

'Well I'm off home for my tea now,' Billy said as he reached up for the old plaid blanket that he draped over the horse's back after he'd groomed him. 'See yer at the usual time tomorrow.'

Patsy nodded, but said nothing. She felt too choked to speak. She'd been looking forward all day to having a chat with Billy. It mattered almost as much to her as seeing Samson.

Billy Grant was almost three years older than her, sturdy and capable with thick brown hair, light blue eyes and a square jaw with a cleft in the centre of it.

Patsy liked being with Billy because he always treated her as an equal and they had become very good companions. Unlike the other boys she knew at school he never made any derogatory remarks about her red hair or her freckles. In fact, he never teased her at all.

He seemed to understand how much she cared about Samson and didn't laugh at her for bringing the horse an apple or a piece of carrot every night. He encouraged her to tell him what she'd been doing and sympathised with her when, like today, her mam was so hungover that she had to stay in bed.

They met up and talked to each other nearly every day and she often wished he was her brother. She felt she could tell him anything and he always seemed to understand her problems even if there was nothing he could do to help her.

What was more, he confided in her, telling her things he said no one else in the world knew. She knew exactly how he felt about school and his teachers, which ones he liked and which he hated. And he told her about his mates and warned her which ones to avoid because they were bullies.

Billy had also told her that he intended to leave school the minute he was fourteen and old enough to do so. It worried Patsy because she was afraid she wouldn't see very much of him once he went to work.

'Why don't you let my dad know when you'll be leaving school and ask him if you can work for him full time?' she had suggested.

Billy shook his head. 'He probably couldn't afford to employ me full time,' he told her. 'I want a job where I can earn a really good wage because I'm saving up for something special.'

It had taken her almost a week of deft probing to find out exactly what it was that Billy was saving up to buy. She'd turned it into a guessing game, naming everything from football boots to a cricket bat, or even a wireless set, but he'd shaken his head each time and his lips had remained sealed.

Then one day, out of the blue, he said he was going to tell her what it was. First, he swore her to secrecy. He said he didn't want anyone to know what he was saving up for, certainly not his sister Janie who would be bound to tell his mum and dad.

'I won't tell a soul. Cross my heart and hope to

die,' Patsy promised and held her breath waiting to hear what it was.

'I'm saving up to buy a Harley-Davidson,' he confided.

'A Harley-Davidson?' Patsy looked blank, then her green eyes danced with excitement. 'You mean a motorbike?'

Billy nodded. 'That's right, but not any old motorbike. I want a Harley-Davidson. I know they cost an awful lot of money, but since I'm not old enough yet to ride one, that doesn't matter. I want to have the money saved up ready, though, so that on the day I am old enough to ride one I can go out and buy it.'

'They're those great big powerful bikes!' Patsy exclaimed in awe.

Billy's face lit up with enthusiasm. 'A Harley-Davidson is the most expensive motorbike in the world and that's because it's the very best motorbike in the world, too.'

Patsy frowned. It seemed a pretty daft thing to her. 'Have you ever been on one, Billy?' she asked dubiously.

He shook his head. 'Not on a Harley, but I have ridden pillion on a Rudge. The Harley is ten times better though.'

'How do you know it is if you've never been on one?'

'A chap who has been on both of them told me so.'

'Will you give me a ride on it when you get it?' she asked hopefully.

He laughed. 'Yeah! I'll make sure it has a Buddy

seat fitted so that I can take you for a spin on it,' he promised. 'You'll love it.'

'Ta! You would still consider working for my dad full time when you leave school if he was to pay you a proper wage, though, wouldn't you?' she persisted, her eyes anxious.

Billy looked thoughtful. 'Well, I might consider it,' he grinned.

'Samson would like that,' she insisted.

'What about you?'

'Yeah! I want you to,' Patsy told him eagerly. 'I'd miss you a lot if you left.'

'Well, that's nice to know,' he said. 'Afraid you're going to miss me now as well, kiddo, because I'm off home to get me tea. Come on,' he went on as he propelled her towards the door. 'I want to lock up the stable.'

Despondently Patsy now walked back across the cobbled yard that separated the stable from the street. She couldn't bear the thought of not seeing Billy every day. He was so very much part of her world, the best friend she had ever known.

She cheered up slightly when she saw that Maureen Murphy was sitting on the front doorstep waiting for her.

'Been sneaking out to the stable to see Billy Grant then?' Maureen teased.

Patsy blushed, her face flaming, making her freckles look like a sprinkling of brown dots over the bridge of her nose. "Course not, I always take an apple or something over to Samson at this time every day.'

'Oh, yeah? And what about an apple for Billy?

61

Or perhaps he gets something better, like a kiss and a cuddle,' she said archly.

'Don't talk daft!' Patsy said crossly.

'You telling me you've never kissed him or had a bit of a cuddle?' Maureen persisted, tossing back her long dark hair and staring at Patsy intently with wide blue eyes.

'Of course I haven't,' Patsy told her indignantly, her own eyes flashing angrily.

'Why not? He's ever so handsome. I bet you'd like to kiss him,' Maureen sniggered.

Patsy looked thoughtful, holding her lower lip between her small white teeth. 'Not really,' she said slowly, 'but I like him as a friend.'

'Yer daft, you are!' Maureen told her. 'He's in our Megan's class at school and she said most of the girls are dotty about him.'

'Your Megan would be dotty about anything in trousers,' Patsy scoffed.

'Oh no she's not!' Maureen defended her. 'She wouldn't even give Billy Grant a second look. He might be good looking but he's too scruffy. He smells, too, of that horse. You wouldn't notice that, though, because you stink of that old horse the same as he does.'

Patsy shrugged her scrawny shoulders. 'What are you doing here, anyway?' she asked as she hunched down on the front doorstep alongside Maureen.

'Waiting for me mam. She's having a jangle with your mam. Probably wants to know what's up with her this time.'

'Me mam's got one of her bad heads,' Patsy muttered evasively.

Maureen gave her a sideways look. 'Do I look that daft that I'm going to believe that?' she smirked. 'C'mon, what's really wrong with her?'

'She's got a bad head!'

'I heard what you said first time,' Maureen snapped. 'I ain't stupid, you know, nor deaf.'

Patsy didn't answer, and she avoided Maureen's sharp look.

'You weren't at school again today,' Maureen said accusingly. 'Miss Richardson was asking where you were.'

'Me mam was bad in the night so me dad said I might as well stay home as someone ought to be with her.'

'My mam says if her headaches are as bad as she makes them out to be then she should be in hospital being properly looked after and getting her head examined and put right.'

'She is properly looked after,' Patsy said defensively. 'I look after her better than they would in any hospital. Anyway, it's only headaches she gets and she'd sooner be at home than in one of those places.'

Maureen shrugged. 'I don't suppose they'd take her anyway. The headaches she keeps on getting are because she has hangovers all the time and that's because she drinks too much.'

'What do you mean by that, Maureen Murphy?' Patsy drew in her breath sharply and her expression changed to one of anger. 'I suppose that's why your mam's here, isn't it? Poking her nose in! Come to read me mam the riot act, has she?' Her voice rose hysterically. 'She needn't bother!

Father O'Brian and me dad can do that without any help from anyone else.'

Tears of outrage spurted from her eyes and she wiped them away on her sleeve. Then she scrambled to her feet and pushed past Maureen.

Blindly she stumbled up the stairs to the front bedroom where Mrs Murphy was sitting by the bedside talking to her mother. She paused in the doorway of the darkened room, her breath catching in her throat as the smell from the vinegar-soaked compress that her mother insisted on having on her forehead stung her throat.

'Is that you, Patsy?' her mother asked in a tremulous whisper. 'Could you get me a drink, lovey, I'm absolutely parched. It must be all this talking.'

Patsy nodded, too choked to speak. When she returned with the mug of water she noticed that there were dark shadows beneath her mother's green eyes, that her hair was mussed into a straggly mess, her cheeks drained of colour and her skin a sickly yellow.

'Give it here, chuck.' Bessie Murphy held out her hand for the water.

Short, plump with very dark straight hair, blue eyes and a round florid face, she contrasted so sharply with the woman lying in the bed that for a minute Patsy hated her. Why should Maureen and Megan's mother be so fit and healthy when her own mother was so sickly? It didn't seem fair, Patsy thought rebelliously. Deep down, though, she knew her own mam could be as fit and well as anyone else if she didn't drink so much.

'There, come along then, let's prop you up so that you can take a sip of this,' Bessie Murphy encouraged Maeve as she slid an arm under her shoulders and effortlessly raised her into a half-sitting position.

'You go on down and talk to our Maureen then, Patsy, I'll only be another minute or so. Your mam and me are having a little talk, private like.'

Patsy bit her lip. She knew now why Bessie Murphy was there and she didn't like the idea one little bit. She wanted to be the one by her mam's side, holding her hand and comforting her. She wanted to be the one to tell her that she must stop drinking because next to her dad she mattered more than anything in the world. Even Samson wasn't as important to her as her mam.

She loved her dad best because since he'd stopped going to sea she felt so safe and happy. If he ever went away again she didn't know where she would be. Sometimes, though, she found it was hard work trying to please him all the time.

She wondered if it was the same with her mam. Perhaps the drinking bouts were her way of dealing with things when living up to what was expected of her, and keeping her feet on the straight and narrow, became too much for her, Patsy reflected. She wasn't really a bad person, it was just that she couldn't be bothered about day-to-day things, like keeping the house clean and having meals on the table, things that other people considered important. She sighed. And sometimes her mam would lose her temper and lash out for no reason at all.

Her casual way of doing things had started when her dad had been at sea. Without him coming home at regular times she'd lost the habit of keeping to a routine. She simply did what she had to, but only when she felt like it.

When I was a very little girl, Patsy mused, whenever my dad was coming home on shore leave Mam would dress me up in a lovely new dress bought specially. When he arrived home I'd sit on his knee, all clean and pretty with a bright ribbon in my hair and I'd be wearing shiny black shoes and white socks, and feel like a princess.

For the first few days that he was at home it was like a wonderful party and friends and neighbours would pop in at all hours to see him and join them in a drink.

Then, Patsy recalled, just as she was growing used to this tall stranger with the smiling face and deep warm voice he would go back to sea. Her mam would be in tears for a few days and then things would drift back into chaos again.

At night, after she'd been sent to bed, she would lie in the dark thinking back on all the fun and laughter there had been while he'd been at home.

Within a week or two her mam would become moody and miserable. She would start going out at night or bring friends home. So many different ones that Patsy had never been able to remember their names so they were all 'uncles'.

It all seemed so long ago, yet it was only a little over a year since her dad had decided it was time to give up going to sea and had bought Samson. His haulage business moved cargo from ships when they docked at Liverpool to the warehouses along the quayside, or transported loads to the other side of the Mersey to businesses in Wallasey or the Wirral.

Patsy thought back to the old days when sometimes she didn't even bother to wash her face and her hair had been tangled and dark for want of washing. Her dresses had been stained and grubby too and their home had been dirty and smelly a lot of the time.

All that was in the past, she reflected. Since he had hired Billy Grant her dad had more time to notice these things. Their home was probably one of the cleanest in Paradise Place and she had more clothes than Maureen Murphy or Janie Grant so she was always nicely turned out.

Her dad had restored order and routine to their lives. They went to Mass together on Sundays and when the weather was nice they went out as a family on trips to the park or over to New Brighton.

Mrs Murphy's mouth pursed impatiently as Patsy still lingered by her mother's side. 'Go on, then, do as I say,' she reiterated sharply, breaking into Patsy's thoughts. 'Go and talk to Maureen, there's things your mother and me want to say to each other that are not for your ears.'

Resentfully, Patsy did as she was told, but inwardly she was seething at being sent away.

She didn't want to talk to Maureen, not after the things she'd been saying about Billy Grant. She'd always thought of Billy as being like a brother and now Maureen had spoiled it all by talking all soppy about kissing and cuddling with him. Patsy's face flamed just thinking about it.

Chapter Seven

John Callaghan was a very happy and contented man. It was his thirty-sixth birthday and he was more than proud of the fact that since he had stopped going to sea some four years ago he had managed to build up a haulage business as good as many men would have achieved in a lifetime.

Being handed a list of possible customers by Samson's previous owner had been a stroke of good fortune, of course. It was still the nucleus of his business, but he had more than doubled the number of customers that he'd had in those early days and he was still expanding. He'd never advertised; it had all happened by word of mouth. Fair prices and reliability and his attention to detail had all helped.

Billy Grant was another great asset. He'd been quick to learn, he was polite and efficient and always looked clean and smart. He didn't say a great deal, but people liked him. And so did Samson. He and Billy made a splendid team.

Things on the home front had gone well too over the last four years, John reflected. There had been a rough patch with Maeve at first. She'd resented losing her freedom, but he was sure that in her heart she understood his reason for staying ashore and knew it was the right thing to do.

Another couple of years and young Patsy would have been completely uncontrollable or in trouble with boys or the police. It wasn't that Maeve didn't love her, but she seemed to have no idea about how to bring up a child. She'd let Patsy run wild and she'd neglected her.

Now, she was thirteen and she had grown into a little beauty with Maeve's green eyes and red hair, but Patsy's hair was a darker red and a riot of curls. She was taller than her mother, tall and lean like him. She wasn't doing as well at school as he would have liked, but then that wasn't entirely her fault. She did try hard, but she had missed out on so much of her schooling in the early days that it seemed it was impossible for her to catch up.

That did bother him, because he would have liked her to be a teacher or perhaps work in one of the big shipping offices in Liverpool, but he knew she'd have to be pretty bright to do either of those things.

He didn't want her to leave school and become a Nippy in a Lyons tea shop like Billy's sister had done and he didn't want her working in a factory, as so many of the girls from Paradise Place ended up doing. When it was a little closer to her fourteenth birthday he might ask around at some of the firms where he made deliveries to see if there was any opening for her as a receptionist or telephonist or even as a typist. She'd have to start at the bottom, of course, and she would probably have to go to night school in order to train for such work, but it would be a real step up in the world for her.

He'd tried talking to Maeve about it, hoping she would be of the same opinion and have a word with Patsy, but she'd not really agreed with him over Patsy's future.

'With her looks and figure she'd be better off going for something more glamorous like being a dancer. I can see her as an actress. She's got my looks and she's tall so she'd be perfect as a show-girl. That's if she doesn't get married first. I can see the lads will be round her like bees round a honeypot once she stops messing about in the stable with that old nag of yours. Her clothes stink to high heaven most of the time after she's been there feeding it and letting it rub its face against her.'

Maeve still didn't like Samson. 'Great lumbering creature,' she called him and nothing would persuade her to go within six feet of him.

'If he accidentally put one of those great hooves down on you then you'd be crushed to death and if he turned nasty then with those great teeth of his he could bite your arm off before you knew what was happening.'

Nothing Patsy or John told her about how gentle Samson was made any difference. Grudgingly she admitted that he was an asset as far as work was concerned, and that without him there would be no haulage business, but that was as far as her acceptance of Samson ever went.

Maeve could be very stubborn when she wanted to be, John thought resignedly. He'd found that persuading her to conform to what he expected from her as a wife and mother had been hard work.

The trouble was that her friends were not his friends. He liked a drink as much as the next man did and he wasn't averse to a game of darts, but he didn't want to spend every evening doing that. He liked to read, to listen to his wireless set or simply to sit and talk over the day's happenings.

This was never enough for Maeve. She craved excitement and she needed to be laughing and joking with an admiring crowd all around her. He sensed the constant restlessness in her and the frustration she felt most of the time because she could no longer carry on like that.

For all her faults, he still loved her as desperately as he had done when they'd first met in Dublin. She'd been a slip of a thing then, her red-gold hair halfway down her back and her green eyes challenging.

He'd spent his brief shore leave with her and she'd agreed she'd be waiting for him when he returned. She'd kept her promise. Eight months later when his ship had put into Dublin she was on the quayside to greet him, only this time she wasn't the slim, lithe girl he'd kissed goodbye. In fact, if it hadn't been for the flowing red hair and vivid green eyes he wouldn't have recognised her. She was as plump as a suet duff and he suspected the worst even before she flung herself into his arms, tears streaming down her face, and announced that she was expecting his baby.

'I was so afraid you wouldn't be back in time

to marry me before it was born,' she sobbed as she clung to his arm.

He felt as if he had been hit midships by a northeasterly gale. He was only twenty-two; he'd no intention of marrying and settling down for years. He loved his present life too much! Going to sea had been his dream ever since he'd been a young boy. The life was strenuous, but he enjoyed the company of the men he sailed with and the excitement of putting into strange ports and seeing new sights. He'd already sailed halfway round the world, but there were still places he hadn't visited.

Settling down ashore and being saddled with a wife and family was for older men, not for young blokes like him. Anyway, there was a whiff of trouble in the air and they might well be at war within the next few months. Life would be hazardous enough at sea without having responsibilities at home.

Yet he knew his conscience wouldn't let him desert her. If, as she said, it was his child she was carrying then he had to do something about it, but marriage was out of the question. He drew the line at that.

Three weeks later, though, they were married. It had been a quick, simple ceremony. His parents were dead and hers, being strict Catholics, had turned her out the moment they knew she was pregnant.

They'd left Ireland immediately.

'We'll start afresh in Liverpool,' he told her. 'I'll see you settled in somewhere before my next trip.'

'Promise me you won't go until after the baby's born,' she pleaded in a little-girl voice that he hated, but found hard to resist.

One of the men he had known on his last ship had come from Liverpool. The name of the place where he lived, Paradise Place, had always intrigued John Callaghan so they went there first to see if he could recommend anywhere they could find a place to live.

'You've come at just the right time, boyo,' Davy Williams greeted him. 'The wife has decided she doesn't want to stay on yer in Liverpool. Too lonely, see, with me away so much. She wants to move back to Cardiff, to be near her own family. We're in the throes of packing up our things and I was about to hand in the rent book.'

'So how does that help us?'

'I'll put a word in for you with the landlord, boyo. He'll want a new tenant, now won't he?' He winked broadly. 'He's bound to prefer one who comes with a reference for being a good sound payer rather than take on a complete stranger.'

Davy Williams's plan had worked. The day he moved out of Paradise Place John and Maeve moved in. Maeve had been like a little girl playing at house. They'd bought new curtains and rugs and bits and pieces of furniture until his wallet was almost empty.

'I'll have to go back to sea and earn some more if we go on like this,' he'd warned.

Her face had clouded and she'd pouted and clung to him with tears in her eyes. 'You can't leave me all on my own, not now when the baby is due any day.'

He'd promised he would stay until after she'd had the baby and he'd kept his word. When Maeve had gone into labour on a scorching hot August day the full realisation of what was happening, and the enormity of his responsibility, hit him like an avalanche as he went with her to the hospital.

As he paced to and fro outside waiting for news the thought of taking off, getting a ship and disappearing out of her life was so strong that he had to force himself to go back into the hospital.

When they told him he had a baby daughter he wanted to run a mile. He was a man's man, a sailor, and the thought of having a wife and a daughter was too frightening for words.

He was told he could go in and see them both, but his legs felt leaden. He'd faced all sorts of dangers and strange situations both at sea and abroad, but none of them compared to this.

Maeve, her hair fanned out on the pillow like an exotic shawl, looked pale and exhausted after her ordeal. His heart thudded with love as he bent to kiss her. He was glad he hadn't succumbed and taken flight.

'It's a little girl,' she whispered. 'Is that what you wanted?'

John felt perplexed. He hadn't given it any thought until that moment. A baby was a baby, a shawl-wrapped bundle that cried when it was hungry and slept the rest of the time.

Then he looked at the baby in the bassinet at her side and his heart not only thudded, it turned over. The baby was asleep and it looked like a life-sized doll. It had Maeve's heart-shaped face and its head was covered with a soft red down.

As he'd stood there gazing down at the tiny bundle, trying to collect his thoughts, the baby had suddenly moved and stretched. Opening her eyes she had looked straight at him and it was as if an invisible thread was joining them. He felt a huge surge of protective love for the fragile little creature that he had helped to create.

They'd named her Patsy and for the next few weeks life took on an entirely new meaning. Nights as well as days seemed to revolve round the baby.

It was with the greatest reluctance he went back to sea, but they needed the money and it was the only life he knew.

During the time he was ashore they had got to know some of their neighbours in Paradise Place. There were several families with babies almost the same age as Patsy so he knew Maeve would have company and people to call on if she needed help with the baby.

He had managed to get a short run and was home again before Christmas. Maeve was looking fit and well and Patsy, now almost four months old, was a complete joy. He was happy to take her out, or sit and watch her as she lay cooing and gurgling to herself in her cradle. Maeve seemed to be besotted by her so he went back to sea in the New Year with a contented mind.

Patsy was a year old when he next came ashore. An active lively little thing, who, now that she could crawl, didn't stay in one place for more than a few minutes.

Maeve made it quite plain that she found Patsy a handful and was adamant that she didn't want any more children. Because he was so besotted by his little daughter, John promised he'd have one more trip and then he'd come ashore for good.

War intervened. All shore leave was cancelled. Then the ship he was on was torpedoed and after drifting for days in an open boat he was finally washed up off the coast of India. Getting another ship home was impossible. He couldn't even get word through to Maeve. All he could do was hope and pray that she was receiving the allowance he had made over to her so that she had enough money to live on and to feed and clothe Patsy.

He was stranded in India until the war ended. When he finally docked in Liverpool he was almost four years older, Patsy was already at school and Maeve almost a stranger.

If she had missed him she made no mention of it. The soft kittenish manner had been replaced by a brittleness that he found disturbing. She'd even changed the colour of her hair. The fiery red was now a strawberry-blonde shade and she wore far too much make-up.

At first their reunion was strained. It was almost as if she resented him coming home. Then she flung herself into a whirlwind of activity, organising a constant round of parties, and inviting her many friends in. Repeatedly he told her that all he wanted was to be with her and Patsy and to relax; to get used to his freedom and adjust to being back at home again. But Maeve took no notice.

Patsy had accepted him without any questions about his absence. He knew she couldn't possibly remember him because he had been away for the greater part of her young life.

Apart from the shock of red curls and the huge green eyes, she too had changed completely. Instead of being a chubby round-faced baby she was now a skinny little girl with bony knees and sharp elbows. It saddened him that she had such a grubby unkempt air about her and she appeared to be extraordinarily self-sufficient for a five-year-old.

At first whenever he spoke to her she simply hung her head, or looked the other way. She was fiercely independent and didn't like being kissed or cuddled. Whenever he went to pick her up she shrank into herself or shivered violently as if she couldn't bear to be touched. He blamed this on his long absence and although it saddened him he took great care not to force her into accepting him.

It irked him when she called him Uncle instead of Dad, but as he met up with Maeve's wide circle of men friends, and saw the way Patsy called all of them Uncle, he gradually began to understand the situation more clearly.

He didn't know how to handle it or how to rectify it. It wasn't his fault that he hadn't been able to get home. He supposed, if he was honest, he had to admit that it wasn't altogether Maeve's fault either that she had adopted a lifestyle that he didn't like.

None of the other women in Paradise Place had been left on their own for such a long time, not even those whose menfolk had been called up into the army. Their husbands had come home on leave from time to time, as well as writing home regularly. He'd not been able to do any of these things. As far as Maeve was concerned, receiving the allowance he made her regularly was the only sign she had that he was still alive.

As soon as possible he had gone back to sea. He felt he needed space, the wide sea and the open sky to sort his mind out and decide what he was going to do about the future.

Almost as soon as he was out of port he wished he could go back. Leaving Patsy behind tore at his heartstrings. He knew she needed his care and protection and that he was deserting her.

He had the same feeling of guilt when it was time to leave on each of his next home visits. By then, he and Patsy had not only accepted each other, but the bond between them had become increasingly stronger. The moment he saw the mute pleading look in her eyes when he said goodbye, he felt sick with apprehension because he knew the sort of life he was condemning her to while he was away.

Patsy was running wild and it was up to him to do something to change that before it was too late and Patsy ended up in trouble. It was not something he could accomplish in a few weeks, or even months, which was why he had stuck to his determination to take a shore job and be a proper father to Patsy.

In some ways he had been more successful than he could have ever hoped and their special outing tonight to celebrate his birthday was proof of that. He was taking Maeve and Patsy to see a show at the Empire Theatre.

Chapter Eight

Regardless of the fact that she was wearing the new blue-and-white spotted voile dress her dad had bought her specially for their celebration night out, Patsy flung herself down on the pile of straw in the corner of Samson's stable and buried her face in her arms.

Tears that had been threatening for the last hour gushed from her eyes and rolled down her cheeks unchecked.

'So what's up now, kiddo?'

Patsy jumped as if she'd been shot.

She'd thought she was alone in the stable and for a moment as she looked up at the tall broad figure of Billy Grant, who was standing only a few yards away from her, regarding her with concern, she felt angry about the interruption.

'What are you doing here at this time of night, Billy Grant?' she snuffled crossly.

'I dropped by to see how Samson was. His ribs got a bit of a bashing when we were down at the ferry today. The boat pulled away a bit sharp like and he wasn't standing four square and he caught himself against the deck rail. He seems to be OK now though, don't you, old boy?' He reached up and fondled the horse, patting its thick neck affectionately.

Samson blew down his nostrils and whinnied in appreciation as he nuzzled against Billy's shoulder.

'What are you doing in here anyway lolling around on the straw when you're all dressed up to the nines?' Billy asked, staring at Patsy. 'I thought that with it being your dad's thirty-sixth birthday you were supposed to be going to the Harry Lauder Show at the Empire Theatre.

Patsy sniffed back her tears and wiped her eyes with the back of her hand. 'We did go to the Empire.'

'Then why are you so glum? Wasn't Harry Lauder any good?'

'Yeah, he were absolutely great! The whole show was good!'

'Why the tears, then?'

Patsy shrugged. 'It was after the show ended that things began to go wrong. Me dad took us for a fish and chip supper and that's when me mam started griping. She wanted to go to the Grafton afterwards for a bevvy and he said he'd sooner go home. They started arguing and she said he was ruining everything because all her mates were waiting there for them.'

'So he gave in and they came back to the pub?'

'Yeah!'

'And you got sent home because they won't let kids of your age in the Grafton?' Billy said softly.

'That's right,' Patsy snuffled. 'A smashing evening out and then I get sent home to bed on my own. Me dad wanted to come with me and make sure I was orright, mind, but me mam grabbed his arm and said I was big enough to put meself to bed without a nursemaid.'

'And so you are,' Billy grinned. 'Anyway, you've been putting yourself to bed while your mam goes off down to the pub for years, so why are you making such a fuss?'

'No I haven't! Not since me dad's stopped going to sea.'

She stood up and brushed away the straw from her dress, then walked over to fondle Samson.

'Come on, I'll walk back to your place with you,' Billy offered. 'I'll even put you to bed if you like,' he added with a wide grin.

Patsy's face flamed. 'You needn't bother, you cheeky bugger! If I told my dad what you said he'd boot you out,' she added threateningly.

'He couldn't manage without me.' Billy grinned flexing the muscles of one arm.

Patsy's lip curled. ''Course he could!'

'How do you make that out?' Billy demanded.

'I'd help him, wouldn't I!'

'Huh! I'd like to see you lifting bales of cotton up into the cart or trying to handle some of the other heavy loads,' Billy teased.

Patsy tossed her head, making her red curls dance around her ears. 'I could hold Samson's head while me dad loaded up.'

'Oh yeah?' Billy's grin widened.

'I do now when I come out with you on Saturdays and in the school holidays, don't I?'

Billy nodded solemnly. 'I was only teasing you, kiddo, trying to get you to stop crying and give us a smile. I like it when you come out with us.

We have some good times, don't we?'

'Yeah,' Patsy agreed. 'And as soon as I can leave school I'll be coming out with you and me dad all the time.'

'You sure about that?' His blue eyes held hers in a puzzled stare and he looked uneasy.

'Yes, why shouldn't I be?'

'Well . . .' Billy ran a hand through his thick brown hair. 'I think your dad has other ideas about what sort of job you'll be doing.'

Patsy frowned. 'How do you know that?'

'He talks to me a lot when we're working.'

'So? What's he been saying then?'

Billy rubbed his chin doubtfully. 'I'm not sure whether I should be telling you or not.'

'Go on,' she prompted impatiently. 'What's my dad been saying?'

'I think he has plans for you to stay on at school and pass exams so that you can become a teacher or something.'

'Oh, no!' Patsy's eyes clouded. 'He's not serious about that, is he?'

'He sounds serious to me. He seems to be very proud of the fact that you won't have to go and work in a factory like Megan Murphy, or a shop, or even become a Nippy like our Janie.'

'What's wrong with being a Nippy?' Patsy asked in surprise. 'Your Janie seems to love it. She looks real posh in her uniform. She's always going on about what a good time she has at work and about all the interesting people she meets.'

'Don't forget about all the money she earns and the tips she gets,' Billy laughed.

'Well, there you are then.'

'Yeah, but she's only been working a couple of weeks, hasn't she. She mightn't think it's so wonderful once the novelty has worn off. Anyway, it's not what your dad wants for you. He has plans for you to do something much grander.'

'Well, I don't. I want to come out with him and you and Samson.' She looked up at the horse and patted his broad neck.

'Forget it, Patsy. Your dad doesn't want to see you working down at the docks every day with us and I bet your mam wouldn't be very pleased about it either.'

'She'd probably love it if she thought me dad was against it,' Patsy said glumly. 'She likes nothing better than winding him up.'

'She loves winding most people up,' Billy grinned. 'My dad says she's always doing it when she's in the Grafton, especially when she's had a few drinks too many.'

Patsy bit her lip to stop herself saying anything. Billy knew quite a lot about what went on between her and her mother, but she didn't want him or anyone else critising her mam or feeling sorry for her.

Things had been pretty good at home lately and so she preferred to forget about the past when her dad had gone to sea and her mam's moods had swung madly from one extreme to the other.

A shudder went through her as she thought back to when she was small. One minute her mother would be kissing and cuddling her and brushing her hair and dressing her up in fancy frocks. Then she'd be off down the pub and forget all about coming home to give Patsy something to eat or put her to bed.

Even worse had been all the men friends her mam had brought home. Thin men, fat men, little men, big men – she'd lost count of them. She'd hated every one of them.

Patsy sighed. She still couldn't understand why her mam needed to go out to the pub. In the past she'd always said that she only liked going to the pub and bringing the uncles home because she was lonely. Now that her dad was home she couldn't be feeling lonely any more so why couldn't they have a normal sort of life like the other families in Paradise Place?

She was pretty sure that her dad felt the same way about it as she did. In the evenings after a hard day at work all he wanted was for them to sit round the fire and read the *Liverpool Echo* or listen to the wireless.

She'd gone with him to buy the wireless and it had been the most expensive one they had in the shop. The man explained that it was battery powered and that it cost so much because it had an Armstrong TRF superheterodyne receiver to ensure better fidelity. Neither of them had been too sure what that meant, but it sounded impressive.

How exciting it had been when they took it home and connected it up to the accumulator and he had let her be the first to turn the tuning dial! It had been like magic moving from one wavelength to another. Sometimes there was music, at other times people were talking, and in between there was a swishing sound like waves on a far-off shore.

Her mam didn't think very much of it, especially when it began oscillating and sending out high whistling sounds so that for a minute or two they couldn't hear the music or what people were saying. Her dad thought even that was interesting and would sit there moving the dial a fraction one way and then the other until he had fine-tuned it and it was working perfectly again.

Whenever he started doing that, her mam went and put her coat on and announced she was going out to the pub where there were real people to talk to and music as well if old Sammy was there with his fiddle, or Phil with his squeeze-box.

'Well, are you coming, Patsy? Do you want me to walk as far as your door with you or not?'

'I dunno!' Patsy came back to the present with a deep sigh.

'Well, I do. Come on, or you won't be home let alone in bed before your mam and dad get back and then you'll be in trouble.'

'Do you have rows going on all the time in your house?'

Billy shook his head. 'No! What me old man says goes. He's boss and nobody ever argues with him.'

Patsy turned this over in her mind. Joe Grant was about the same age as her dad, a heavily built man with a bald bullet head. He looked more like a boxer than a docker with his prominent nose and a cleft in the centre of his square jaw. She'd heard her mam say that he was aggressive and pig-headed.

Billy must take after his mam, Patsy decided. Elaine Grant was a plump, motherly woman with a fringe of fair hair framing her grey eyes. She had a smile and a cheery greeting for everyone although she always seemed to be bustling about looking after her family.

As well as Billy and his sister Janie there was a younger boy. Freddie was something of a terror at school, but his mother would never believe it and always took his part no matter what mischief he'd been involved in.

'Does your mam ever go to the pub on her own?'

'She never goes to the pub. Me dad wouldn't stand for it. He likes his beer, mind you, but he only goes to the pub on a Saturday night and he never gets plastered.'

'Do you go to the pub, Billy?'

He laughed and shook his head. 'Can't afford to go drinking.'

'Why not? You don't have to give your mam all your wages, do you?'

Again he shook his head. 'I'm saving up for the Harley-Davidson, remember? It will be ages before I can afford to buy it. Don't you tell anyone, mind, not even your dad. Promise?'

Patsy nodded solemnly. 'Am I still the only one who knows your secret, then?'

Billy grinned. 'You and Samson. I tell him all my secrets, the same as you do. He never argues or lets me down. Come on, he needs his sleep even if you don't,' he told her, pushing her towards the door.

As they walked across the cobbled yard and the short distance to her front door in silence, Patsy was suddenly conscious of how tall and broad Billy had become in the last few months. She could see from their shadows that he was half as tall again as she was. He might be kind and gentle like his mam, but he was built like his father, she thought, as she glanced sideways at him. Not for the first time she wished he was her brother instead of someone who only worked for her dad.

'Well, your place is in darkness so either your mam and dad are still both down the boozer celebrating his birthday, or you're so late back that they're home and in bed,' Billy commented.

Patsy pushed her hand through the letterbox and retrieved the doorkey that was hanging there on a piece of string.

'They're probably still at the pub,' she said glumly.

'So do you want me to come in and keep you company until they get home?' Billy asked.

'Gerroff! Do you think I'm daft?'

She would have liked to ask Billy to come in, but she thought it best not to. If her mother was tipsy when they came home there was no knowing what she might say or do and it would be embarrassing for Billy to see her mam like that.

'Tara, see you tomorrow then,' Billy said and began to walk away. He paused and called back over his shoulder, 'By the way, you look smashing in that frock, kiddo. It suits you!'

Patsy felt her cheeks burning. No one had ever paid her a compliment like that before and she didn't know what to say so she pretended not to have heard.

She dashed upstairs and undressed as fast as she could. She wanted to get into bed as quickly as possible so that she would still be able to hear his voice saying 'you look smashing in that frock, kiddo,' as she fell asleep.

Chapter Nine

It was a cold murky Saturday morning in late March. John Callaghan had agreed to collect a heavy consignment from a factory in the Wirral, bring it back to Liverpool and then have it loaded on to the SS *Maybury* before the ship sailed on the mid-morning tide.

'You can come along as well and give a hand with Samson while Billy and me handle the load if you like, Patsy,' her father told her.

'Yes!' Her face lit up. There was nothing she liked better than to sit perched up on the long narrow seat of the cart, wedged in between Billy and her dad. While they loaded or unloaded she would hold Samson's head and talk to him, calming him if there were any sudden noises.

'It's going to be a six o'clock start and there's no hanging around waiting for you if you're not ready, so you'd better get an early night,' he told her.

'You give me a shout when you get up and I'll be out in the stable harnessing Samson before you've got your boots on,' she told him with a wide grin.

'There's no need for you to do that. Billy will be coming in well before six to get Samson fed and ready. You'll still need to be up early, though.

It's a cold night so it will be frosty in the morning. Make sure you've time to get a good breakfast inside you.'

'And you'll both have to get it yourself,' Maeve told them peevishly. 'I'm not getting out of bed to cook anything for you at that ungodly hour.'

Patsy pulled a face, but John signalled to her with a shake of his head to say nothing. They knew that Maeve never got up in the morning to cook them breakfast whether it was John going off for the day around seven or Patsy going to school an hour or so later.

'Wear something warm, remember,' her dad told her. 'It's freezing cold at that time of the morning.'

Their trip went extremely well. They caught the six-fifteen ferryboat and were in Wallasey soon after six-thirty. The river was as still and grey as the sky so the crossing was calm.

It was bitterly cold and damp so John Callaghan insisted that Patsy went inside one of the salons to keep warm. He and Billy took it in turns to shelter in there with her while the other one stayed with Samson.

Half an hour later they were at the factory gates. Their consignment was ready for them and there were two burly men to help load up the wagon.

'With any luck we'll be back in Liverpool docks again before eight o'clock like we promised,' Billy said confidently, as they climbed up on to the cart.

'Don't be too optimistic,' John warned as he picked up the reins. 'There seems to be a mist starting to creep in from the sea.'

He was right. Even before they reached Seacombe ferry the mist had thickened and slowed down their progress. The River Mersey was shrouded in fog and warning klaxons and ships' hooters sounded from all sides.

'We'll miss the eight o'clock sailing at this rate,' John said worriedly.

Fortunately for them there were very few travellers on the ferry at that time of day. One of the crew on the *Royal Daffodil* saw them coming down the slipway and waited for them.

'Too early to have the roads aired,' John joked with a deckhand as the ferryboat pulled alongside the Liverpool landing stage and they started to tie up.

'Yeah, and it's a tidy old load you got there,' the man told him, eyeing the piled-up cart. 'You'll need an extra horse to get that lot up the floating roadway. If you hang on a minute I'll see if they've got one working yet. They don't always start very early on a Saturday.'

Their luck was in. A carthorse far bigger than Samson was brought out from the stables under the floating roadway and hitched up in front of Samson. The deckhand led him forward, leaving Billy and John to make sure that Samson walked directly behind him and that their load remained steady.

Patsy scampered on ahead of them and was breathless by the time she'd reached the top of the steep slope. She liked to be there to watch when they unhitched the carthorse, gave him a slap on the rump and left him to turn round and take himself back down the narrow gangway. It was a routine he did a dozen or more times a day, but she still marvelled at how clever he was to be able to make his own way down the long narrow passage at the side of the floating roadway on his own.

Safely on land, John and Billy checked over the harness before making their way along the dock road to where the SS *Maybury* was waiting.

'Youse lot is bloody late,' the gaffer snarled when they eventually drew up alongside the boat.

He signalled to a couple of dockers to give them a hand to unload and get the cargo aboard. It was an exhausting hour's work for them all, but they managed to meet their deadline with half an hour to spare.

'I think we've earned ourselves a break,' John told Billy and Patsy. 'Come on, there's a café just along the front here with space outside where we can tie Samson up for half an hour. The place is a bit rough, but they do great bacon butties and a decent cuppa char.'

'I put a nosebag on board for Samson. He didn't have time for a full feed before we left,' Billy told them, 'so he'll be glad of the chance to stoke up.'

The bacon butty was every bit as good as her dad had said it would be and although the tea was much too strong for her Patsy didn't complain. She was content to be sitting there in the small, overheated shack with them.

Thinking back to the conversation she'd had with Billy on the night of her father's birthday Patsy wondered how she could break it to her dad that this was the life she wanted. She didn't want to be a teacher or to work in an office where she would have to go all dolled up every day.

She knew it was going to be hard to convince him that she liked wearing thick woollen stockings, a tweed skirt and a heavy coat with a muffler around her neck for extra warmth. She liked riding high on the cart, holding Samson's head while they loaded and unloaded, and, above all, she enjoyed being with her dad and Billy.

They made a wonderful team, she thought as she watched them enjoying their food and tea and talking about the work they would be doing in the coming week.

Not for the first time, she wished Billy was her brother. He could well have been, she thought as she studied them more closely. Now that he was fully grown he was more or less the same size as her dad in height and in a few more years, when he'd finished filling out, he'd probably be much the same size.

There were other similarities too, she noticed. They both had thick hair that they brushed back from their forehead; though Billy's was much fairer than her dad's. They both had blue eyes, but Billy's were a lighter, brighter blue. They had long faces with square chins and looked solid and dependable, and when they smiled there was a warmth and kindness in their expression.

She could have sat there all day, studying them and letting her thoughts wander, but her dad had other ideas.

'Come on,' he ordered, draining his cup and standing up. 'Time we were making a move.'

As they emerged on to the dockside the damp and coldness shrammed them. While they'd been inside the café the sea mist had crept in and now it mingled with the grey city smog so that they could hardly see a few feet in front of them.

Billy made his way over to where Samson was tethered, a bulky grey shape in the yellow half-light. He removed the horse's nosebag, which was now completely empty, and than climbed up on to the wagon.

'You get up there and ride with Billy,' her father told Patsy. 'These cobbles are as slippery as glass with this mist on them and since you can hardly see your hand in front of your face I'm going to lead Samson until we get back on to the main road.'

Their progress was slow as the icy cold, damp fetid mist shrouded them. Samson plodded along snorting uneasily, as if in protest at the strange noises from all around them. Strident warning sirens and blaring klaxons sounded from the ships on the river and these made him shy, prick up his ears and whinny noisily as if in fright.

'Come on, Samson, let's get out of here and up on to the main road,' John Callaghan muttered, urging the horse forward. As they turned into the main stream of traffic, however, the conditions grew even worse. Huge Green Goddess trams loomed up out of nowhere, their bells clanging noisily. As John guided Samson out of their way they found themselves in the path of cars and motorised lorries that came so close that they almost scraped the sides of the cart.

The clamorous blare of one horn spooked Samson and he reared up. The animal threw his head back so hard that although John Callaghan clung to the reins with all his strength, he lost his balance. His feet sliding on the slippery road surface, he fell right in the pathway of an enormous lorry.

From her seat high on the cart Patsy heard the dull impact and her first thought as she peered through the dense smog was that Samson had been hurt. Scrabbling down to the roadway she ran towards the front of the cart.

She stopped in horror. Samson was unharmed but a man's body lay pinned under the rear wheel of the lorry and her head reeled with shock when she realised that it was her dad.

From then on Patsy felt she was living in an ever-increasing nightmare. There was commotion around her as people came running from all directions and for a few minutes there seemed to be utter chaos.

Several policemen arrived on the scene and traffic was brought to a stop as they shouted orders and moved the crowd back. An ambulance was sent for and decisions were made about what to do next.

Patsy felt Billy's arm go round her shoulders and she turned her face away so that she couldn't see what was happening. She didn't want to accept that it was her dad lying there motionless, pinioned beneath the wheels of the lorry.

A crowd of dockers, under police supervision, manhandled the lorry off her father's crushed body moments before the ambulance arrived. Even without medical knowledge it was obvious that there was nothing they could do for John Callaghan. The doctor who had arrived with the ambulance, after a cursory examination, declared him to be dead.

Dry eyed, but numb with grief, Patsy turned to Samson. He stood dejectedly between the shafts, his head down, as though he knew he was partly to blame for the accident.

Patsy fished around in her coat pocket to find the apple she'd brought out to give him and as he munched stoically on it she patted his broad neck. 'It wasn't your fault,' she whispered, burying her face in his mane.

Billy placed a hand consolingly on her arm. 'I'd better get Samson back to his stable,' he told her. 'Are you coming home with me or are you going in the ambulance to the hospital?'

'No!' Patsy shuddered. 'There's not much point, is there?'

'Billy put his arm around her shoulder again. 'Come on then, you ride and I'll walk. Samson is probably feeling nervous so I'll lead him until we're clear of the main streets.'

Shrouded in fog and gloom, Patsy had no clear idea of their journey back to Paradise Place. When Billy pulled into the small yard and opened up the stable doors she remained where she was, frozen in body and mind.

'Come on,' he said as he helped her to the ground. 'You'd better go and tell your mam what's happened.'

The colour drained out of Patsy's face. 'I can't do that on my own,' she protested. 'You'll have to come with me.'

Billy hesitated. 'I ought to see to Samson, he's soaking wet, cold and probably frightened by all that's gone on this morning,' he prevaricated.

'Then I'll stay and help you,' she told him.

Before he could protest she had started unhitching the cart.

'Leave that,' he said, pushing her to one side. 'You put down some dry straw and fill up his feeding trough and see there is fresh water for him.'

Working together they made the horse as comfortable as they could. Patsy picked up the curry-comb ready to start grooming him but Billy took it from her.

'We'll just dry him down and put a blanket over him, then leave him to rest and settle down. I'll clean him up properly later on,' he told her. 'Come on,' he said. He propelled her towards the stable door. 'It's time we faced your mam and let her know what has happened.'

Patsy hung back, shivering and shaking her head. 'I can't do it,' she whispered.

'You've got to,' Billy insisted. 'I've said I'll come with you, if you like.'

She stared at him, her eyes dull with despair and the freckles across the bridge of her nose standing out like a brown band against the chalky whiteness of her face.

'I'm not even sure that it's true,' she shuddered. 'That . . . that thing lying there in the road, not

99

moving, not breathing, that couldn't be my dad!' she exclaimed shrilly.

'Oh, Patsy!' Billy held her close, smoothing down her red curls. 'I know how terrible this is for you, it's been an ordeal for all of us, but you've got to be brave. You must tell your mam what has happened.'

She looked up into his face pleadingly. 'Couldn't you tell her?' she begged.

He shook his head. 'I'll come with you, I'll be there to give her the details if she wants to know them, but you should be the one to tell her,' he said firmly.

Chapter Ten

For Patsy the days that followed the accident were a long, never-ending nightmare. She and Billy had to make statements to the police. There were countless messages of condolence to be acknowledged, from the companies John Callaghan had acted for as carrier. At the same time there were constant visits from neighbours in Paradise Place, all of whom wanted to help.

Bessie Murphy came in several times a day to see if Maeve was all right or if there was anything she could do. Her husband, Daniel, even went across to the stable to see if Billy needed a hand.

Maeve Callaghan was bearing up remarkably well. When Patsy and Billy had first told her what had happened she was too stunned to speak. A short time later the police arrived and Maeve gave way to a fit of uncontrollable weeping.

She was quite hysterical after they left and Patsy was so concerned that she asked Billy to send his little brother Freddie to fetch Father O'Brian and the doctor.

'Let's hope that one or the other of them will be able to pacify her,' she said worriedly.

By the time a reporter and photographer from the *Liverpool Echo* arrived on the doorstep half an hour later Maeve had made a swift recovery. She insisted on renewing her make-up before she saw them in case they wanted to take a picture of her and then proceeded to deliver a voluble account of what had happened and how she felt about it all.

On the day of the funeral, Maeve dressed from head to toe in deepest black and concealed her face with a heavy black veil.

At first Patsy had said she wasn't going to attend the funeral, but Father O'Brian had been shocked and insisted that it was her duty to be there to support her mother in her hour of grief.

Eventually she agreed, but only on condition that the coffin was carried on their cart with their own horse pulling it. She insisted on helping Billy to drape the cart with crape and to groom Samson for the occasion.

They worked in silence until Samson's coat gleamed and his harness glittered. Patsy washed the fringes around his fetlocks and even blackened and polished his hooves so that he looked as though he was entering for some championship prize. Between them they decorated his massive head with black ostrich plumes that dipped and swayed as he plodded majestically towards the church, led by Billy.

It was a magnificent turnout. Patsy and her mother walked directly behind the cart, followed by almost everyone in Paradise Place. Dockers and deckhands who had grown to know and like John Callaghan joined them as they approached the church.

Father O'Brian, resplendent in his full regalia,

conducted a sung Mass which took over an hour. Then the cortège moved to the newly dug grave in the adjoining cemetery. Later the *Liverpool Echo* carried pictures of the impressive funeral procession and another lengthy report of the accident.

After the internment Maeve seemed quite composed though very pale. Throwing back her heavy black veil she invited Father O'Brian and everyone else there to take part in the wake that had been organised in honour of her husband's memory.

Silent and distressed, Patsy accompanied Billy as he took Samson back to the stable. She found immense comfort from being with them and ministering to Samson's needs. Even after they'd fed and watered him she wanted to stay on in the stable, but Billy insisted she must leave and offered to see her home. She looked so sad and unhappy that he longed to take her in his arms and comfort her.

The wake was still in progress. Loud voices, peals of laughter and bursts of song assailed their ears as they reached Patsy's house.

'I can't go in there,' she muttered, turning away. 'How can they be laughing and drinking and carrying on like that when me dad's lying dead in his grave?'

'It's the way some people cope with grief,' Billy told her gently. 'Your dad was a wonderful man, a lot of people were very fond of him and this is their way of celebrating his life and saying goodbye.'

Patsy shook her head, her green eyes burning

with anger. 'Well, it's not mine,' she said stubbornly.

Before Billy knew what was happening she had taken off, running down the street and disappearing into the distance. He made a half-hearted attempt to go after her then decided that perhaps it was better to let her have some time on her own. She needed to come to terms with what had happened, say goodbye to her father and grieve in her own way, he thought sadly.

Although Patsy had appeared to remain dry eyed and stoic ever since the accident, as if determined to remain in control of her feelings, Billy knew how upset she was. To carry on like that and keep all her emotions bottled up inside her would serve no purpose, he reflected. She needed to purge them from her system and convince herself that even though she was missing her dad desperately her life still had to go on.

He thought about all the dreams and plans her father had nurtured for her. What did the future hold for her now, Billy wondered? Or for himself, if it came to that. His future was as much in the balance now as Patsy's was, he thought uneasily.

Tomorrow he would call on Maeve Callaghan and, if she was sober enough to talk about such things, see if he could find out what she intended to do about the haulage business. He had been working for John Callaghan for four years now, counting the time when he'd still been at school. He'd been over the moon when he'd been old enough to leave school and work full time. He'd been so happy that he'd never considered looking for any other job.

John Callaghan had always treated him very fairly and he'd learned a tremendous amount from him. He'd been a splendid boss and they'd made a first-class team. Now the thought that it might all be ending worried him greatly.

What would happen to Samson if Maeve decided to give up the business? He was such a docile and reliable creature that it would be terribly sad if he was sold off to someone who wouldn't care for him like he did, Billy thought. He could hardly sleep that night. He went over and over in his mind the things he could say to Maeve Callaghan to try and persuade her to keep the business going. If she did agree to do so, would he be able to manage all the carting and keeping track of all the accounts and orders? He wasn't used to paperwork. John Callaghan had handled all that side of things himself.

He wouldn't have to let Maeve Callaghan know that, of course, Billy decided. He'd been pretty bright at school so he was confident that he could pick it all up if he had to. Anyway, Patsy would probably be able to help him.

Thinking of her diverted his thoughts into another channel. He wondered what time she'd come home and where she'd gone when she'd run off like that. Her dad had been everything to her so he knew how she must be hurting. Running away wouldn't solve anything, though. He'd have to talk to her tomorrow and try and make her see that.

Next morning, Billy felt at a loss about what to do. He went through the normal routine of feeding and grooming Samson and mucking out the stable, but he knew he ought to go and talk to Maeve before he went down the docks.

He waited until Patsy would have left for school before knocking on their door. He wanted to see Patsy, but he felt it would be more sensible to talk over business matters with Maeve first.

He knocked twice and was about to walk away when Maeve opened the door. She had make-up on and her hair was combed, but she was wearing a bright red silk wrap and he could see she was still in her nightclothes.

'Sorry, Mrs Callaghan, I didn't mean to disturb you' he mumbled awkwardly, 'but I thought I ought to speak to you before I took Samson . . .'

Maeve cut him short. 'Look Billy, if it's business you've come about I'm not interested,' she told him sharply and started to close the door.

'Hold on, there's arrangements John made and I don't know what to do about them.'

'If it's things to be collected and delivered then go ahead and do it,' she snapped. 'Don't bother me about it now. You can come back later and talk to me when you've done them.'

This time the front door was firmly slammed shut with such force that that the frame rattled.

Billy didn't know what to think. Did this mean she was going to carry on the business? Did it mean that he was in charge? If he couldn't cope on his own would she let him hire someone to help?

The questions buzzed round in his head like a swarm of wasps as he hitched Samson up to the cart and set off for the docks.

As he had told Maeve Callaghan, there was work already booked so he went to attend to it. The gaffers were pleased that he had turned up because there had been no time to find anyone else to do the work. They were as co-operative as they could be, making sure he had help with both loading and unloading, but he knew they were making this special concession because of what had happened. In the near future he would have to find someone to help him as there was no way he could manage single-handed.

He made his way back to Paradise Place at the end of the day with these thoughts uppermost in his mind, and puzzled over the best way of explaining it all to Maeve Callaghan.

Perhaps he had done the wrong thing in going to see her when she was on her own. It might after all have been better if Patsy had been there. She would have made sure that her mother listened to the things he had to say. What was more, she would have been able to support him when he explained to her mam that he was going to need help of some kind.

As soon as he had tended to Samson he made his way to the Callaghans' house again. This time Maeve had the door open almost before he could knock. She still wasn't interested in anything he had to say about the business; it was Patsy's absence that she was concerned about.

'Are you saying that she hasn't come home from

school?' Billy asked, twisting his cap uneasily in his hands.

'Come home from school! She hasn't even *been* to school! In fact, I haven't set eyes on her since the funeral yesterday. The last time I saw her she was walking over to the stable with you and that damn horse. Now where is she?'

Billy shook his head. 'I've no idea, Mrs Callaghan. I walked her back to the house after we'd settled Samson, but she took herself off for a walk because she didn't feel she could face all the people that were here.'

'Huh! She couldn't face them! What about me? I had to face them, didn't I? I had to give them all food and drink, and listen to their maudlin conversation until almost midnight. Selfish little madam, clearing off like that and leaving me to look after them.'

Billy looked puzzled. 'So are you saying that Patsy didn't come home at all last night?'

'I've already told you she didn't!' Maeve snapped. 'Can't you listen to what I'm saying? Here I am worried out of my senses and you stand there and keep asking me the same question over and over again.'

Billy shook his head in despair. 'I'm sorry. It's just that I find it hard to take in. Have you any idea where she could be?'

'That's what I'm asking you, isn't it,' Maeve snapped. 'I thought she might have decided to take the day off school. You know, play truant and go out with you and that horse like she's sometimes done in the past.'

'I haven't set eyes on her, not since last night when she said she was going for . . .'

'Oh shut up, you great oaf, you've already told me that a dozen times,' Maeve snarled, her green eyes icy.

Billy was uneasy. He suspected that either Maeve was still under the influence of all the drink she'd had at the wake, or that she had been hitting the bottle again this morning. Either way, it wasn't helping them to find Patsy.

As if reading his thoughts Maeve made a valiant attempt to pull herself together.

'If you want to help, Billy, then the best thing you can do is get out there and look for Patsy,' she told him.

'I'll do that willingly, Mrs Callaghan, but I've no idea where to start. Have you any idea about where she might have gone?'

'If I had I'd be out there myself bringing her back home, wouldn't I,' Maeve told him exasperatedly. 'Surely you must know where she goes, who her friends are and what she gets up to when she's not at school.'

'Have you asked any of her school friends if they know where she might be?'

'Only Maureen Murphy, and she's about as useless as you are. Anyway, according to what Maureen tells me you see more of Patsy than she does.'

'The only time I see Patsy is when she comes to the stable with an apple or carrot for Samson or when she comes out on the cart.'

'Well, there you are then. Try and think of some

place you visit where she might have gone. Just do something! Don't stand there with that hangdog look on your face! Go and find her.'

'Perhaps we should tell the police that she's missing?'

'Call in the scuffers? You must be out of your bleedin' mind,' Maeve told him. 'Don't you think I've got enough on me plate without having the law sniffing around?'

'They might be able to help,' Billy repeated doggedly. 'She might have been in some sort of accident and been taken to hospital, they'd know about that.'

'If she'd been in an accident they'd have been hammering on my door long before now.'

Billy rammed his cap back on his head. 'I've no idea where to start, but I'll take a look around,' he promised.

'Yeah, well you do that. Use your brain if you've got one, but don't go asking the scuffers anything. Understand?'

Chapter Eleven

For several days Billy searched every imaginable spot where he thought Patsy might be. He had hardly any sleep for worrying about whether or not she was safe. At the back of his mind was the fear that she might have done something foolish like stowing away on a boat and he might never see her again.

John Callaghan's funeral had taken place on a Thursday. Billy had spent most of Friday unaware that Patsy was missing, doing the deliveries that John Callaghan had booked in before his accident. When Maeve told him on the Friday night that she hadn't seen sight nor sound of Patsy since the funeral he had spent all day Saturday, and again on Sunday, searching for her, but he could find no trace of Patsy.

On Monday morning Billy was so tired through lack of sleep, and so worried about having to try and cope with running the haulage business single-handed, that he found it difficult to concentrate on what he was doing.

Hitching Samson up to the cart he set off, leaving the tin of sandwiches his mother had made up for his midday snack behind in the stable. By the time he realised what he had done he was already driving along the dock road to make his first pick-up. Going back for them was out of the question.

'You're going to be in luck, Samson, when we get back,' he told the horse. 'They'll be an extra treat for you tonight.'

When he returned that evening, though, the sandwiches had vanished. He looked for the tin but couldn't find it anywhere. Puzzled, he decided he must have forgotten to pick it up from the kitchen table before he'd left home that morning.

His mother was equally baffled. 'Where's your snack tin then?' Elaine Grant asked when she cleared away the evening meal and began making up the family's sandwiches for the next day. 'Have you left it behind in the stable?'

Billy frowned. 'Are you sure I took it with me this morning?'

'Of course you did! I packed you up two bacon butties and a cheese and pickle one. And I put an apple in so that you could give half of it to that old horse,' she added with a smile.

He shook his head in bewilderment. 'I thought I took it with me, but when I got down on to the dock road I couldn't find it so I thought I'd left it in the stable. Then when I got back there I looked high and low and couldn't find it so I thought I must have forgotten to pick it up from the table before I left this morning.'

Billy knew it wasn't like him to be forgetful, particularly where food was concerned and the problem flickered in and out of his mind all evening.

Next morning he made sure his snack was safe

in his coat pocket, then at the last minute, before he left the house, he picked up a couple of extra apples to take along with him. He'd promised Samson a treat so he'd make sure that this time there would definitely be one at the end of the day.

When he left the stable half an hour later Billy placed the apples on a ledge where he could see them so that he wouldn't forget to give them to Samson when they got back.

Working single-handed became harder as the day wore on. The loads seem to become either heavier or more difficult to handle. He found memories were short. Many of the men who had given him a hand freely on the previous Friday now held out their hand for a reward after helping him.

He knew he would have to talk to Maeve Callaghan and try and explain the situation to her, but at the moment, with Patsy missing, he didn't think she'd listen. Anyway, he wasn't sure she would understand what he was on about. Patsy would, because she had been out on the cart with them so many times in the past.

'If ever a horse deserved a reward then you do,' Billy told Samson as he unhitched him and led him into the stable at the end of the day.

He went straight to the ledge where he'd left the apples then frowned when he saw it was empty. He searched in the straw on the ground underneath in case they had fallen off, but there was no sign of them. He couldn't understand it. He was quite sure he'd put them there first thing that morning.

On his way home he called in to see Maeve Callaghan but she still had no news about Patsy.

'Nothing else I can do,' she shrugged. 'If she wants to run off then that's up to her. You go on looking for her if you want to, kiddo, but I've got my own life to get on with.'

Billy had noticed the moment she'd answered the door that she was heavily made up, but he'd thought that was to put a brave face on things. Now, though, he saw that she was dressed up to the nines in a knee-length green silk dress, silk stockings and high-heeled shoes that made her look more like a flapper than a grieving widow.

'You off out somewhere?'

Maeve Callaghan tossed her head indignantly. 'Yes, I am, not that it's any of your bloody business, Billy Grant,' she told him tartly.

He flushed darkly. 'I wasn't meaning to be rude, Mrs Callaghan. It's just that I wanted to talk to you about the business . . .'

'Oh damn the bloody business,' she snapped. 'I'm in too much of a hurry to talk about it now. If you can't manage on your own then pack it in, but don't come here whining to me because you're on the dole. I don't give a damn! Understand.'

'If the business packs up what will you and Patsy live on?'

'That's also none of your business, Billy Grant. Anyway, what's really griping you is the fact that you'll be out of a job when I sell that old nag, which is something I intend to do any day now,' she announced vehemently.

'I'm sure I could keep the haulage business

going if I had some help,' he told her quickly. 'There has to be someone to hold the horse steady while I load up, like Patsy used to do . . .'

'Then you'd better find her, hadn't you,' Maeve said and started to close the door.

Billy walked away, his hands in his trouser pockets, his head down on his chest. He knew he'd handled it badly. He was very much afraid that if Maeve Callaghan could find a buyer then she would sell Samson without a moment's hesitation. And if she did that he'd be on the dole like she said, he thought dejectedly.

'To hear Maeve Callaghan going on you'd think we hadn't even tried to find Patsy,' he told his father despondently as he related what had happened. 'Patsy hasn't been out of my mind for a single second, but I had to see to the deliveries. Let down any of those gaffers who run things at the docks and they've got memories like elephants; that's what John Callaghan used to say.'

'He was right there,' Joe Grant agreed. 'Bloody gaffers! They think they're God Almighty because they have the say-so when it comes to allocating the work. You should hear the way they treat us men.'

'Don't you get started on that Joe,' Elaine Grant murmured. 'You know it only gives you indigestion and pains in your chest when you gets yourself all worked up about things.'

'What do you know about it, woman!' he muttered. 'You haven't got to stand on the dockside in all weathers, herded together in a bunch like cattle, hoping to catch the gaffer's eye so that you'll be amongst those who are picked for the day's work. Sometimes, when it's stinking fish, or that bloody fertiliser muck they call guano, the smell chokes you to death and you wish you hadn't been one of the lucky ones.'

'Well, it does no good at all to let it worry you. Instead of grumbling it would be better if you spent your energies looking for some other kind of work.'

'Like what?' Joe's jaw jutted out. His stocky frame seemed to double in size as he squared his broad shoulders aggressively.

'Perhaps you should go and have a talk with Maeve Callaghan. If our Billy says she's thinking of selling up then perhaps you could take over. You and our Billy working together might manage to make a go of it.'

Joe ran a heavy calloused hand over his bald head.

'Are you out of your bloody mind, woman? Where the hell am I going to get the money to buy a business?'

'Perhaps if you asked you could work alongside our Billy. He said he needs help,' Elaine pointed out.

'Ask a favour of Maeve Callaghan? She wouldn't give you the time of day unless you paid for it. I wouldn't work for her if I were starving, so let's hear no more about it.'

Billy barely listened to them arguing. His mind was concentrating on where Patsy might be. He'd asked everyone who knew her if they'd seen her, but no one had set eyes on her since the day of her dad's funeral. Somewhere at the back of his mind he felt there was a clue as to her whereabouts. Something someone had said, or something that had happened. But what?

It came to him the moment he woke up the next morning. He felt almost lighthearted as he rushed his breakfast and picked up the tin of food his mother had prepared. He would have liked to ask her to double the quantity, but he was afraid his idea might be wrong and he didn't want to raise false hopes about finding Patsy.

When he reached the stable he went through his normal routine of feeding and grooming Samson and hitching him up to the cart. Before he left, he placed his snack tin and his bottle of cold tea on the ledge where he'd left the apples the day before.

All day his thoughts kept wandering back to the stable. He could hardly wait to get back there to see if the food and drink had vanished as he thought they might do.

Although he was on tenterhooks to find out he took his time in the yard unhitching Samson and rubbing him down before leading him into the stable.

Then his eyes went straight to the ledge. The food had gone! Someone had also drunk the tea but returned the empty bottle. As he fed Samson, Billy's ears strained to hear the slightest movement, but there seemed to be none.

He began searching the stable. It wasn't all that big a place but there were nooks and crannies where they stored fresh hay and the bran and other food for the horse as well as a deep recess where they kept spare sacks, tools and tack.

There was no sign of anyone in any of these places. Then, as he was about to leave, Billy sensed a movement on the platform above the bales of straw. When he glanced upwards he thought he could make out a dark shape or bundle that he was sure hadn't been there before.

Lighting the candle lantern that was hanging behind the door for emergencies, Billy clambered up on top of Samson's stall, holding the lantern aloft so that it threw a beam of light into the space above.

As the light shone on Patsy's dirt-streaked white face he almost toppled backwards.

'Patsy! Have you been hiding up there all the time?' he exclaimed, aghast.

When she didn't answer he called up to her angrily: 'I've been searching everywhere for you! I asked everybody I knew if they'd seen you and you've been right here all the time!'

Waving the light at her he said firmly, 'Come on down then, right this minute. Do you hear me?'

When she made no move a shiver of unease crept over him. Was she hurt and unable to move? Then he remembered that she had obviously been able to come down and take the food he'd left on the ledge so he stood firm.

'If you don't come down then I'll come up there and get you,' he told her.

To his relief there was a movement above his head, a flurry of dust and straw and then a pair of legs in thick black stockings appeared over the edge.

'If you jump I'll catch you,' he offered.

She didn't answer, but began climbing on to the top of Samson's stall then down to the ground beside him.

Billy's relief at seeing her safe and sound turned to anger. 'What on earth were you playing at? You must have known your mam would be worried sick and I've spent days looking for you.'

His heart contracted as he saw how dirty and miserable she was. Her red curls were matted with dust and cobwebs, her face was streaked with dirt where she'd been crying and her clothes were crumpled and grubby. She looked hungry and she was shivering with the cold.

He took off his jacket and wrapped it round her shoulders, then awkwardly he took her in his arms and hugged her.

'Have you been here ever since you ran off after the funeral?' he asked her quietly.

Patsy sniffed and nodded.

'But why?'

'I told you I couldn't go back there with all them people singing and carrying on and me mam acting as if it was a party.'

'That was almost a week ago. Where have you been since then?'

'Hiding out here in the stable.'

'So it *was* you who scoffed my sandwiches, and the apple that was meant as a treat for Samson,' Billy grinned.

'I gave him the core,' Patsy said defensively. She gave a forced giggle that ended in a sob. 'He let me have some of his bran!'

Billy shook his head in mock despair. 'Stealing

from the horse, eh? You must have been pretty hungry, kiddo, to do that!'

'I was absolutely starving,' Patsy admitted. 'I still am, if it comes to that.'

'Then you'd better let me walk you home so that you can get out of those mucky clothes and get a square meal inside you.'

Patsy shook her head. 'I'm not ready to do that yet.'

'So what are you going to do then?'

'Stay here while I sorts me head out proper,' she told him.

'How long is that going to take?'

'I don't know,' Patsy shrugged. 'You can help me. You can fetch me some clean clothes and something to eat.'

'How am I going to do that? If I ask your mam for clean clothes for you she'll want to know where you are.'

'Then bring me some of your Janie's clothes,' she pleaded. 'We're about the same size so they'll fit me. Tell her I don't want to borrow her Nippy outfit,' she added with a weak grin. 'Anything will do, it's only a loan for a few days while I work things out.'

Billy stared at her in silence. He didn't want to get involved because he knew once news of it reached Maeve Callaghan's ears she'd blame him for Patsy going missing all this time.

'If I do that will you do something for me?' he asked.

Her green eyes fastened on his face questioningly. 'Like what?'

'Help me over the business.'

'How can I do that?'

'I can't manage on me own. I need someone to work with me, even if it's only to hold Samson's head when I'm loading up. You're good at that.'

Patsy looked doubtful. 'You mean leave school and come out with you every day?'

Billy hadn't thought through the implication of his words but now, eager to keep her interest, he nodded quickly.

'I had something like that in mind,' he told her. 'Your mam isn't interested in the business. She wouldn't even listen when I told her I couldn't manage on my own. All she could talk about was of getting rid of Samson.'

Patsy shook her head sadly. 'She's never liked him, not from the first day me dad brought him home.'

'You're not going to let her do that, are you?' Billy persisted. 'What will you and your mam live on if she does that? What's more, if the business goes then all your dad's hard work will be lost. And I'll be out of a job as well,' he added morosely.

Chapter Twelve

In the months that followed John Callaghan's death life took on a new meaning for Patsy.

In the past she'd had to drag herself out of bed to go to school because her heart wasn't in it. As she sat at a desk listening to things that held no interest for her and which she didn't really want to know about her thoughts had drifted.

Usually they'd been with Samson. She wondered where he and her father were working and if Billy was treating him as well as he should. She knew Billy loved the great dray horse almost as much as she did, but she was also aware that he made him work hard.

It was Billy's job to persuade Samson to pull the heavily loaded cart up steep hills or along slippery cobbled roads down at the docks. It was also left to Billy to see that his nosebag was hitched into place whenever they took a break and that there was water for the horse when puffing and panting had left him parched.

After school each day, instead of going home, or out with Maureen Murphy and Janie Grant, Patsy would rush home, change into old clothes and then go straight to the stable. There was always something she could do to make sure Samson was well looked after. Often she mucked out his stall and spread fresh clean straw in readiness for his return at the end of the working day. If she had time she would scrub out his trough and replenish it with clean water for him to drink.

Billy always welcomed her with a wide friendly grin when he drove into the small yard. While they unhitched Samson from the cart he would tell her about what sort of day they'd had. Then he would leave her to lead Samson into the stable while he cleaned out the cart so that it was ready for work next morning.

Now, all that had changed. Instead of going to school she worked alongside Billy all day. Although she had to be up much earlier she found that was no problem at all. She was eager to be out of bed and start the day each morning. The apathy she'd felt when facing a day at school was a thing of the past.

As the cold, frosty days of April gave way to the milder days of May, with their sudden bursts of sunshine, the whole world was a bright and welcoming place.

The black patch, which had drawn her into its deepest depths after her dad's accident, was relegated to the back of her mind. She still missed him a great deal, and she knew she always would, but after the first few weeks of overwhelming grief she realised that she couldn't sit around thinking about him for ever.

She had Billy to thank for her change of attitude. He had made her see that unless she joined forces with him the business her dad had worked so hard to build up would simply disappear.

Her first battle had been persuading her mam to keep the business going. It hadn't been easy.

'Don't talk such a lorra rubbish, Patsy,' Maeve Callaghan had said derisively when Patsy told her about Billy's idea. 'You're still a kid and Billy Grant's only sixteen so what do either of you know about running a business?'

'We can soon learn!' Patsy told her. 'He knows all the gaffers down the docks that me dad used to do work for and he knows all the foremen and bosses at the factories where me dad collected loads. They all say he was so reliable in the past that they'll give him a chance to go on handling their goods.'

Maeve remained unimpressed. 'The best thing to do is sell out while they still remember who John Callaghan was. If we can find someone who wants to buy the business then that sort of good-will will probably fetch more than that old nag. All he's good for is the knacker's yard, but whoever buys the business can find that out for themselves.'

'There's nothing at all wrong with Samson!' Patsy defended him hotly.

Maeve's mouth curled. 'Then why did he cause the accident that killed your dad, tell me that?'

'The accident wasn't Samson's fault,' Patsy said wearily. She had heard this point of view from her mother over and over and had often tried to explain to her that it wasn't the horse's fault but Maeve would not listen.

'If your dad hadn't been walking along the road because he had to lead the stupid creature then he wouldn't have ended up under that lorry,' Maeve repeated stubbornly.

'It was a real pea-souper of a fog, Mam, I was there, remember! You couldn't see your hand in front of your face, that was why me dad was leading Samson. If he hadn't been doing it then Billy or me would have been leading him.'

'Well, like I say, the sooner we dump him the better,' Maeve insisted doggedly.

'If you sell Samson and get rid of the business then what are we going to live on?' Patsy questioned.

'We'll have the money we get for the horse and business, of course!'

'That won't last very long, especially the way you're living it up these days,' Patsy pointed out.

'Less of your damn cheek!' Maeve scowled. 'I've spent years stuck at home on me own, looking after things for you and your dad. I need company, you should know that.'

'Only too well,' Patsy retorted bitterly. 'I can still remember what it was like when I was a little kid and me dad went to sea.'

The thought of getting rid of Samson greatly distressed Patsy. Without her dad to talk to there was only Samson and Billy. Although Samson couldn't answer she was sure he understood. When she was feeling particularly unhappy he would nuzzle her shoulder, or blow down his nose at her as if to say 'Cheer up, I'm still here for you'.

'If you let me and Billy run the business,' Patsy went on determinedly, 'then you'll have money coming in regularly.'

The argument went on for over a week and Patsy was in despair. There seemed to be no sign of her mother weakening. Then suddenly out of the blue, she gave in.

'Go on, then. I know I'm daft to trust the two of you to run the business, but I'll give you three months to prove you can do it.'

Together all of them had visited the bank and explained to the manager, Mr Mantel – a bald little man with horn-rimmed glasses, who wore a navy blue pinstriped suit and a bright yellow tie – that they were now in charge of the company John Callaghan had set up.

Patsy's heart had sunk into her boots when the first thing Mr Mantel told them was that things would have to be done legally and that because of her age she would not be eligible to run a company or act on behalf of her father. When he insisted that it must all be done in her mother's name she was almost on the point of abandoning the whole idea.

'Couldn't Billy Grant take over my dad's business?' she asked, fighting back her tears of frustration.

Mr Mantel shook his head when he heard that Billy was only sixteen. 'I'm afraid that won't be possible either,' he pronounced gloomily.

Maeve seemed amused by their dilemma. 'You didn't expect the bank to let you two kids run a business, did you? she laughed. She smiled archly at the bank manager. 'Don't worry, Mr Mantel, I'll sign the cheques.'

'You will have to provide proper accounts and

I shall require receipts for every penny you spend,' he told her officiously.

Nevertheless, by the time they left his office, he'd agreed to provide them with banking facilities for the foreseeable future and Patsy could hardly contain her relief.

'Right,' Maeve told them, 'I'll pay you the same wages every week, Billy Grant, for as long as you do a good day's work. You'll have Patsy there to help you, but if I catch you slacking or cheating me in any way then out you go and the business gets sold. Understand?'

Patsy had left school immediately even though she wouldn't be fourteen for another five months. She loved working alongside Billy and they quickly adapted to each other's rhythm and became a perfect team. In next to no time they were working side by side on the docks unloading ships and carting goods to one warehouse or another or transporting them to places in the Wirral, as they'd done when John Callaghan had been in charge.

In the beginning, Patsy tended to Samson while Billy coped with the loads. He was young and strong, but often the load was so heavy or big and cumbersome that she had to give a hand. Often at the end of the day he was almost too tired to talk to her as they drove home.

'I'm knackered, that's all,' he would grin when she asked if he was all right, 'and I bet you are too only you won't admit it.'

She was tired, she had to agree, but she was so keyed up by the excitement of it all that she didn't mind.

After the first couple of weeks, Patsy gave up wearing skirts and now wore trousers. It was not only easier for getting in and out of the cart, but it stopped the wolf-whistles and cat-calls she'd had to put up with when she'd first turned up as Billy's co-worker.

Riding on the cart with her father had been different, because everyone thought she came along for the ride. Actually working alongside Billy, not only holding the horse but even helping him to load up when necessary, gave her a different standing altogether. As far as they were concerned she was fair game for taunting and teasing.

The next thing she'd done was to cut her red curls as short as possible so that from a distance, in her dark blue corduroy trousers, dark donkey jacket and black cloth cap she looked like a boy.

She couldn't disguise her pretty face, hide her big green eyes, or her wide smile. Nor could she help the way when she blushed the peppering of freckles over her nose stood out.

Yet she managed to turn these to her advantage when it came to sounding out the gaffers and foremen over new work. She would do the asking, then Billy would assess what the job would cost and between them they would clinch the deal.

On Saturday evenings and most of Sunday Patsy spent her time writing out the bills-of-lading and the invoices. Billy checked them carefully before putting them into envelopes ready for delivery the next time they were down at the docks, or they would put them in the post to firms in the Wirral.

Patsy hated the way her mam kept them under her thumb yet refused to do anything at all to help, but there was nothing she could do about it. She lived in hope that once her mam grew tired of the novelty of acting like a boss she would leave them to their own devices.

She had to admit that in many ways Maeve played fair. When he realised that he wouldn't be in sole charge Billy began to look for ways of getting a better return for his day's work and insisted that Patsy receive a proper wage. Maeve refused to put his wages up or pay Patsy, but after a lot of arguing she did agree that she would pay them a small commission on all the orders they fulfilled.

This inspired both of them to work even harder. They took on jobs that no other carrier wanted to handle. They were always willing to work away from the Liverpool area, taking loads across on the ferryboat to places in the Wirral where other carriers didn't want to go.

Patsy loved these trips. Leaning on the rail of the ferry, staring out across the Mersey at the great liners docked alongside or being towed out to the Bar in readiness to sail on the next tide, she would let her thoughts wander, wondering where they'd come from and where they were going. Stories her father had told her about his many voyages filled her mind and sometimes she imagined herself on one of them. It was a fantasy that was broken the moment the ferryboat grated alongside the floating roadway at Seacombe or the pier at New Brighton.

It pleased Billy to let her indulge in these flights of fancy. He too had his dreams. He would have liked nothing better than to take them both away to some far-off exotic destination where they could explore new places and see strange sights.

As it was, the nearest they ever came to doing that was when they took a load across to New Brighton. Whenever that happened they always tried to make time to visit the Tower Fairground where there was a menagerie. Patsy loved the great lumbering elephants with their tiny wise eyes. Billy preferred the sleek leopards or the ferocious lions that roared menacingly whenever they went near their cage.

They were such frequent visitors, either conveying or collecting goods or spending a few minutes of relaxation looking at the animals, that they became quite friendly with some of the men who worked there.

It was in this way that Patsy met Bruno Alvarez.

Bruno was in his mid-twenties, a dashing olive-skinned Spaniard with flashing dark eyes and jet black hair. He looked as fit and supple as the lions and tigers he trained.

Whenever they stopped off at the fairground Bruno seemed to appear from nowhere and engage them in conversation. He spoke quite good English, but also used his flashing white smile and expressive hands to convey his message or emphasise his feelings.

Patsy found him intriguing and entertaining, but Billy disliked his bravado.

'Bit of a pansy that Bruno chap,' he commented as he and Patsy made their way back to Seacombe ferry. It was a glorious day in May so they'd decided to take the road which ran alongside the river from New Brighton to Seacombe. He reined Samson to a stop when they reached Egremont Promenade and sat staring moodily out across the Mersey to where the Isle of Man boat was steaming up ready to sail on the next tide.

'You didn't believe any of that guff he was spouting, did you?' he asked, giving Patsy a sideways look.

'You mean about the way he trains the tigers?'

Billy nodded. 'Big cats!' he muttered derisively. 'Who does he think he's kidding? I bet he'll have a couple of whips in his hand when he goes into the cage and a couple of chaps armed with big sticks on the outside ready to rush in to help him if the "big cats" as he calls them start getting nasty.'

'Well, that makes sense to me,' Patsy defended him. 'He knows they can be dangerous so he takes precautions. Anyway –' she pulled a couple of tickets out of her coat pocket and waved them in front of Billy – 'I'll be able to see if you're right or not when I go to the show.'

'Where did you get those from?'

'Bruno gave them to me!'

'You're not going to use them?'

'Of course I am!'

Billy looked taken aback. 'You never go out in the evenings, Patsy. You always say you are too tired.'

Patsy sighed. 'I know, but I think it's time I made an effort. Everyone else seems to have fun at the weekends and all I do is stay at home and catch up with paperwork.'

Billy was silent for several minutes. 'Look, if you're fed up with doing the bills then I'll do them. I used to help your dad with them, but I thought you wanted to do them.'

'I can manage. I'm just saying that it's time I did something else on a Saturday night, that's all.'

Billy felt uneasy. Was Patsy waiting for him to offer to go with her? She had made the point that she had two tickets, but he wasn't sure if that was because Bruno had given her two or whether she had asked for two so that he could go along as well.

Biting his lip he asked hesitantly, 'Do you want me to come with you?'

Patsy shook her head. 'No thanks, Billy. I'm going to ask Maureen Murphy.'

Billy looked shocked. 'You can't come over here on your own on a Saturday night!'

Patsy raised her eyebrows. 'I won't be on my own if Maureen is with me now, will I?' she giggled.

'Two girls coming over here in the evening on their own?'

'Oh, come off it, Billy. You sound like someone's grandmother. What's wrong with Maureen and me coming over here? Safer than some of the places we could go to in Liverpool on a Saturday night. It's not even as if it will be dark when the show finishes, not at this time of the year.'

Chapter Thirteen

Patsy's visit to New Brighton Tower Fairground the following Saturday night was the first of many similar excursions.

She sat enthralled as Bruno appeared, resplendent in a uniform of tight white breeches and a red jacket bound in black silk that was lavishly trimmed with gilt buttons and braiding.

With a sweeping flourish he doffed his white peaked cap, also bound with black silk and heavily encrusted with gold braiding, and then bowed low to the audience before entering the tigers' cage.

There was a tense silence as he proceeded to put the two tigers through their paces. Under his instructions they climbed on to cream and gilt stools, jumped through spangled hoops and performed several other tricks.

When he finally emerged from their cage, which was quickly bolted and barred behind him by the uniformed attendants who had been standing there throughout his performance, there was thunderous applause from the audience.

Patsy and Maureen sat entranced. Patsy would have liked to see it happen all over again, but almost immediately the immense cage was wheeled out of the ring. Five gaudily dressed clowns came rushing into the arena to perform their tumbling act and amuse the audience while the sawdust was raked over ready for the next act. This starred a young girl performing tricks on the back of a white Arab horse.

More exciting acts followed and the entire show lasted for almost two hours. There was an interval halfway through and as people began to make their way to the bar Patsy felt a hand on her shoulder. Wheeling round in her seat, the colour flooded her cheeks as she found Bruno standing there.

'You came to see my act, then?' he smiled. 'Now you tell me you like it, yes?'

'Like it! I thought it was wonderful,' Patsy assured him enthusiastically. Smiling happily she introduced him to Maureen, who giggled self-consciously when he raised her hand to his lips and kissed it.

'Perhaps I take you both for the lemonade, yes?' Bruno suggested. 'Come, this way. We go to the back to be served so that we do not have to wait like all the others.'

The interval was over all too quickly. Bruno had to return to the ring where, he told them, he'd be performing once more, this time with lions.

'You will wait for me after the show has ended so that we take the stroll along the promenade, yes?' he asked, his dark eyes fixed on Patsy.

She hesitated, remembering the pile of invoices and bills-of-lading that she had pushed to one side in order to come out for the evening, then shook her head. 'I'd like to do that, but it would make me very late getting home and then I would be in trouble,' she told him.

'Then you will come again. This time not to see the show but to see me, Bruno. Yes?'

'Billy and me will probably be over this way again with the cart some time next week.'

'No, no, you do not understand!' He gesticulated. 'It is not you and Billy I want to see, Patsy. It is only you! I want to see you again when you are like a young lady, not in the trousers and cap. Understand?'

Patsy understood quite well and she was excited and flattered by his attentions. It made her feel very nervous to be chatted up by someone quite a bit older than her; older than Billy, even. Apart from Billy, no boy, or young man, had ever showed any interest in her before, and she wasn't too sure what to say or do.

She was glad that Maureen was with her, even if Maureen simply stood there as if she'd been struck dumb and was grinning like a Cheshire cat.

'On Sunday there is no work at the fairground, except to see to the animals. People come and walk about and look at the animals in their cages, but there is no performance. You understand?'

Patsy felt her colour rising. 'Yes,' she mumbled.

'Tomorrow is Sunday. So you also come? Not to see the animals but to walk about with me. Yes?'

Patsy shook her head. 'I can't. Not this Sunday,' she said emphatically.

Bruno looked disheartened and his smile vanished. 'You no want to walk about with Bruno?'

'Yes, of course I do,' Patsy told him quickly. 'I

can't come tomorrow, though. Next Sunday perhaps.'

'Yes? That is good. Next Sunday then!'

His good humour restored, he took Maureen's hand and kissed it then he held Patsy by the shoulders and kissed her on both cheeks before showing them back to their seats and disappearing behind the scenes.

Patsy sat through the rest of the show in a daze. She was still trying to get her breath back, and come down to earth, when they boarded the ferryboat.

'You're a dark horse, Patsy Callaghan,' Maureen told her as they found themselves seats in one of the salons. 'Fancy you knowing a chap like that!'

'He's nice, isn't he?'

'Nice! He's absolutely gorgeous! He can kiss my hand any time – or my cheek,' she added, giving Patsy a sly sideways glance.

Patsy looked embarrassed. 'That's just foreigners' way of doing things,' she mumbled.

'So where does he come from then?'

Patsy shrugged. 'I don't know. Billy thinks it may be Spain.'

'So Billy knows him as well, does he?'

'We both know him, we've talked to him a few times when we've been making deliveries to the fairground,' Patsy explained.

'So that's what he meant by "trousers and cap"? If he's only seen you before when you're working then it's a wonder he recognised you when you're dressed as a normal person.'

'Wearing skirts and stockings is not very practical

when you have to climb up and down into a cart all the time and help heave loads around,' Patsy pointed out.

'You could get a normal job and let Billy Grant run the haulage business on his own,' Maureen said.

Patsy shook her head. 'No, it's not the sort of thing that you can run single-handed.'

'He could always find a young lad to help him, couldn't he?'

Patsy bit her lip. 'You don't understand, Maureen. It was my dad's business and I'm doing it for him. He worked so hard to make a go of it and I don't want to see it go under.'

'You like Billy Grant, don't you! You always have. Even as a kid you used to go straight to the stable to see him even before you went home at night. Are you still soft on him?'

'We're business partners, nothing else,' Patsy said sharply.

'Oh yes! I bet he doesn't know that you were coming over here tonight to see Bruno.'

'Well, that's where you're wrong. If you must know, Billy was there when Bruno gave me the tickets.'

'So why didn't he come with you, then?'

'For the simple reason that I thought you would enjoy it. Now, though,' Patsy said crossly, 'since you've done nothing but criticise and pick on me, I think I'd have been better off asking Billy Grant after all.'

Maureen wasn't to be silenced so easily. She was far too curious about Patsy's relationship with Bruno.

'Does your mam know you've come over here tonight?'

Patsy shrugged. 'I said I was going out with you, I didn't bother to say where we were going. She's probably not interested. Too pleased to know I'd be out of the house all evening.'

'You mean so that she can entertain one of her men friends.'

The minute the words were out, Maureen clamped a hand over her mouth. 'Sorry, kiddo, I shouldn't have said that,' she muttered contritely.

'It's what everyone else in Paradise Place says, isn't it?' replied Patsy.

Maureen looked uncomfortable. 'Well, she has been carrying on a bit for someone who has not long lost her husband. She's down the Grafton most evenings, or so my dad says.'

'Well, he should know. He goes there every night himself.'

'He drops in for a quick pint on his way home, that's all,' Maureen bristled.

'And no one thinks any the worse of him for doing that,' Patsy said wryly, 'but when a woman goes in for a drink she's suddenly thought of as a Judy or labelled a Mary-Ellen.'

'I never said that,' Maureen declared hotly.

'You didn't need to, luv, I can hear it in your voice.'

'It's not what I meant at all,' Maureen muttered sulkily.

'Look,' Patsy said, and put her hand on Maureen's arm, 'I don't give a damn about what me mam does or about what people say about her.

She likes plenty of company and a good time, that's all there is to it.'

'She likes flirting and all! She's always chatting up the men in the Grafton and letting them buy her drinks.'

'It's her life. As I said, it's nothing to do with me, kiddo.'

'So are you going to tell your mam that you're meeting Bruno next week?' Maureen asked.

Patsy looked thoughtful. 'I don't know. I mightn't go, anyway.' She grinned. 'I've got all week to make up my mind now, haven't I?'

'He's a real hunk, you'd be daft to turn him down,' Maureen declared. She shot a sideways glance at Patsy, 'If you don't want to meet him next Sunday then I will.'

Maureen was right about Bruno and Patsy knew it. She had no intention of turning down his invitation.

She lived in a private dream all the following week. Her absent-mindedness irritated Billy. He suspected it was because she was thinking of Bruno and he felt uneasy about it. Bruno was not only a foreigner, but he was so good looking that in Billy's estimation he was bound to be a flirt. He was convinced that if Patsy wasn't careful Bruno would break her heart and he didn't want to see that happen.

A further point – which Billy wouldn't admit, even to himself – was the fact that he was jealous of Bruno.

He'd had strong feelings for Patsy ever since she had first started coming out on the cart with him and her dad. He knew that in those days she thought of him as the brother she didn't have. As they both grew older he'd secretly hoped that her feelings for him would change and, if he was lucky, become more like those he had for her.

After John Callaghan had died, and Billy had managed to persuade Patsy to leave school and help him full time to run the business, his hopes about their relationship had soared, but he'd decided it wasn't the right time to speak out.

Now he wished he had said something. If he'd told her then that he loved her and that he wanted to marry her, but that he was willing to wait until she was older, she probably wouldn't have given Bruno Alvarez a second glance.

If he said anything to her now about his feelings for her she would think he was only doing it because she had shown an interest in Bruno and had confided in him that she was going across to New Brighton to see him.

Billy felt that the problem was insurmountable. Worrying about what the outcome might be made him tetchy and short tempered. Patsy didn't seem to notice. All week she remained in her dazed trance. The most he could hope for was that her meeting on Sunday with Bruno would turn out to be a flop.

As far as Patsy was concerned it was one of the most wonderful occasions in her life. It was a glorious June afternoon and she was able to wear her favourite dress. She'd bought new white gloves to wear with it and with her curls brushed until they glowed she knew she looked completely different from her hoydenish appearance when she was working alongside Billy.

As the ferryboat sailed up the Mersey towards New Brighton she went up on to the top deck, leaned on the rail and pretended she was travelling to an exciting foreign land.

Bruno was waiting for her by the pier and she saw his dark eyes gleam in appreciation as he took in her changed appearance.

He looked different too in his grey flannel trousers, white shirt and dark blazer. Not nearly so flamboyant as he did when he was working, but still devastatingly handsome with his shock of black hair and olive skin.

He kissed her on both cheeks, making her blush, then tucked her hand into the crook of his arm and suggested a stroll along the Ham and Egg Parade.

'It is a very strange name for a road,' he smiled.

'It's called that because at all the boarding houses along there they serve ham and eggs to their customers,' Patsy explained laughingly.

'Ham and eggs is a speciality? You must come to Spain where I will serve you not one speciality but many. We have wonderful fish, delicious fruits and so many different wines that you would not be able to taste them all if you lived to be a hundred.'

'It all sounds marvellous!'

'There is more, much more!' He waved his hands expressively. 'It is a warm sunny land, full of exotic flowers and wine and so everyone is relaxed and happy because they sit in the sun, drink wine and enjoy themselves.'

'So why did you leave such a wonderful place and come to England?'

'I come here to work,' Bruno explained. 'I want to earn the big money, make myself wealthy, but soon I go back to my home in Almeria.'

'So you are missing Spain and feeling lonely?'

Bruno shrugged expressively. 'In my country people are friendly and oh so welcoming. Here they do not talk to each other very much and they do not like strangers.'

'That's because we like to be introduced to people before we talk to them,' Patsy explained.

Bruno looked puzzled. 'But you talk to me before we were introduced,' he pointed out.

'I know, but look at the number of times we have seen each other when I've been with Billy delivering things to the fairground,' Patsy said. 'That makes a difference.'

'Billy?' Bruno frowned. 'Ah yes! Is this Billy your brother or your boss?'

Patsy laughed. 'Neither! We are partners. We work together.'

Bruno looked puzzled. 'You mean you are married to him?'

'No, nothing like that,' Patsy smiled. 'We're business partners. It's a long story . . .'

'Come.' He took her arm and led her down a slipway on to the shore. 'We will sit here on the warm sand and tell each other all about ourselves. Later, I will take you and buy you the afternoon tea. Yes?'

When Patsy had finished telling him all about herself, and how she and Billy came to be working together, Bruno talked again about the wonders of Spain.

'One day, you will come with me to my home in Almeria and see these things for yourself,' he promised. 'You will meet all my family and all my many friends. You they will love.'

Patsy sighed blissfully as he took one of her hands and cradled it between his. His strong brown fingers stroked her bare arm, sending delicious shivers right through her.

'So you will come there with me?' he persisted.

Patsy smiled but looked doubtful. 'You make it all sound so wonderful, but I have to work too. I have a living to earn the same as you do, Bruno, so it may be a long time before I can ever visit Almeria.'

Chapter Fourteen

During the long warm summer Sunday afternoons of July and August, Patsy became more and more enchanted by Bruno Alvarez and even admitted to herself that she was crazily in love with him.

He was utterly charming, very romantic, and so handsome that he swept her off her feet. He was her first boyfriend and quickly became her lover.

His seduction routine was so smooth that it had happened almost before Patsy realised what a tremendous step she had taken.

During their first two or three meetings Bruno was so restrained that Patsy felt completely at ease in his company. As they walked along the prom-enade, stopping occasionally to watch a liner being guided by fussy little tugs down the Mersey and into dock at Liverpool, he talked enthusias-tically about Almeria.

'Soon I return there when the season here is over. You will come with me, yes?'

His dark eyes were pleading, but his voice was so teasing that she assumed he was joking and happily went along with the game she thought he was playing.

So often she wasn't sure when he was being serious and when he was fooling around. Except when he kissed her. That was serious. When he held her close to his hard muscular body and his firm lips covered hers, the excitement was almost unbearable and she felt her entire being quiver with emotion.

So much so that she felt embarrassed when he suddenly sometimes stopped as they walked along the promenade and took her in his arms and kissed her.

'You mustn't do that,' she protested, pushing him away.

His dark brows drew together in a puzzled frown. 'Why is that, my pretty Patsy? What is it that I do wrong?'

'Someone who knows me might see us kissing.'

'This would matter to you? You have feelings for me the same as I have for you so what is so wrong with my kissing you?'

She wasn't sure why she was so concerned about being seen. There was no one, except perhaps Billy Grant, who really cared what she did or what happened to her. Her mother was too engrossed in her own life. And she could hardly pass judgement, since the things she got up to were far worse.

The only other person who might care was Maureen Murphy and that was only because she was infatuated with Bruno herself even though she had only met him once. She was always trying to persuade Patsy to take her along with her when she went to meet Bruno on Sundays.

'Two's company, three's a crowd,' Patsy would remind her.

'I know that, but surely Bruno must have a friend. We could make up a foursome. Be safer,' she added with a snide smile.

'I'm safe enough as I am,' Patsy told her. 'Bruno is a perfect gentleman,' she added, her colour rising.

Yet she knew that wasn't quite true. On the previous Sunday he had persuaded her that, since it was such a hot day, instead of strolling along the promenade, which was very crowded, they should walk further on towards Leasowe Light-house and find somewhere quiet where they could sit and watch the river.

They'd found a secluded spot in a convenient dip in the sandhills and made themselves comfort-able. For the first few minutes they merely kissed and cuddled, but then Bruno became more amorous.

At first Patsy made no objection when he lay down full length in the sandy hollow and pulled her down alongside him.

Lulled by the sun's warmth, the gentle murmur of Bruno's voice and the sensual caressing from his long-fingered hands as they stroked the contours of her face and buried themselves in her red curls, she felt totally relaxed, even to the point of closing her eyes. She barely noticed when his hands began to slide gently down her throat and he started fondling the curves of her breasts.

Finding she made no resistance, Bruno became bolder. He unfastened the bodice of her dress, gently cupping each of her breasts in turn, murmuring his pleasure at their warm softness.

Then he buried his dark head between them and delicately circled each of her nipples with his tongue.

'You are so beautiful, Patsy, your skin is so smooth and creamy,' he murmured huskily.

Before Patsy was fully aware of what was happening he had lifted the skirt of her cotton dress and his hands were moving over her bare flesh in an intimate manner that sent warning shudders through her.

Shocked by what was happening she tried to remonstrate with him and to push his hands away, but it was too late. Bruno became even more passionate. His mouth covered hers, silencing her protests. Her own blood pulsed wildly, thundering in her ears; waves of excitement coursed through her as his hands glided over her body exploring every secret crevice.

She knew it was wrong, but now she wanted Bruno every bit as much as he needed her. Her surge of happiness was overpowering, and she found the sensations he was extracting from her body exquisite.

With a blissful sigh she stopped resisting and gave herself up entirely to his touch, revelling in the magic of the moment. It was her very first experience of physical love and there was a moment of sharp, agonising pain when Bruno entered her, but this only heightened her desire.

When he was finally sated and moved away from her she was too overcome by the enormity of what had happened between them to move a muscle.

The true magnitude of their actions didn't register in her mind until much later. That night, lying in bed, letting the memories of the day glide through her mind before she fell asleep, the realisation of what she had done seared her mind, making sleep impossible. Supposing she became pregnant? She pushed the thought away. Refused even to contemplate such a thing.

She wondered what Bruno would think of her for giving in to him so easily. He'd said nothing about marrying her so would he lose interest in her now? Or would he take it as a sign that she really was in love with him and wanted to go back to Almeria with him when his season was finished in New Brighton?

The thought of leaving Liverpool, even for somewhere so wonderful, threw her mind into turmoil.

Yet what had she to lose? she asked herself. Here she was working a long, gruelling day yet most of the money she and Billy earned went to her mother, who spent it on buying drinks for herself and all and sundry at the Grafton.

In Almeria, if what Bruno had said was true, life would be so much more easygoing. The sun shone, the people laughed, danced, drank wine and gossiped with each other. It sounded heavenly and if she was there with Bruno what more could she ask from life?

The only thing that worried her was – could she bear to be parted from Samson? He was so much more than a mere dray horse. She shared her secrets with him; he listened to all her troubles.

He was there for her from first thing in the morning and her loyal companion all day. He was her link with her dad.

Billy would look after Samson, of course, because Billy loved him almost as much as she did, but leaving him behind would create a gap in her life that nothing else could fill.

She'd be leaving Billy behind as well, she reminded herself. They'd been such close friends all these years that it would be a wrench to do that, too. Billy had been the one who had comforted her and stood by her when her dad had died. It had been Billy who had made her see sense and realise that unless she pulled herself together then the business her dad had worked so hard to build up would simply disappear.

Billy was such a wonderful friend. Her feelings for him were so deep and so strong that she sometimes forgot that they merely worked side by side and that there was no other tie between them.

Over the next few days these thoughts surged around in her mind. She was so much on edge that once or twice Billy wondered if she was ill or sickening for something. Usually she sang or chattered to him as they loaded up, or while they drove from the docks to wherever they were taking their load; now she was silent and lost in thought.

He suspected that it was to do with Bruno Alvarez, but was afraid to ask in case she told him something he didn't want to hear.

He had warned her against Bruno often enough. He had seen trouble brewing from the very first time they'd met him. Maureen Murphy had told him all about what went on the night the two of them had gone over to see the show at New Brighton Tower Fairground. She'd let slip the fact that Bruno had asked Patsy to go out with him again the following Sunday.

Since then, Billy knew, she had been going over regularly on a Sunday to see Bruno. All dressed up in her best, her red curls brushed until they gleamed, and wearing white shoes and gloves, she looked so totally different from the boyish young girl in shabby trousers and jacket who accompanied him on his rounds each day.

When he'd mentioned it casually one Monday morning she'd bitten his head off.

'What's it to you, Billy Grant, what I do on a Sunday?' she'd snapped, her face colouring up so much that her freckles stood out like a myriad of dots.

'I was only asking because I wondered if you had a nice time?' he told her mildly.

'We walked along the prom and then we had tea in one of the cafés in Victoria Road and then I got on the boat and came home.' She tossed her head defiantly. 'Is there anything else you want to know?'

He shrugged. 'Not unless there's anything else you want to tell me.'

'Well there isn't!'

'Oh, come on! It's not like you to be secretive. Where does he come from? Is it Italy, France . . .'

'He comes from Almeria in Spain. He told me all about where he lives and it sounds wonderful. It's hot and sunny and there's flowers everywhere and the people sit around drinking wine when they're not singing and dancing. Will that do?'

Although he tried to make light of the matter, inwardly Billy felt churned up. He was so worried about her. He didn't trust Bruno for a second. He was much too old for her, flash, far too handsome and he was a foreigner. What was more, Billy was pretty certain that like most showmen Bruno didn't stay anywhere longer than one season.

He had painted Patsy a romantic picture of his home in Almeria, but Billy guessed that his life there was little better than the one he had in Liverpool. It might be sunny for most of the year, but it was probably just as hard to make a living there. Otherwise why had he bothered to come to England?

Billy wished he'd had the sense to tell Patsy how he felt about her before she had met this Spaniard. Normally they worked in such harmony, but now there was a distinct sense of unease between them. He'd held back because he'd thought she needed time to get over her dad's death and also because he felt she was still too young for a serious relationship. He'd been afraid that if he spoke out it might cause an uncomfortable rift between them.

He couldn't bear the thought of losing her, but he knew he had to tread carefully if he was going to manage to convince her that her future lay here in Liverpool with him.

If her relationship with her mother had been on a sounder footing he would have asked Maeve for advice, or persuaded her to speak to Patsy on his behalf. As it was, to do that would only make matters worse.

Maeve was no help to either of them. She did nothing to help them with the business. In fact, these days she was rarely sober and she was getting a very bad reputation. Other women in Paradise Place objected strongly to the way she flirted with their husbands and Billy was sure that sooner or later she would end up in a fight.

She had never been the motherly type. Even after John Callaghan had given up the sea she had only made a pretence of caring for her home and looking after him and Patsy. Now, although she still lived under the same roof as her mother, Patsy fended for herself so there was nothing really to hold her in Liverpool.

Except him. And, of course, Samson. She loved the old horse dearly – but when it came to a choice between Samson and Bruno Alvarez, Billy had a sick feeling in his gut that it would be Bruno who would win.

Unless he could do something to change the situation. If only he could turn the tables, win her back, show her that he cared even more for her than Bruno did. Show her that he could offer her a good life here in her own familiar surroundings.

His offer to take her to the pictures startled her.

'Whatever do you want to do that for?' she asked him, her eyes wide with surprise.

'I thought you might like a night out at the Trocadero,' he told her.

She hesitated and he could see she was torn between accepting his offer and being disloyal to Bruno if she went out with him.

When she shook her head his spirits fell. He could see it was going to take more than an invite to the pictures to persuade her to go out with him. Most girls would have been won over with a bunch of flowers or a box of chocolates, but Billy felt that it would cheapen his cause to offer such inducements after she'd turned down going to the pictures.

Over the next few weeks the atmosphere between them became more and more tense. Billy sensed that once again her thoughts weren't with him or the job, but with Bruno.

In that he was right. Ever since that warm Sunday in July, Bruno's passion had dominated their meetings. Patsy wasn't sure if she was pleased about this or not. When she was in his arms and he was making love to her everything else was forgotten. But when she got home and relived what had taken place, guilt and apprehension overwhelmed her.

Several times she thought she ought to make him stop. That sort of behaviour should wait until after they were married, or at least engaged.

When she tried to remonstrate and explain this to Bruno he looked bewildered.

'One day we are to be married so why is it wrong?'

'Because we are both Catholics and we both know it is a sin,' she told him primly.

Bruno took her face between his hands and gently kissed her. 'When the season ends, which will be very soon now, you will come back to

Almeria with me. There my family will make you welcome and I will make you my bride.'

'If I'm going to be married then I want it to be here in this country, in Liverpool,' Patsy told him firmly.

He shrugged eloquently. 'We do whatever it is that you wish,' he agreed smoothly. 'You like to have your mother and friends there to see you marry? Yes? Then we will do it in the church here and then we will marry again when we get to Almeria so that all my own family can rejoice in the sight of my beautiful bride.'

Patsy had thought that wonderfully romantic. So much so that she insisted that on the following Tuesday he must come and meet her mother.

Chapter Fifteen

Today, 27 August 1929, was going to be the most exciting day in her life, Patsy Callaghan decided. Not only was it her sixteenth birthday, which was a landmark in itself, but she had promised Bruno that today he would meet her mother.

Patsy could think of nothing else. Dressed in a man's blue cotton shirt and denim trousers, her curls hidden under a cloth cap, she whistled cheerfully as she worked with Billy on the dockside, loading up a consignment of cotton bales.

The midday sun was at its hottest and it blazed overhead, turning the dull Mersey into a sheet of glittering gold. They'd been hard at work since seven o'clock that morning and they were feeling exhausted and ready for a break.

'Let's get this load across on the ferry and then we'll find a shady spot somewhere over on the other side to eat our snack,' Billy suggested.

'Suits me,' Patsy agreed, running her arm across her brow to wipe away the sweat and grime.

'Not much of a way to spend your birthday, is it?' Billy grinned. 'If you're not planning to do anything special tonight then what about the two of us going out somewhere?'

Patsy bit down on her lower lip, her eyes full

of dismay. 'Sorry, Billy, I've already got something planned,' she said.

'Yer mam's throwing a big party for you, is she?' he asked sardonically.

'Well, no, not exactly . . .' She hesitated wondering whether to go on. The idea of asking Maureen Murphy and Billy if they'd like to come to her home for a meal after they finished work had been in her mind all week. The idea of taking Bruno to meet her mam tonight had seemed such a good one when she'd issued the invitation on Sunday, but ever since then she'd wondered if it was going to work out.

She'd never actually confided in her mam about how serious going out with Bruno had become. She'd mentioned his name once or twice, and said he came from Spain, but that was all. She'd never mentioned that they were planning to be married. Or told her that she intended going back to Spain with him when the New Brighton season ended.

Now that the moment of introduction was almost upon her she was beginning to have butterflies in case her mam didn't like him, or in case when he arrived at the house her mam was in one of her moods and was downright rude to him.

Patsy knew she should have told her mam a great deal more about Bruno, but there had never been the opportunity to do so. Lately her mam had been going out earlier in the evening and staying out so late that Patsy was in bed and asleep long before she came home.

Her mam was never up in the morning before Patsy left for work and on the few occasions when they were both at home in the early evening her mam was usually in a foul mood. Lately her moods had been as bad as anything Patsy remembered from the past when she'd been a little kid and her dad had been away at sea.

With Billy and Maureen there at least she could count on Bruno having someone to talk to, and they'd help smooth out any awkward moments. The only problem was over inviting them. Would Billy come? Maureen would jump at the chance, but if Billy wasn't there then Bruno would have three women for company and he might find that a bit overwhelming.

She knew Billy didn't approve of her going out with Bruno and wondered if he already suspected that she might be thinking of going back to Spain with Bruno at the end of the season.

The feeling of excited anticipation she'd had earlier in the day slowly began to evaporate. By late afternoon, when they were on their last delivery, she felt so miserable that she was on the verge of tears. The only way to recapture that feeling of well-being, she told herself, was to ensure that things did go well. To do that she must enlist Billy's help.

'Billy, you know you suggested that the two of us should go out tonight?'

'Yes, it's still on,' he told her eagerly, his blue eyes lighting up. 'Where do you want to go? Anywhere at all. A meal, then pictures or the theatre? Or we could go dancing. It's entirely up to you.'

'Well, it's a bit difficult. I had planned to do

something else, but I would love it if you came along as well.'

Billy's jaw jutted out. 'You mean a trip to New Brighton to watch the famous animal trainer at work, I suppose,' he said grimly.

'No, not that, although it does involve Bruno,' Patsy said quickly.

'Go on.' Billy kept his eyes fixed on the road ahead, his lips clamped together in an uncompromising line.

'Well,' she hesitated, unable to find the right words. She didn't want to hurt Billy's feelings in any way because she so desperately needed his support.

'If it's going to be a mystery tour then don't spoil it by telling me,' Billy said sarcastically.

Patsy paused. Then in a rush she said, 'I've invited Bruno over to meet my mam and I'd like you to be there as well.'

'What the bloody hell for?'

It was so unusual for Billy to swear, at least in front of her, that Patsy was struck dumb. He sounded so aggressive that she wondered if she was doing the wrong thing after all in even mentioning it to him. It was too late now: she'd told him enough for him to know what was happening and so she'd have to go through with it.

'I thought it was time they met and my sixteenth birthday seemed to be as good a time as any,' she said lamely. 'I thought of asking Maureen Murphy as well,' she added.

'Why should you want him to meet your mam?'

He shot a sideways glance at her. 'Unless, of course, you're serious about him?'

'We . . . we're friends, you know that.'

Billy was silent for a minute. 'Closer than us?'

'It . . . it's a different sort of friendship,' she said defensively, her colour rising.

His good-looking face hardened. 'Like that, is it! Then I don't see why you need me to come along. Your mam won't want me there for a start.'

'Rubbish, she thinks the world of you,' she grinned. 'She's always saying what a wonderful chap you are and how hard you work.'

'And how much money I hand over to her so that she can afford to go to the pub every night and drink herself silly and treat all her men friends?' he commented bitterly.

'Billy!' Patsy had never heard him talk like this before and it shocked her.

'Well, it's true and you know it is.'

She did know, but she didn't want to talk about it and antagonise him further, not at this moment when she needed his help so much.

'So will you come?'

He shook his head, his jaw set stubbornly, refusing to answer or meet her pleading look.

'Please, Billy. You are my dearest friend.'

'Friend perhaps, but not your lover!'

Her cheeks burned. She'd hoped he didn't suspect quite how serious matters were between her and Bruno. Now that he did there seemed to be nothing else to hide so she might as well come out into the open with him about her future plans.

Billy went chalk white when she said that she

was planning to marry Bruno when the season ended in New Brighton and that she was going back to Spain with him.

'Are you really serious about that? Do you know the sort of life you will be living over there?'

'Oh yes!' she smiled brightly. 'Bruno has told me all about Almeria. The people are friendly. A land of song and sunshine, he called it.'

'You don't want to believe a word of that,' Billy sneered. 'Almeria may be in southern Spain where the weather is warmer than here, but what he hasn't told you is that a lot of the people are so poor that they live in caves on the outskirts of the town.'

Patsy stared at him in annoyance. 'And what makes you think that is where Bruno's home is?' she demanded.

'I'd stake my life on it. That's where the Spanish gypsies live and anyone can see that he is a gypsy.'

'You're only saying that to turn me against him,' Patsy said angrily. 'Of course he's not a gypsy. For one thing, if he was a gypsy, like you say, he wouldn't be able to speak such good English.'

Billy shook his head. 'He probably would, because the kids are taught to beg from the time they can crawl. They hang out round all the ports asking for money and they can do it in half a dozen languages. They're also thieves and vagabonds so you want to watch out.'

'I don't believe a word of that!' Patsy railed.

Billy shrugged. 'It was your dad who told me about what all these foreign places were like. I bet he told you the same things only you've forgotten them.'

'You're making it up to try and make me change my mind about Bruno,' she declared, her eyes filling with tears. 'I don't care what you think or say, though, I'm in love with Bruno and I'm going to marry him.'

'You're going to give up on our business arrangement then as well, are you?' Billy asked in disbelief.

'You'll find someone else to help you on the cart. It will mean you'll be the boss and they'll have to do what you tell them,' she added with a grin, trying to lighten the atmosphere.

Billy was not in the least amused. He stared straight ahead, as though he hadn't heard. Then he gave vent to his feelings by slapping the reins down hard on Samson's back, startling the tired horse into a fast trot. Patsy waited anxiously for him to speak. When he did she was completely taken aback.

'Yeah, kiddo, I'll come to your bash,' he told her in a light-hearted tone. 'Don't bother to ask Maureen, though. Me and your mam, you and Bruno. A cosy little foursome, eh? So what are you planning on doing to make it a special evening?'

'I . . . I don't know, I hadn't thought that far ahead,' Patsy admitted.

'I tell you what, why don't we have a fish and chip supper, that'll give Bruno something to remember about Liverpool. Afterwards, to please your mam, we'll all go to the Grafton and get pissed out of our minds. How does that sound to you?'

'Well . . .' Patsy felt uneasy. It wasn't like Billy to want to go to a pub.

He slapped the reins again. 'That's it! Settled! I'll come round to your place as soon as I've scrubbed the muck off and put on a clean shirt. How about that? What time is Bruno going to be there?'

'He's coming across on the seven o'clock boat. He's arranged to take the night off.'

'Really?' Billy gave a long low whistle. 'He must think it's going to be a pretty special occasion then.'

When they reached the stable Billy insisted that he would see to Samson. 'I may as well get used to doing it all on my own again,' he remarked as he unhitched the cart and led the horse towards the stable.

'Billy, please!' Patsy ran after him, grabbing at his arm. 'Don't be like that,' she begged.

He shook her away. 'You dash off home and get yourself ready. It's bound to take you a lot longer than it will me because you'll want to be all dressed up to the nines,' he told her.

'By the way,' he called after her, 'it might be a good idea to warn your mam in advance that this is a very special occasion and that before the evening is out she's going to hear some very special news!'

'I thought I would wait and introduce Bruno to her first before telling her about our plans,' Patsy said uneasily.

Billy shrugged. 'It's up to you, kiddo, how you handle things. It's your big night. I'm just coming along to referee the show!'

Maeve Callaghan looked rather amused when

Patsy told her about the arrangements she'd made for the evening.

'So my little girl is growing up at last and Bruno Alvarez is a serious boyfriend, is he? You never told me that before.'

'I have mentioned his name. I told you he was someone I met when we were delivering in New Brighton. He works at the fairground. He trains the lions and tigers.'

Maeve's light green eyes widened in surprise. 'So is he a foreigner? He must be with a name like that.'

'Well he comes from Spain, but he's very nice. I know you'll like him.'

Maeve raised her eyebrows questioningly. 'So why ask Billy Grant along as well? Are you playing them off against each other, or trying to make Billy jealous?'

'Of course I'm not trying to make Billy jealous, why on earth would I want to do that! I thought it would be better if there were four of us rather than just three,' she explained lamely.

'And we are all going for a fish and chip supper and then to the Grafton for a bevvy?'

'Does that sound all right to you, Mam?' Patsy asked anxiously.

'Suits me. It's your birthday after all so we'll do whatever you like.'

'So you will come out with us, Mam?

'Yeah. If that's what you want,' Maeve agreed. 'Hope you're going to get yourself dolled up a bit,' she added, surveying Patsy's working clothes with distaste.

Patsy grinned. 'Of course I will! It's my birth-day.'

'So what's so special about this foreign fella? Training animals is not much of a job. What does Billy think of him?'

Patsy shrugged. 'I think he likes him all right,' she murmured evasively.

'I bet he doesn't!' Maeve laughed gleefully. 'You *are* playing them both along aren't you, my girl? Take after me, don't you?'

Patsy opened her mouth to deny what her mam had said, then she shut it without saying a word. Never, never would she turn to drink and men like her mother had done ever since her dad had gone to sea.

Now was not the time to criticise her mother or to make comments about anything that might start an argument. She desperately wanted her mother to accept Bruno, to like him, and to approve of them marrying.

She'd warn Bruno not to say anything about her going back to Spain with him. She'd break that piece of news to her mam later.

Chapter Sixteen

Patsy found it hard to believe how well her mam and Bruno were hitting it off. She had been afraid that her mam might be critical, unfriendly even. She had been so nervous that she had left it to Billy to introduce them to each other.

To her relief, Maeve had greeted Bruno warmly. In fact, she'd turned on the charm to such an extent that he seemed to be absolutely captivated by her.

As the evening progressed, Patsy didn't know whether she should be pleased or worried at the obvious attraction between them. If Billy hadn't been there she would have felt even more upset, because the two of them practically ignored her.

She should have suspected that her mother was going to go all out to grab his attention when she spent ages getting ready to go out. Maeve had taken a great deal of trouble with her hair and make-up and put on a low-cut black dress that showed her ample cleavage and skimmed her curves like a second skin.

Alongside her mother, even though she was wearing her pretty blue and white spotted voile dress, Patsy felt extremely gauche. She was a good six inches taller than Maeve and because of her very active life her beanpole figure had none of the ripe sexual allure of her mam's plump curves.

She was not able to compete with Maeve when it came to being seductive either. Whatever subject was being discussed, Maeve made full use of her carefully made-up green eyes and her wide smile. Bruno hardly seemed to notice that there was anyone else there.

'Patsy has told me such a lot about you, of course, Bruno,' Maeve gushed, 'but I had no idea that my little girl had such a fascinating friend.' She gave a sexy little shudder. 'I couldn't believe my ears when she told me you were a lion tamer!'

'Lions and tigers,' he told her, smiling.

'Really! How thrilling.' Her green eyes locked with his smouldering dark ones. 'I'd love to see you in action,' she murmured.

'You must come over to New Brighton very soon,' he told her. 'I cannot understand why Patsy hasn't brought you over to see my show before now.'

'Probably because she is so anxious to keep you all to herself,' Maeve smiled.

She focused her whole attention on him, letting shivers of fear and murmurs of awe escape her lips as he told her about his act in great detail.

'And you trained to do all this in your own home country?' she breathed in feigned amazement.

'From a very young age. My father, he too is a lion tamer, one of the most famous in Spain,' Bruno boasted.

'Spain?' Maeve's eyes widened. 'You come from Spain! So romantic!' she said enviously. 'It's a country I've always dreamed of visiting.'

Patsy subsided into bewildered silence as Bruno extolled the wonders of Almeria. She'd heard it all before but watching the simulated rapture on her mother's face was unbearable.

Billy tried to help by introducing other topics but each time he did so Maeve ignored him and turned her attention back to Bruno, fluttering her eyelashes at him, and inviting him to tell her more about himself.

Bruno was so eager to comply that Patsy felt utterly miserable. She could see that Bruno was dazzled by her mam. She felt so miserable and defeated that she wanted to creep away into a corner and hide. In Bruno's eyes her mam must appear self-confident, glamorous and sexy whereas she was simply a gawky naïve kid.

Patsy could only hope that when they moved on to the Grafton, and her mam was surrounded by her own friends, Bruno would realise how much older than him her mam was and that he didn't stand a chance with her.

By the end of the evening he would see her for what she was, a middle-aged woman who liked to drink more than was good for her, Patsy thought uncharitably.

Billy was almost as concerned as Patsy was about the immediate affinity between Maeve and Bruno. He had heard his father constantly criticising Maeve's behaviour in the pub because of the way she flirted and upset a lot of the wives in Paradise Place, but he'd not taken very much notice.

His mother had always been more charitable.

'It's because Maeve Callaghan is lonely that she behaves like that,' Elaine Grant would argue. 'She's a very attractive woman, you have to admit that, with her reddish hair and green eyes and that lovely peaches and creamy skin. She's so very young to lose her husband, she's still only in her thirties, remember.'

'If she's all that wonderful then why doesn't she find herself another husband, not try and pinch some other woman's man,' Joe Grant would argue.

Looking at what was going on between Bruno and Maeve, Billy felt a shiver run down his spine. He saw trouble ahead and he was sure there was going to be heartache for Patsy.

He knew he should be feeling glad, because with any luck it would push Patsy into his arms for consolation, but that was not the way he wanted things to be. He loved Patsy intensely and he wanted her to return his love as a spontaneous gesture not as a last resort.

As the evening progressed, Patsy became more and more despondent. She had always been worried about introducing Bruno to her mam, but for very different reasons. She had thought she might be scornful about her having a boyfriend, might make sneering remarks that would make Bruno uncomfortable, or simply consider the whole thing ridiculous and ignore Bruno.

She had never expected that Maeve would be so attracted to him that she would monopolise him. She watched with growing concern and heaviness of heart as she saw her mam's hand resting possessively on Bruno's sleeve as she emphasised some point in their conversation. Then, as she saw the way her green eyes exchanged unspoken signals with his dark ones, almost as if there was no one else in the room, Patsy looked away in despair, feeling betrayed.

She wanted to go home; to creep into bed and hide her head under the covers and give way to the pent-up tears that had been threatening all evening. She felt an overwhelming sense of relief when the landlord called 'Last orders, please!' She edged close to Bruno, intending to take his arm the moment 'Time' was called so that they could at least spend a few minutes together before he had to dash for the last ferryboat.

Maeve forestalled her by inviting him back for a nightcap before he returned to New Brighton.

'If he does that then he'll miss the last boat,' Patsy said quickly.

'Does that matter?'

Maeve addressed the question to Bruno, her eyes challenging.

He gave an exaggerated shrug. 'I do not have to give a performance until it is the evening. I have only to feed the animals in the morning.'

'So you could stay here overnight and catch an early morning boat?'

'I could, if I had somewhere to sleep,' he agreed.

Maeve gave him a teasing smile. 'Then it's all settled. You stay.'

Patsy could take no more. Turning away, ignoring the hand Billy stretched out to stop her, she made for the door. Tears streaming down her face she headed back to Paradise Place, to the sanctity of the stable.

There, in the darkness, she leaned against Samson's sturdy body and let the tears roll unchecked down her cheeks.

Samson snorted and nuzzled his warm nose into her shoulder as if trying to comfort her.

Running away was only giving in to her mam's wiles, she told herself despondently. Drying her eyes, she made her way home. When she reached her front door she could hear her mam's tipsy laughter.

Determined not to let her mother win Bruno away from her, Patsy straightened her shoulders. She was adamant that she would hold on to him.

They both looked surprised when she walked in.

'I thought you'd come home and gone to bed,' Maeve exclaimed. 'Where have you been? Surely it hasn't taken you all this time to say good-night to Billy?'

'No, and I have no idea where Billy is,' Patsy said sharply. 'He was still in the pub with you when I left. I went over to the stable to make sure that Samson was all right.'

'Samson!' Her mother raised her eyebrows and smiled at Bruno. 'Patsy worries more about that old horse than she does about me,' she pouted. 'He comes first with her every time. He's your secret love, isn't he, darling?'

'He's reliable and can be trusted,' Patsy retorted and then wished she hadn't risen to her mother's taunt because her reply sounded so childish.

'Are you staying here tonight, then?' she asked, turning to Bruno.

'Of course he is! The last boat's gone, what do you want him to do – swim across the Mersey?' Maeve simpered.

'So where is Bruno going to sleep?' Patsy asked bluntly.

Maeve winked at Bruno. 'On the sofa, of course. Why don't you go and find a couple of blankets for him.'

By the time Patsy returned with the blankets Maeve was pouring out a glass of brandy for herself and Bruno.

'A nightcap before we turn in,' Maeve said, waving the bottle unsteadily in the air. 'I know you don't want one because you don't approve of drinking, do you my darling. I'm sure she will change when she's more grown up,' she added as she smirked at Bruno.

Patsy plumped the blankets down on a chair and turned away. She could hardly speak for the lump in her throat.

This was her sixteenth birthday and it was to have been a very special occasion. She felt so miserable that it should end like this. She had intended to tell her mam that she and Bruno were planning to be married and that she was returning to Spain with him. Now all those wonderful plans seem to be in jeopardy, she thought bleakly.

She stared across the living room at Bruno and wasn't even sure she knew him. The way he had behaved tonight, he was not at all like the man she had thought him to be.

When he returned her stare his look was so uninterested that she felt she was being tossed away like an empty cigarette packet.

'Good-night,' she whispered.

Neither Bruno nor her mother answered. Long after she'd undressed and crept into bed she could hear their voices. She dozed fitfully, plunged into nightmarish dreams that left her soaked in perspiration.

When the first streaks of daylight appeared at the side of her curtains she crawled out of bed and pulled on her working clothes. There was no point in lying there tormenting herself. She'd go over to the stable. Samson hadn't been groomed the night before and if she did it now it might take her mind off her problems.

She crept down the stairs as quietly as she could, hoping that Bruno was still sleeping on the sofa. The living room door was ajar and as she peeped in, to make sure she hadn't wakened him, her breath caught in her throat. The sofa was empty. The blankets she had brought down for him were still on the chair where she had dumped them.

She stood in the doorway as if frozen. He could have decided to go back to New Brighton after all, she told herself over and over. She knew it wasn't true. It couldn't be true because the last boat had sailed and there was no other way he could get there.

He probably went down to the landing stage and waited in one of the shelters for the early morning mail boat, she told herself. She knew that wasn't true either.

Holding her breath she crept back up the stairs and stood for several minutes outside her mother's bedroom wanting to look inside but afraid to do so.

Finally, unable to stand the suspense any longer, she turned the handle and opened the door.

What she saw confirmed her worst fears. Her mam and Bruno were both there, in bed together. The bedclothes were in wild disarray and Maeve's bare arm was across Bruno's bare chest.

Covering her mouth with her hand to suppress the bile that was rising in her throat, Patsy rushed headlong down the stairs and out into Paradise Place.

The dark stable was warm and comforting with its familiar smells of hay and horse. Samson neighed a greeting, nuzzling her hand in search of an apple or a piece of carrot.

'Sorry, my old luv,' she whispered. 'I haven't anything special for you.'

She reached for the curry-comb and brush. The rhythmic movement as she groomed him was soothing. Gradually her rapid breathing slowed to normal and her reeling senses calmed. As she talked out loud to Samson about her troubles and problems the bitterness within her slowly dissolved.

Then she froze, not daring to even breathe. There was someone else in the stable.

'Who's there?' she gasped, her heart thundering. To overcome her fear she clung tightly to Samson's mane.

'It's all right, Patsy, it's only me!'

Her breath escaped in an explosion of relief as Billy emerged from the shadows.

'I didn't hear you come in,' she gulped.

'You left the door unfastened. What are you doing here at this hour of the morning?'

'I couldn't sleep.'

He grinned. 'Me neither. Too much to drink last night, I suppose. I'm not used to it, but since it was your birthday bash . . .' He stopped as Patsy broke into sobs.

'Hey, hey! What's the matter? What have I said?' He gathered her into his arms, stroking her red curls as if she was a small child.

'Nothing, nothing,' she sobbed, burying her face in his shoulder.

'Didn't things go well when you got home?' he asked softly. 'Come on, tell me what's gone wrong,' he persisted gently as her tears flowed faster and her body was convulsed by sobs. 'I heard some of what you were saying to Samson so I know there's been trouble. Is it to do with Bruno . . . and your mam?'

Patsy tried to answer, but her voice was too choked and her sobs too violent.

Billy drew her down on to the stack of clean straw waiting to be put down in Samson's stall. He held her close, stroking her hair and kissing the top of her head.

'Oh, Billy, I'm so miserable,' she whispered, resting her tear-streaked face against his. 'How could she do this, my own mother?'

Billy felt afraid to answer. He held her tighter, gently pushing her curls back from her damp brow, stroking her face to try and soothe away her misery. After a while, she began to relax. Her sobs diminished to the occasional shoulder-heaving gulp as she nestled close to him, finding comfort from being in his arms.

For Billy it was utter torment. He loved her so deeply that he hated seeing her so upset. He wanted to tell her how he felt about her, but he was afraid to do so in case it made her pull away from him.

Of their own accord his hands began to move over her body, stroking her shoulders and then moving down her back. When she made no objection he grew bolder. He slipped one hand up under her jumper, his fingers closing over her small firm breasts, gently caressing first one and then the other.

As she turned her face towards his and their lips met he threw all caution to the wind. He returned her kisses with fervour and all the time his hands were exploring her body more and more intimately. He pulled away the cotton trousers to stroke the firm contours of her hips and thighs.

Their passion mounted. He knew he couldn't stop now, whatever the outcome might be. He remembered all the dreams he had harboured of them making love together and in a breathtaking moment of passion he slid into her body. The blissful sense of happiness felt awesome, greater than anything he had ever experienced in his life before.

He would have lain there for ever, cradling Patsy in his arms, but she broke the spell by pulling away from him and sitting bolt upright, a look of astonishment and dismay on her tear-stained face.

'Billy, what have we done?' she gasped.

He reached out, wanting to pull her back into his arms again, but she struggled free. Her face flushed with shame, she avoided his eyes as she moved away from him and straightened her clothes as quickly as she could.

He wanted to assure her that they'd done nothing wrong, that he loved her with all his heart, but it was as if there was an impenetrable wall between them that stopped either of them saying a word.

In icy silence they went about preparing for the day's work ahead. As they set off for the docks, sitting stiffly side by side on the cart, Billy wondered if they were ever going to speak to each other again.

Chapter Seventeen

As September's balmy days turned into October's wet and chilly ones, and the holiday season at New Brighton came to an end, Patsy waited expectantly for Bruno to tell her what he was planning to do and say when he intended to return to Spain.

When the funfair closed down in mid-September the animals had been moved to their winter quarters so she couldn't understand why he had said nothing to her about their date of departure.

She tried talking to him about it, explaining that there was so much she had to do before she could leave home. She had to let Billy know in good time so that he could make arrangements for someone to help him in the business. She had to break the news to her mother that she would be leaving home, she pointed out.

No matter what she said, Bruno remained evasive. Even when she asked if he had changed his mind about returning to Spain he merely shrugged his shoulders, flashed the brilliant smile that could churn her stomach with desire, and told her, 'Later, later, we will talk later, my little flower. Not so much of the hurry. Stop worrying your pretty little head, I will tell you all in good time.'

Patsy did worry, though. She worried about the

way Bruno refused to talk about their future and she worried even more about their relationship. He was still as eager as ever to make love the moment they met on Sundays, but there was a restlessness between them afterwards that concerned her.

She tried to blame it on their surroundings. Inclement weather made it impossible for them to find privacy amongst the sandhills at Leasowe and deserted beach huts, or promenade shelters, didn't have the same ambience.

Recently, even when they made love she sensed that all was not as it had been between them in their first rapturous encounters.

There were so many guilty secrets in her heart. They had never mentioned the night he had spent at her house in Paradise Place. She had never told him that she knew he had slept with her mam and he had never spoken Maeve's name. He never asked after her, never referred to that night at all, and this gave Patsy a vague, disquieting feeling. It was as if it had never happened.

Patsy wished she could adopt the same attitude, but she found that was impossible. When they met on a Sunday, the moment they started to make love, uppermost in her mind was the memory of opening the bedroom door and seeing Bruno lying there in bed with her mam. And what had happened the following morning in Samson's stable also haunted her.

She knew she shouldn't have let Billy make love to her, but she had been half out of her mind with distress at what she had witnessed. The feel of his arms around her had been so comforting, and he had been so gentle that she had been carried away.

It had been a very precious moment, one she couldn't forget. His lovemaking didn't set her afire like Bruno's did, but she had found it wonderfully consoling. It had temporarily alleviated her sadness and shock. Afterwards, although she had felt both guilty and astonished, she had felt at peace. Only Billy and his deep love for her had carried her through the next few days.

When she saw Bruno the following Sunday, she had expected him to confess that he had slept with her mother, and when he did she fully intended to tell him that it was all over between them.

Bruno hadn't said a word. She'd felt terribly confused because no matter how hard she'd tried she'd not been able to broach the matter. She even began to wonder if it *had* all been a figment of her imagination, a result of the wine she'd had to drink.

She blamed the wine for what had happened between her and Billy too. It had been difficult trying to explain that to Billy: he was so convinced that it meant as much to her as it did to him.

She'd tried to let him down gently, but he'd been so angry, so insistent.

'It had nothing to do with having a glass or two of wine. You feel the same way about me as I do about you, only with working together we've always been so close that you haven't realised it,' he protested.

'I think the world of you, Billy, but that's not the same as being in love.'

179

'And do you think the world of Bruno Alvarez?' he asked, mimicking her voice.

Patsy's eyes softened. 'What I feel for him is different to anything I've ever felt before,' she said dreamily.

'Because he's a foreigner and has a glamorous job,' Billy scoffed. 'You let him treat you like dirt and it makes me sick!'

'I do not!' Her voice rose in indignation.

'You can still claim you think the world of him even after he's slept with your mam?'

Patsy's face reddened. 'He'd had too much to drink as well; he didn't know what he was doing.'

'If you believe that then you'll believe anything,' Billy said scornfully.

'It's what happened! It was all a terrible mistake.'

'Like letting me make love to you was a mistake,' Billy said bitterly.

Patsy reached out and touched his arm. 'I'm sorry, Billy. I never intended to hurt you.'

'I wonder sometimes if you have any feelings at all, Patsy Callaghan,' Billy muttered. 'You know that Bruno spent the night in your mam's bed, but you carry on seeing him as though nothing has happened.'

'I've told you, I love him! If I make a fuss about it I might lose him, and I couldn't bear for that to happen,' Patsy said quietly.

Her mam hadn't mentioned Bruno's name either. She'd not even asked about him the next day. Patsy felt sure that when she'd left the house the following Sunday to go to New Brighton her mam must have known she was going to meet Bruno, yet she never said a word.

There hadn't even been any coolness between her and her mam, Patsy reflected. Life had continued in its usual pattern. Her mam was still in bed when she left for work in the morning, and she was usually getting herself ready to go out when she returned at night.

Her mam didn't say where she was going, but then she never did. Patsy assumed she was off to the Grafton as usual, but she never checked. She was usually in bed before her mam came home so she never knew if she brought anyone back with her or not.

It was as if they were all living in tight little worlds of their own, Patsy thought sadly. Following their one and only lovemaking Billy seemed to be harbouring the dream that she was in love with him, but she was more convinced than ever that it was Bruno she loved.

Unable to stand the uncertainty about the future any longer, Patsy finally asked Bruno outright when they were leaving for Spain. As usual he tried to evade the issue, but she refused to accept his negative shrug.

'I need to know, Bruno. Are we going at the end of this month or next? I keep telling you I have to make plans, tell my mother and Billy.'

Bruno took her face between his hands, forcing her to meet his dark gaze. 'I want to take you home very much, yes? I need to earn the money though to keep you happy, yes? I can earn so much more better money here in England than in my own country so I must stay here a little longer, yes? You understand?'

Patsy pulled herself free, her green eyes blazing. 'That is not what you said back in the summer. You said you would be going home when the season ended,' she reminded him.

'Yes, but my mind I have changed. It is very much for the best.'

'Whose best? Yours or mine?'

'You have the red hair temper showing,' he told her, amusement in his voice.

'I am not in a temper, I am concerned because it means changing all my plans.'

Bruno snapped his long brown fingers. 'Your plans, pouf! It is *my* plans that count. I need to earn good money so I stay.'

'The season is over, there's no work for you here in New Brighton now so how can you be earning money?'

'It will start again soon. It is all arranged. There is to be a circus here at Christmas and my animals will perform. I will be well paid for my act. You will see.'

Nothing she said made any difference so Patsy resigned herself to the fact that all her plans had fallen through. Things had changed between her and Bruno too.

She was sure it had something to do with her mother. The fact that Maeve never mentioned Bruno's name, never asked after him, didn't even enquire if she was still seeing him, filled Patsy with suspicion.

Added to that, Maeve's whole attitude had

changed. She still went out every night but she was dressing with more care. She seemed quieter, more content, less given to moods. Often she was singing to herself, or smiling as if contemplating pleasant secret thoughts. Patsy wondered if she was in love and it troubled her because she had an underlying suspicion that the man involved might be Bruno.

Patsy made vague excuses to Billy about her own change of plans, but he was so relieved and happy to find that she wouldn't be going to Spain that he didn't probe.

Although he'd accepted her pronouncement that what they had done the morning after her sixteenth birthday had been wrong he'd seemed to regard her in an entirely new light ever since then. Whenever the opportunity arose he would take her hand and give it an affectionate squeeze. Often while they were grooming Samson he would kiss the nape of her neck or her cheek.

The look of love in his eyes unnerved her. Things were not going as smoothly as she would have wished between herself and Bruno, but she didn't want to build up Billy's hopes again.

Patsy also had another reason for concern. She'd suspected it for the last couple of months, but now, as the year drew to a close, she knew for certain. She was pregnant.

At first she had thought she'd imagined it, or miscalculated her dates because she was in such a state of uncertainty about her future. She tried to think back; to calculate as accurately as she could, but it only increased her confusion. She waited another month, and then another, and then she knew it was as she feared. She was also aware that she had left it far too late to get rid of it.

She wanted to tell her mother, but Maeve was so secretive, so immersed in her own life that she could never find the right time to do so.

She knew there was only one other person she could confide in and she couldn't bring herself to talk to him about it. She was afraid that if she told Billy she was expecting he might jump to the conclusion that the baby was his.

The only thing she could do, she realised, was to conceal her condition. With it being winter Billy was hardly likely to notice if she wore baggy trousers and even baggier jumpers. He would think it was the sloppy clothes she was wearing to keep warm that made her look fat and shape-less.

She avoided Maureen Murphy and Billy's sister Janie. With their sharp eyes they might guess her secret.

The only time when she was worried that her changing shape might be noticed was on Sundays when she went over to New Brighton to see Bruno. Sometimes she wished he would comment that she was getting fat so that she could tell him why, but either he didn't notice or said nothing even if he did.

Even that no longer became a problem when, towards the end of November, he told her he was going to Blackpool for three weeks to train his group of animals in readiness for the Christmas circus.

'Why do you have to go there?' she asked resentfully. 'If the circus is to be here in New Brighton then why not train the animals here?'

He shrugged. 'Blackpool is the home for the big cats in winter. It is more convenient to do it there.'

Patsy felt bereft. The first Sunday he was away she mooned about the place wondering how to spend her time then finally made for the stable and cosseted Samson.

On the second Sunday she stayed in bed for most of the morning glad of the opportunity to have a rest. Keeping up appearances and not letting Billy know she wasn't really fit enough to do her share of the heavy work was beginning to take its toll. Her legs and back ached badly and often kept her awake at night. Sometimes she felt almost too weary next morning to climb out of bed.

When she came downstairs around midday to make herself a drink before she started to get dressed Maeve was already up and in the kitchen. She stared at Patsy open mouthed as if seeing her for the first time.

'What the hell has happened to you?' she gasped.

'What do you mean?' Patsy rubbed the sleep from her eyes and frowned in bewilderment.

'Look at you!'

'Stop fussing, Mam, I felt like a lie-in. I'll get dressed in a minute,' Patsy yawned. 'There's only us two here, isn't there?'

'Just as well!' Maeve exclaimed cynically. 'God knows what they'd think if they saw you!'

Patsy looked puzzled. Slowly it dawned on her why her mother was so concerned. Desperately she tried to button up the coat she'd pulled on over her nightdress but the edges would barely meet.

'You daft little bitch, you've gone and got yourself up the chute, haven't you?' Maeve spat at her.

Patsy shivered, but made no answer. She didn't know what to say. She knew she should have found a way to tell her mam. Being pregnant wasn't the sort of secret she could keep for ever.

Maeve's face was contorted with rage. 'You feckless Judy,' she railed. 'How could you be so bloody stupid?'

'I . . . I don't know how it happened,' Patsy choked.

'For God's sake!' Maeve's lip curled and the colour drained from her face. 'You don't know how it happened,' she mimicked. 'Don't come that Little Miss Innocence act with me! Of course you bloody well know what you've been up to. You're not a kid and you're not a bloody virgin either, by the look of you!'

Patsy stared at her, speechless. She had never seen her mam in such a rage. She had hoped that when she did eventually get round to telling her she was pregnant her mam would understand and be sympathetic.

'So whose is it? You've been sleeping with that oaf Billy, haven't you, you silly slut!' Maeve screamed.

Dumbly Patsy shook her head. 'Billy doesn't know a thing about it,' she whispered brokenly.

'Then the sooner you bloody well tell him and find out what he's going to do about it the better,' Maeve yelled.

'Mam, it's got nothing to do with Billy,' Patsy protested. 'He's not like that!'

For a moment Maeve looked taken aback. 'Are you telling me that he's a cream poof?' she gasped.

'No, of course he isn't,' Patsy said hotly, 'but my being pregnant has nothing to do with him.'

'Oh yes it bloody well has and the sooner the two of you tie the knot the better. I'm not having any little bastards living under my roof. Your dad would turn in his grave with shame.'

'But, Mam . . .'

'I don't want to hear any more. Just look at you. How many months gone are you? And you have the gall to stand there and tell me you didn't know what was happening? Get up those stairs, get yourself dressed and go and let that stupid oaf know that he's going to be a dad any day now. Tell him he'd better face up to his responsibilities or he'll have me to deal with and . . .'

'But, Mam . . .'

'Sort this mess out before the rest of Paradise Place knows what's been going on. Do you hear me? Does that Maureen Murphy know about this?'

Patsy shook her head, too choked to speak.

'Right! That's something, I suppose. You'd best go down on your knees to Father O'Brian. Billy Grant and his lot aren't Cat'licks, but nevertheless you'll marry him, my girl, I'll make sure of that.'

Chapter Eighteen

Patsy's eyes were still red and swollen when she went to work on Monday morning. Several times while they were fixing Samson's harness she saw Billy looking at her questioningly, but each time she avoided his eyes and quickly turned her head away.

'What's wrong with you today?' he asked jokingly as they hitched the horse up to the cart. 'Too many late nights over the weekend?'

'Something like that,' she mumbled. 'I think I might be going down with a cold.'

'Perhaps you ought to take the day off, then. Why don't you go home and go back to bed, Patsy,' he suggested, his voice full of concern. 'You certainly don't look too good.'

'Perhaps I should,' she agreed.

He sounded so solicitous, so caring, that she had to rub the back of her hand across her eyes to brush away the tears. She wondered what he would say if she told him the truth about exactly why she was not looking too good.

She wanted to tell him and to warn him about her mother's reaction, but she was afraid to do so in case Billy turned against her and then she would have no one to confide in.

She had been stunned by her mam's attitude.

It wasn't as though Maeve was strait-laced or particularly moral herself. Patsy was so dog-tired at night that her mam could have taken umpteen men up to bed and she wouldn't have known. Since she'd found Bruno in with her she'd never opened her mam's bedroom door ever again. What she didn't see didn't bother her.

So why had her mam been so outraged? Patsy wondered. Was it because she feels I should have told her sooner, or was it really because of what she thinks Dad would have thought if he was still alive?

She knew he would probably have regarded it as a heinous sin, because he'd been such a good Catholic, but her mam wasn't. She never goes to Mass these days, Patsy mused, and she never checks on whether I do or not.

The way her mam assumed that it was Billy's baby bothered her. What would she have said if I'd told her that Bruno Alvarez was the father? Patsy wondered.

In the end, Patsy came to the conclusion that her mother was so incensed by the news because the truth had been kept from her for so long and some of the neighbours might already know. Patsy felt guilty about that, but one of the reasons why she hadn't spoken out before was because deep down she wasn't sure whether her mother and Bruno were still seeing each other. It was something she tried to blot from her mind because she had no idea how to handle the situation if they were and she was still so much in love with Bruno that she didn't want to lose him, even though things were far from right between them.

If he noticed that she had put on weight he never mentioned it. They hadn't made love for ages because of the cold weather and since she was always heavily wrapped up against the biting winds that came in off the Mersey her changing shape was well hidden.

She blamed it all on the miserable winter weather. On Sundays there was nothing for them to do except go for a cup of tea in one of the few cafés that remained open in Victoria Street. Having nowhere to go took away all the glamour and excitement.

Sometimes he seemed to be almost indifferent to her. The fire had gone from his kisses; she no longer thrilled to his touch. It was this as much as anything else that made it so difficult to tell him about the baby.

'If you hadn't decided to change your plans then we would both have been in Spain by now,' she said wistfully when they met one Sunday. Bruno had been grumbling about the cold and seemed to be in a more surly mood than usual.

'I had no choice but to stay. My animals are here and there was a show at Christmas time,' he reminded her.

'We could have left for Spain as soon as that was over. The show only lasted for two weeks,' she pointed out.

'I try to tell you that I need the big money. And now I am getting things ready for the new season,' he said curtly. 'It cost too much money to go running back to Spain for a couple of weeks, yes?'

'I thought we were going to be married and we were going to live in Spain,' she reminded him, tears of disappointment welling up in her eyes.

Bruno said exasperatedly, 'The plans, they have to change. It is the money that is important.' He shivered and turned his coat collar up around his ears. 'Next year, perhaps, yes?'

'Next year, the year after, who knows,' Patsy argued miserably. 'You say next year, but what if you change your mind again?'

'I go when my pockets are full and not before.'

'We don't have to wait until you are ready to go back to Spain in order to get married,' Patsy pointed out querulously.

When he spread his hands wide in a dismissive gesture, Patsy felt uneasy. She was alarmed by his apathy. She desperately needed to tell him about the baby, but wasn't sure if this was the right moment to do so. Her thoughts were so jumbled that she couldn't find the right words.

'I'm beginning to think you already have a wife in Spain,' she blurted out.

He laughed dismissively. 'If I have a wife in Spain what would I want with another one here?'

'That's the point I'm trying to make,' Patsy said uncomfortably. 'You don't seem to want a wife here. All you want is someone to make love to while you are in England.'

His dark eyes narrowed and he stared at her calculatingly. 'I cannot understand what your words mean,' he prevaricated. 'You say too much, you confuse me,' he told her as they started to walk up Victoria Road to the café.

Patsy stopped. 'I am not feeling well, I'm going home,' she stated and felt resentment well up inside her when his only reaction was to give one of his infuriating shrugs.

'You have the headache?'

It was the first time since she'd known him that she had ended their meeting early and he showed such little concern that her anger spilled over.

'Headache, backache, my legs ache and so do my feet.' She wanted to add: and my heart aches most of all, but she felt too unhappy to carry on talking to him. Although they had barely spent more than half an hour in each other's company she told him she was going to get the next ferry-boat back to Liverpool.

He didn't try to stop her. Merely raised his eyebrows, then turned and walked back with her towards the landing stage where the *Royal Daffodil* was about to leave.

Patsy had thought he was going to come with her, but he simply stood at the bottom of the gangway and waved farewell as the boat pulled away. He hasn't even kissed me goodbye, she thought bitterly.

All the way back to Liverpool she had felt annoyed with herself that she hadn't told Bruno that she was pregnant. She had to do it and the sooner it was out in the open and he knew, the better.

'Go on then, Patsy, off with you,' Billy's voice cut into her thoughts and brought her back to the present with a jolt. 'Home to bed! Perhaps if you nip this cold in the bud you'll be feeling all right in the morning. If you're not, then stay tucked up where you are.'

She wondered if she dared take Billy up on his offer. She wouldn't go home to bed. If she took the day off she'd go over to New Brighton, find Bruno and do what she should have done yesterday: explain the situation to him. He was a Catholic and once he knew she was pregnant she was confident he would want them to be married before the baby arrived.

'Are you sure you'll be OK on your own?'

'You watch me!' Billy grinned. He put an arm round her shoulder. 'Go on, push off. Of course I can manage without you. There's only a couple of local deliveries to do, not enough to keep us both occupied. I must get going though because the first load has to be picked up from Edge Hill before nine o'clock.'

Patsy decided not to waste time going home to change out of her working clothes. Her mother might be up by now and she didn't want to face another row. She waited until she heard Samson clopping down the road and knew Billy was out of the way then headed for the ferry and New Brighton.

Easter was only a few weeks away and then the season would be opening so there was a great deal of activity in the fairground. It took her some time to find Bruno.

He stared at her for a moment as if he didn't know who she was. 'You are dressed for work so you are feeling better again,' he greeted her. 'Today I not have time to stop and talk with you.'

'What I have to say will only take a minute,' Patsy told him, 'but there is something I must talk to you about.'

'If it is about marrying or going to Spain we must leave such talk for another time. I am busy, yes?'

'No, you are not too busy to hear what I have to tell you,' she insisted stubbornly.

He frowned darkly. 'Come quick and spit it out then.'

This wasn't the way she wanted to tell him her news, Patsy thought. She'd imagined that at least they could find somewhere private. She didn't want to tell him here in the middle of a busy fairground with workmen all around them.

'Can we go somewhere quieter, where there is not so much noise and banging?' she asked.

He took her to a far corner of the fairground. 'Now what is this news that is so important that you must come and interrupt me?' he asked curtly.

She bit down on her lower lip, not sure how to break it to him. 'It is news to make you happy, to make us both happy,' she told him quietly.

He looked puzzled. 'Go on!'

'I . . . I am pregnant, Bruno. I am expecting your baby. It will be born very soon now.'

He stared at her in stark disbelief. 'I do not understand?' His heavy dark brows drew together in a ferocious frown. 'What is this that you are trying to tell me?'

'I am expecting your baby, Bruno.' She pulled aside her jacket. 'Look, see for yourself. Surely you must have noticed that I was putting on weight,' she added crossly.

He drew back, shaking his head in dismay. 'I do not understand. This cannot be so,' he said harshly.

'It's quite true, Bruno. I wouldn't have said so otherwise, now would I?'

He stared at her as if she was a stranger. 'Why now? Why you not tell me yesterday, or the week before, or even the month before. Why now at this busy moment?'

'Bruno!' She was taken aback. She'd not known how he would react to her news, but she had certainly not expected it to be like this.

He spread his hands wide and shrugged. 'What is it you want me to say?'

'I want you to tell me you are happy that we are having a baby. To agree that we must be married as soon as possible.'

He shook his head, his dark eyes unfathomable. 'Pleased, I am not. Shocked, yes! I must have time to do the thinking.'

Patsy stared at him, nonplussed. She couldn't believe what she was hearing, or understand his hostile attitude. She couldn't think of anything else to say. Not unless she pleaded with him to marry her, and her pride wouldn't let her do that.

Re-fastening her coat over her bulky figure, she turned away. 'Very well, I will give you time to think,' she said dully. 'You know where I live, so come and see me when you have decided what we are going to do.'

Without waiting for him to reply she walked away. When she reached the main road she turned and looked back, half hoping that he would be running after her. There was no sign of him.

In a daze Patsy walked the short distance back to the pier. As she waited for the return boat to Liverpool she deplored her own foolhardiness. Perhaps Billy was right after all when he said foreigners didn't think the same way as they did. If Bruno refused to marry her, what was she going to do? She felt bitter and confused. First her mam and now Bruno seemed to be against her.

Patsy was so engrossed in her morbid thoughts that when she came off the boat at Liverpool she didn't notice the horse and cart at the top of the floating roadway. She was jerked out of her reverie when a familiar voice said, 'You might as well have a ride home with us as catch a Green Goddess.'

'Billy! What are you doing here?'

'I've finished the last delivery for today and was on my way home. I couldn't believe my eyes when I saw you coming off the New Brighton boat. I thought you said you were going home to bed,' he commented as she climbed up beside him.

She shook her head. 'No, there was something else I had to do that was more important.'

He flicked the reins and concentrated on the road ahead. 'More important than getting your-self fit for work tomorrow?'

She shot him a sideways glance. 'It was very urgent. Something I had to do.'

'Well, are you going to tell me what it was?'

'I'm pregnant.'

The words hung in the air between them like a ship's pennant.

'I had noticed,' Billy said quietly, 'and I wondered when you were going to tell me.'

Patsy's jaw dropped. 'You knew!'

'Well, it had to be that or else you were getting ready to be the fat lady in the circus,' he joked. 'Come on, Patsy, I'm not blind, you know. You've been getting fatter and fatter ever since Christmas. Lately there's been days when it's as much as you can do to climb up and down into the cart.'

'And yet you've said nothing!'

'I was waiting for you to tell me. After all, I could have been wrong, you could have been putting on weight and then think how embarrassed you would have been if I'd been the one to mention it.'

Patsy didn't answer.

'Have you told your mam yet?'

'She found out yesterday. She went absolutely crazy . . . she thinks it's yours,' Patsy said awkwardly.

Billy swung round in his seat to stare at her. The broad smile on his face vanished when he saw her expression.

'So you've been over to New Brighton to see Bruno, and tell him it's his, have you,' he said in a cold, noncommittal voice.

'Yeah. A lot of good that did me an' all! He didn't seem to want to know,' she added bitterly.

Billy faced her squarely. 'It's your baby, Patsy, no matter who the father is and you've only to say the word and I'll marry you. We'd be happy together, I know we would.'

Chapter Nineteen

When Patsy reached home and opened the front door she found her mam, her hair all over the place, her face red with effort, a half-smoked cigarette dangling from the corner of her mouth, struggling down the stairs with a heavy sack.

'Mam? What's going on?' Patsy frowned.

'You can put that back on,' Maeve told her sharply as she started to take off her coat.

'Why, do you want me to take that sack somewhere?'

Maeve drew heavily on her cigarette. 'You can take the bloody thing wherever you like and yourself with it,' she snapped, breathing out a cloud of smoke.

Patsy looked bewildered. 'What do you mean by that?'

Maeve straightened her dress and smoothed her hair back into place. 'Exactly what I say, my girl! Your clothes and your bits and pieces are all in there.' She kicked disdainfully at the sack with the toe of her high-heeled shoe. 'Now take it and get out of my bloody sight.'

'You mean you are turning me out?' The blood drained from Patsy's face. She stared at her mother in shocked disbelief.

'I'm not turning you out, kiddo, I'm bloody well

throwing you out!' Maeve took another drag at her cigarette. 'I don't want you here under my roof another minute.'

Patsy felt frozen to the spot. She wondered if her mam had been drinking, then told herself that couldn't be the reason for her being so belligerent. Her mam went out drinking most nights and when she came home again she was usually laughing and singing. If she brought someone home with her then sometimes she behaved in a silly manner, but Patsy had never seen her in quite such an aggressive mood as this.

'Did you hear what I said?' Maeve snapped. 'I want you and all your belongings out of this house right now.'

'Mam, be reasonable, I've nowhere to go!'

'Then you'd better find somewhere, or ask that Billy Grant if you can shack up with him since he's the one who's got you into this mess.'

'Billy has nothing at all to do with what's happened. I told you that before,' Patsy said wearily.

'Oh no? Are you trying to tell me you've been playing the field?'

'No, I leave that for you to do,' Patsy retorted angrily.

Maeve's hand came up and made contact with Patsy's face before she could move a muscle. The impact of the resounding slap sent Patsy reeling.

'Mam!' she gasped, her eyes filling with tears, her head spinning, as she staggered back.

What on earth was happening to them both? she thought in alarm. She realised that her mother was upset by the news that she was pregnant so she'd expected to get a tongue-lashing, that was only natural. Once that was over, though, she'd thought her mam would help her and tell her what to do for the best.

'Mam, don't do this to me. I've never needed your help more in my life,' she pleaded.

'You might need it, but you're not bloody well going to get it.' Maeve came closer, breathing gin fumes into Patsy's face. 'I must have been blind not to see what was going on right under my nose. You think I'm a soft touch because I let you and that Billy run the business just as you like. You think you can trick me all ends up, don't you? Well, you're wrong.'

'Mam, just listen to me for a minute,' Patsy begged. 'This has nothing to do with Billy, he didn't even know about the baby until today.'

'No? So whose kid is it, the Tooth Fairy's?'

Patsy shook her head, her red curls dancing like flames in a fire. 'It's Bruno's!'

Maeve's green eyes were glacial as she stared at Patsy. 'You little bitch! I was waiting for you to say that,' she said. 'Only I know different, don't I.'

'It's the truth,' Patsy said wearily. 'We've been meeting every Sunday since the beginning of the summer. Bruno promised me we would be married as soon as the season ended and after that he would take me back to his home in Almeria.'

Maeve shook her head, smiling cynically. 'That's what you told him you wanted to do. Bruno told you that it was out of the question because you were only a kid and too young to leave home,' she added scornfully.

Patsy shook her head. 'No, Mam, that's not true. Wherever did you hear that?'

'Straight from the horse's mouth,' Maeve told her exultantly, 'and I don't mean that old nag out in the stable. I mean from Bruno himself.'

'Bruno?' Patsy stared at her in disbelief. 'When did he tell you this?'

'Several times. The last time was today, only about an hour ago.' Maeve licked her lips, watching the bewilderment on Patsy's face.

'Bruno's only just left here!' she declared triumphantly. He came over here before his evening show started specially to tell me what you'd been accusing him of and to assure me that he'd never touched you. He said that he'd taken you out a few times, before your birthday, but that was all . . .'

'Mam, that's not true.'

'He'd seen you a few times before your birthday but he had no idea what your age was,' Maeve went on, ignoring the interruption. 'He was shocked when he came over here that first time and found out how young you were. He told me that straight after that he stopped having anything to do with you.'

'He certainly did not! We've seen each other every Sunday since my birthday, the same as we did before,' Patsy told her hotly.

Maeve looked smug. 'Bruno told me you had been over to New Brighton every Sunday afternoon pestering him to take you out, but he wasn't having any.'

'Pestering him! Walking to Leasowe sandhills

and making love was pestering him, was it?' Patsy exclaimed bitterly.

'That's what you wanted him to do, no doubt,' Maeve taunted, 'but he wasn't the least bit interested because he knew you were only a kid.'

'And all the promises about marrying me and taking me back to Almeria, I suppose I imagined he said all that, did I?'

'He told you about his home in Spain, so you probably daydreamed the rest,' Maeve laughed.

Patsy's shoulders slumped. 'I don't know how to convince you, Mam,' she said despondently. 'Why won't you listen to me, try and understand that I am telling you the truth.'

'Why should I do that when I know you're not,' Maeve demanded. 'Take a look at yourself!' she said scathingly. 'What do you look like? Dressed in a man's shirt and trousers and an old cloth cap perched on your head. What fella would give you a second look let alone fancy you? I know Bruno's no longer interested in you because he has been taking me out ever since your birthday!' she gloated.

Patsy's face hardened. 'I've been doing my best to forget I found you in bed with him,' she said. 'Not something for you to be proud of, being in bed with my boyfriend, Mam! You're every bit as bad as the neighbours say. And to think I've always stuck up for you when they run you down and say things about the way you carry on in the Grafton when you're pissed out of your mind.'

The colour drained from Maeve's face. 'That will do, Patsy. How I live my life is my own affair.'

'You mean affairs, don't you. One affair after the other, isn't it,' Patsy taunted. 'I can still remember the string of "uncles" you used to bring to the house when I was a little kid, while my dad was away at sea.'

Maeve raised her hand as if to lash out again, but Patsy was too quick for her. 'Oh no you don't!' she said scornfully, backing away.

Her scalp crawled with sweat as she stared at Maeve wide-eyed. 'What's up with you, Mam?' she asked. 'I've done nothing to deserve this.'

'No?' Maeve's lip curled. 'Getting yourself pregnant and bringing a load of disgrace on both of us is counted as nothing, is it?'

Patsy's shoulders slumped. 'I know what I've done is wrong, Mam, that's the reason why I've been too scared to tell you.'

'And you've not given a thought about what all the neighbours will be saying about the way I've brought you up?'

Patsy stared at her, confused. Then she gave a wry smile. 'When have you ever worried about what the neighbours thought or said, Mam? They've had plenty to talk about in the past.'

'Be that be as it may, but I'm not standing for it now. I want you to go. I want you out of this house right this minute and I never want you to come back. So take that sack.'

Before Patsy could argue further Maeve opened the door and heaved the heavy sack out on to the roadway.

'Go on! All your things are there, now get out,' she shouted breathlessly. Refusing to look Patsy in the face, Maeve stood with one hand on the door, face averted, waiting for her to leave.

The moment Patsy stepped over the threshold Maeve slammed the door, so quickly and so violently that she caught it against Patsy's heel, making her yell out in pain.

Patsy stood outside her home feeling stunned and shivering in the April drizzle. She still couldn't believe that her mam had meant what she'd said, or that she really was throwing her out. She turned round and banged wildly on the door, but there was no response.

'Mam!' she yelled, banging again with her fists, 'open up this door, it's started to rain and I'm getting soaked.'

The silence from inside remained unbroken. Patsy crouched down to peer through the letterbox. She could see her mam was still in the hall so she thumped again on the closed door with her fist, but Maeve remained where she was, standing at the foot of the stairs, holding on to the newel post.

Tears streaming down her cheeks, Patsy grabbed hold of the heavy sack and tried to think where she could go for shelter.

Asking Billy for help was out of the question. For a fleeting moment she wondered if Maureen Murphy would help her, but the thought of all the questions Maureen's mother and sister would ask, and the gossip that would result from anything she told them, put her off.

She stifled her sobs. No, she resolved, she'd deal with this on her own. It was bad enough that her mother had turned her out without it becoming common knowledge for the whole of Paradise Place.

The sack was heavy and what had started as an April shower had now turned to heavy rain. She was getting soaked. There was only one place she could go to shelter, Patsy thought wearily, and that was into Samson's stable.

By now he would have been fed and settled for the night so there was no fear of Billy coming back again until morning. That would give her plenty of time to decide what to do and what to tell him, she thought as she dragged the heavy sack along the ground.

It was still only early evening and she was hungry so before taking off her wet coat Patsy went to the corner shop for buns, milk and some apples and then to the chippy.

As she tucked into her fish and chips she wondered if she ought to go across to New Brighton again to try and explain the situation to Bruno. Surely the fact that her mother had turned her out must change things, she reasoned. Even if Bruno didn't want to go back to Almeria right away they could be married here in England.

He was a Catholic, so he knew all about mortal sin and he wouldn't want the baby to enter the world as a bastard. Or should she go and see Father O'Brian and ask him for help? Her spirits lifted. She might even be able to get Father O'Brian to talk to Bruno and persuade him they should be married as soon as possible. Surely Bruno would listen to a priest and do whatever he advised?

Patsy screwed up the newspaper the fish and chips had been wrapped in. She'd tidy herself up and go along to the church right away.

When she opened the door the rain was lashing down and blowing straight at the stable so she closed it again quickly. It would be madness to go out in that lot, she decided. Another day wouldn't make all that much difference. It would give her time to plan out in her mind what she should say to Father O'Brian.

Samson whinnied expectantly as she picked up an apple and rubbed it on her sleeve. She took one bite then lost interest and gave him the rest of it. As he munched away she laid her head against his warm side with a sigh. 'You're the best friend I've ever had, aren't you, Samson?'

Her mind was in such turmoil that her head felt as if it was going to explode. She couldn't think straight and she had no idea what to do for the best. Troubled memories floated in and out of her mind like scattered debris.

If only she could turn the clock back; if only her dad was still here. She thought about all the dreams and hopes he'd had for her future and it saddened her to know that none of them would ever come true. She would never be a teacher as he had hoped she would be, nor would she ever work in one of the impressive Liverpool shipping offices.

Perhaps it was as well that he wasn't alive to know how badly she had failed him, she thought sadly.

She felt so tired and utterly depressed that tears trickled down her cheeks. Her back was aching so much that she wished she could curl up into a ball and never wake up again.

Struggling to her feet she groped around in the fading light for some clean straw and spread it out in a corner of the stable to make a bed for herself. She kicked off her boots, then lay down on it fully clothed and pulled a horse blanket over her for warmth.

Perhaps after she'd had a sleep she'd feel better and would be able to see things more clearly, Patsy thought hopefully as she stared into the darkness. By next morning her mam might have calmed down and she would be able to go back home again.

Chapter Twenty

Patsy fell into an exhausted sleep within a few minutes of lying down on the makeshift straw bed. She slept soundly until the first pink glow in the sky forewarned another day of unsettled spring weather.

When she did waken she ached all over and for a moment couldn't make out what she was doing in Samson's stable. She closed her eyes again and wondered if she was still dreaming.

Gradually her mind cleared and she remembered what had happened the previous evening. She went back over the row between herself and her mam and all the awful things they'd said to each other. It was the first time she could remember her mam hitting her so hard and the memory of the vicious slap across her face brought tears to her eyes.

She was sure it must have all been a terrible mistake and the sooner she went back home and cleared the air the better. Her mam hadn't been herself. Someone else must have done something, or said something, that had really upset her. It couldn't simply be the knowledge that she was about to be a grandmother. Or could it?

Patsy sighed. Her mam wasn't all that keen on babies or small children, so that could have been what had led to her violent outburst. She'd thought she was going to be saddled with a young baby around the place! As well as all the extra work that would bring she was probably worried that it might cramp her style.

Patsy smiled to herself. Her mam must feel she was too young to be a grandmother. She prided herself on how young she looked. She even boasted that with her good figure, fresh creamy complexion and shoulder-length strawberry-blonde hair, people often said she looked in her late twenties.

Patsy eased herself upright. She felt huge and clumsy as she brushed herself down and straightened her crumpled clothes. She couldn't stay here another night without water or facilities of any kind. There was barely any light when the door was shut.

Now that she had gathered her wits together she was eager to be up and sorting things out. The first thing she'd do, she decided, would be to go and see her mam and make her understand that the baby wouldn't spoil her life in any way. And when she'd made her peace with her mam she'd go over to New Brighton and make Bruno understand that they had to get married right away, before their baby was born.

She was on the point of pulling on her boots when the stable door opened and Billy appeared carrying a bucket of fresh water and a bag of feed for Samson.

His mouth dropped open in astonishment when he saw Patsy and he stopped just inside the door staring at her as if she was a ghost.

He ran a hand through his shock of brown hair. 'What on earth are you doing here?' he said, frowning. 'What's going on?'

Patsy grimaced. 'It's a long story, where do you want me to begin?'

'Well, why you're sleeping in here, that will do for a start.'

'Because last night me mam kicked me out –' she pointed dramatically towards the sack – 'and all me belongings with me!'

'You had a bust-up with her?'

'Yeah, you could say that.'

'Do you want to tell me about it?'

'I suppose I may as well.' Some of Patsy's bravado seeped away. 'You'll probably hear about it anyway. By mid-morning I expect there will be rumours flying all round Paradise Place.'

Billy's face remained impassive. He tipped the bucket of water into Samson's trough and shook out the bag of feed for him.

'Go on then, I'm listening,' he said gruffly.

'It's because of the baby,' Patsy said stiffly. 'I don't think my mam likes the idea of becoming a grandmother.'

Billy's jaw tightened and his blue eyes were challenging as they met hers. 'There's a lot more to it than that, now isn't there?'

'What do you mean?' Her voice was sharp. Her green eyes were icy as she stared back at him.

'Well . . .' He thrust his hands into his trouser pockets. 'She's probably upset because you're so pregnant and you've never said a word to her about it until now. If you'd told her a lot sooner then she would have had time to get used to the idea.'

Patsy's lower lip jutted sulkily. 'How could I tell her when I didn't know myself?'

'You must have had some idea,' Billy argued. 'Women usually know these things quite early on.'

'Oh yes,' she tipped back her head and regarded him cynically, 'I suppose you know all about that sort of thing, do you, Billy Grant?'

Colour stained his face. 'I seem to know more about it than you do,' he snapped.

Patsy's face crumpled. 'Don't shout at me, Billy. I thought you were my friend.'

'I'm not shouting,' he said in surprise. 'I am your friend, you should know that, Patsy. I can't understand why you didn't confide in me earlier, though. How do you think I feel now that I know you've been pregnant all this time and I've been expecting you to carry on working as normal? Helping to lift heavy loads, and giving a hand to control a massive great horse, isn't work for a girl at the best of times and certainly not for someone in your condition.'

'Honestly, Billy, I didn't know I was pregnant, not for a long time,' she said emphatically. 'I thought I was putting on weight because it was winter and I was eating so much stodge.'

'And that's why you've taken to wearing such baggy clothes, I suppose?'

'Partly. I didn't want people to see how fat I was getting.'

'Even when you realised why you were getting fat you didn't talk about it to anyone, not even me,' Billy went on accusingly.

'No,' she admitted. 'I didn't because I didn't want to believe it was true.'

He frowned. 'And now your mam has thrown you out because you're pregnant. So what are you going to do?'

'I don't know,' she mumbled. Suddenly the idea of going back home and confronting her mam seemed futile. 'Stay here until I get things sorted out, I suppose.'

'Here? You mean here in Samson's stable?'

She shrugged. 'He doesn't seem to mind.'

Billy grinned. 'Maybe not, but it's not a very good arrangement, is it?'

'Then I'll try and sort something out with me mam. I was hoping she might be feeling different about things today.'

Billy raised his eyebrows questioningly. 'Would you like me to go round and talk to her?'

'No, no! Don't do that whatever you do,' she entreated.

'Why not? She might listen to me.'

'You wouldn't like what she has to say about you.' Patsy muttered.

Billy looked puzzled. 'What do you mean by that?'

Patsy chewed on her lower lip for a moment. 'Well, I told you she thinks you're the father,' she blurted out, her face scarlet.

Billy gave a soundless whistle. His mind sped back to what had happened right there in the stable the night of Patsy's sixteenth birthday and his heart thudded.

He looked at her speculatively. Could it be his

child she was carrying? It wasn't the first time he'd wondered about that and for a moment he felt elated.

Then common sense took over as he realised not only the improbability of that being the case, since they had only ever made love once, but also the problems it would probably cause for them both if it was true. Unless Patsy agreed to marry him, but would she?

'So what did you tell your mam?' he asked cautiously.

'That it had nothing at all to do with you, of course!'

Billy scowled. Alvarez! Of course, Bruno Alvarez must be the father. How could he have thought otherwise? For a moment he saw red. He loved Patsy so strongly that he hated her. Then the feeling went as quickly as it had come and he had nothing but pity for her and the awful predicament she was in.

'Please don't go to see my mam, Billy.'

'I won't if you tell me what you're planning to do.'

Patsy grinned. 'First and foremost I'm going to pinch some of the water you brought over for Samson, if there's any left, and wash my face.'

'Right! I'll hitch Samson up to the cart while you're doing that and we can work out some sort of plan for the future as we work.' He paused and looked at her awkwardly, his face reddening. 'Do you think you should carry on working in your condition?'

'I worked yesterday so I can work today,' she

told him. 'That is if you give me five minutes to sort myself out.'

'Make it three minutes and I'll treat you to some breakfast at the café on the Dock Road,' he promised as he led Samson outside.

As she bent over the horse trough Patsy sensed that something was wrong. Her back had been aching when she'd woken up, but now there was a griping pain and cramps in the pit of her stomach that made her wince and took her breath away.

Knowing Billy was waiting for her outside in the yard she tried to stand up, but the excruciating pain made her gasp.

At the same time she noticed that her clothing was soaking wet and wondered what had happened. Then her heart almost stopped. It could mean only one thing. Gripped by a fresh wave of pain, her fear increased. The baby was coming.

Again she tried to stand up, but her legs felt like jelly. She crouched back on the straw wondering what to do now. Should she call out to Billy or try to manage on her own?

She tried to think what jobs were booked in, and what time their first call was, but her mind refused to function. All she could think about was the pain and what was happening to her body. Her face was wet with perspiration, her clothes were soaked and she couldn't go home because her mam had turfed her out.

Another wave of pain surged through her body and she yelled out for Billy.

'The baby!' she gasped as he came rushing in from the yard. Then another contraction took over her body and waves of pain left her speechless and her mind a blank.

When the spasm was over she flopped listlessly against Billy as he wiped the sweat from her brow and murmured words of comfort.

'I'm going to fetch your mam, Patsy,' he told her as he gently laid her back on the straw. 'It's for the best, she'll know what to do.'

Patsy grabbed at his coat sleeve. 'No, no, you can't do that, she won't come, anyway. You know she's chucked me out! That's why I'm here, isn't it?'

'I'll go and get my mam then. You need a woman here and she'll come and help you, Patsy.'

'No, no!' She clutched at him wildly as a fresh spasm gripped her swollen body. 'I don't want you to do that. I don't want my mam or your mam. You'll have to help me, Billy!'

He held her, mopping her face, murmuring words of encouragement, trying to pacify her, but all the time becoming more concerned. He had no experience of such things and had no idea what he ought to be doing.

Patsy's mop of red curls was dark with sweat. He brushed them back from her forehead and looked down into her glazed eyes. 'I can't do this, Patsy,' he told her awkwardly. 'You need towels, blankets, hot water.' He paused and shook his head from side to side. 'I don't know what we need, but there's nothing at all here. Let me go and fetch someone. Perhaps you ought to be in hospital?'

'It's too late, Billy. The baby's going to be born

215

any minute. You'll have to help me,' she pleaded. 'Open up that sack – there's bound to be something inside it that we can use.'

'You need a woman here,' he insisted. 'Let me fetch my mam.'

Patsy tried to answer him but a contraction twisted her body in a violent shudder. She clung frenetically to his arm, her green eyes imploring, as she begged him not to leave her.

He took a deep breath to steady his own nerves as he gently loosened her fingers. He was scared. He knew he was out of his depth and that the right thing to do was to get help. Perhaps he ought to send for an ambulance. In hospital she would have all the right care.

As if reading his mind, Patsy grabbed his arm. Her voice was hoarse and frightened as she pleaded with him again.

'All right. I'll do it your way,' he promised quietly. He opened up the sack and tipped out the contents, sorting through her few belongings and putting to one side anything that might be useful. The rest he stuffed back in the sack and moved it out of the way.

Removing his donkey jacket and rolling up the sleeves of his checked cotton shirt, he knelt down beside her and loosened her clothing as another contraction left her gasping for air.

'Try and stay calm,' he said softly. 'It will all be over quite soon.'

She looked up at him trustingly and nodded, but before she could speak her body convulsed violently. She tried to control her screams as pain ripped through her and for a brief moment the world around her was blotted out.

From far off she heard Billy's voice telling her what she must do, but she had no control over her body at all. It was now one seething mass of pain, wave after wave, sending her in and out of darkness.

Then an agitated mewing sound pierced the dark that surrounded her and she wondered why there was a cat in the stable. She drifted in and out of consciousness, tormented by the sound and waiting for Billy to stop the animal from crying.

Vaguely, through a misty haze, she could hear Billy telling her something. He sounded very excited, but Patsy couldn't understand what he was saying. Something that sounded like 'The baby is a boy', but his words meant nothing to her.

She didn't know what he was on about, and she didn't care. Now that the terrible searing pain had stopped all she wanted to do was sleep. She wished Billy would go away and leave her alone. She tried to open her eyes and tell him this, but she was so very tired that it was too much of an effort to do so.

Chapter Twenty-One

For the first three days after the baby was born Billy hardly left Patsy's side. Work was abandoned. He ate and slept at the stable, worrying about the baby, knowing it was probably premature and wondering if he had done all the right things for it when it was being born.

He was torn between whether or not he should tell his mother or someone else about what had happened or whether to comply with Patsy's wishes.

To cover up for his absence from home, and the fact that he was not taking the horse and cart out each morning, he told everyone that Samson wasn't well and that he didn't think he ought to leave him.

No one seemed very bothered, and when he said it was something he could deal with he was left to his own devices. His mother made up a pile of his favourite cheese and pickle sarnies as well as bacon butties each day and left them on the kitchen table for him to collect if she wasn't there when he popped home.

'Can you make me some conny-onny ones as well?' he asked. He remembered they'd been Patsy's favourite when she was little and he hoped they'd tempt her appetite.

'I'll do better than that,' Elaine Grant promised, 'I'll make some wet-nelly and leave you a big wedge of that as well. You've always loved it, ever since you were a little lad.'

When he told his mother that he fancied some soup or stew she expressed surprise, but agreed to have some ready for him next time he dropped in.

'Are you going to sit down and eat it here?'

'No, I'll take it back with me.'

'In that case you'd better take the Primus stove and a saucepan with you so that you can heat it up.'

'Thanks, Mam. I'll take the Valor stove as well if you can spare it.'

She looked puzzled. 'You mean that big one we use to warm the upstairs before we go up to bed in winter?'

Billy nodded. 'You're not using it, are you?'

'Well, no, but it's not like you to feel the cold, son,' she frowned. 'I thought the weather had turned quite mild for April. You be careful where you place it, mind, with all that hay and straw about the place.'

'I'm not the one that's cold. It's to take the chill off the stable . . .'

'You and that old horse,' she laughed. 'You think more of him than you do of your family! Still, I suppose he is almost as important to you as we are. Without him you wouldn't be able to work, now would you.'

Afraid that his mother might become suspicious he didn't dare ask her for any of the other things he required. Instead he visited a junk shop and managed to find a tin bath that he could use to wash the baby, Patsy herself and their clothes in. He also found a shallow wooden chest that he thought would make a cradle.

He needed soap, cotton wool and dozens of other things, as well as warm clothing for the baby. He was scared to buy these from any of the local shops in case someone who knew his mother came in. If they told her what they'd seen him buying she was bound to ask him why on earth he wanted such items.

Billy felt worried whenever he had to leave Patsy and the baby, even if it was only for half an hour. It was risky in case anyone came near the stable and heard the baby crying, but it was something he had to do in order to fetch supplies for them.

Once he'd lined the wooden chest with straw, and then with a warm blanket, he was happy that the baby would be quite safe. It might waken and cry, but it could come to no real harm.

It was Patsy he worried about. For the first couple of days she had a raging fever and drifted in and out of consciousness all the time. In between spoon-feeding Patsy and attending to the baby he put cold compresses on her brow and changed her sweat-soaked nightdress.

By the third day, though, her forehead seemed to be that little bit cooler, her body less clammy. By the afternoon she seemed fully aware of what was going on around her.

While she'd been semi-conscious he'd managed

to persuade her to feed the baby whenever she was lucid enough to do so. He'd placed it in her arms and her response to its cry had been automatic. It was almost as if she was unaware of what was going on, or that it was her own baby she was suckling.

By the third day, however, although she was still so weak that she could hardly sit up, she was fully aware of the baby when he placed it in her arms.

Her expression of gratitude when she saw how well it was thriving embarrassed Billy.

'I still think you should have gone home to your mam, or got someone to come here and help,' he muttered. 'I'm not even sure I did the right things when he was born. You ought to see a doctor, Patsy. You really should if only to make sure you're all right as well as having the baby checked over. He was premature, remember.'

She looked down at the tiny redheaded scrap in her arms. 'There's nothing to worry about, Billy. He's perfect, you can see that for yourself.'

'You don't know that,' he persisted firmly. 'Look, Patsy, how do you think I would feel if anything went wrong with either of you later on? I'd never be able to forgive myself if we found out that it was because of something I hadn't done right when he was born.'

'You're talking daft, kiddo!' she protested weakly. 'There is nothing wrong with either of us.'

'You don't know that for sure,' he repeated doggedly, his square jaw looking stubborn. 'He's a tiny baby and he looks a bit frail to me.'

Patsy laughed out loud for the first time since the baby had been born. 'Listen to yourself!' she teased. 'He's small! Of course he's small. Did you expect him to be the same size as Samson?'

Billy shook his head in despair. 'If you think he's all right then he probably is,' he muttered. 'What are you going to do now, though? You can't stay here for ever.'

Patsy's face clouded and her momentary happiness vanished. Her shoulders sagged and he felt so sorry for her that on impulse he hugged her, holding her close, stroking her curls, and tenderly kissing her brow.

'I'm sorry. I didn't mean to worry you, Patsy, but you will have to make plans for the future, for the baby's sake if not for yourself.'

'You think I should tell my mam, don't you?' she murmured unhappily.

'Your mam or . . . Bruno.' Even saying the name choked Billy, but he tried hard to hide his resentment. 'He should be providing for you and the baby.'

'Yes, I suppose you're right, but then he doesn't know I've had the baby, does he? I intended to go to New Brighton to talk to him before the baby was born.'

'Well, you're in no fit state to make that journey for quite a while yet so why not let me tell your mam?'

She moved free of his embrace and turned to face him, her green eyes pleading. 'I'd sooner you went over to New Brighton and told Bruno about the baby.'

Billy stiffened. Surely she didn't expect him to do that! It was the last thing he wanted to do, even to help Patsy.

'Please, Billy,' she begged.

'I don't know,' he prevaricated. 'I don't think I should be the one to tell him. Anyway, you haven't even given the baby a name yet.'

Her face lit up. 'We'll do it now! You delivered him so you choose a name.'

He shook his head. 'I can't do that!'

Smiling, Patsy pulled back the blanket the baby was wrapped in and studied the child. 'With blue eyes he's the spitting image of me dad,' she said proudly.

'So do you want to call him John?'

She shook her head. 'No, that doesn't seem right somehow.'

They stared at each other blankly. He was afraid she would say 'Bruno' and if she did he would tell her that wasn't the right name for a redhead.

'I like the name Liam,' Patsy murmured.

Billy felt a sense of relief. 'Right, that's it then. The baby is Liam.'

'So now he has a name will you go and tell Bruno?' she urged.

'If that's what you want. It might take me quite some time, though. Will you be all right if I leave you here on your own?' he asked anxiously.

Patsy looked surprised by his concern. 'You've left me here on my own before,' she reminded him.

'I know, only then you were either asleep or out cold,' he told her ruefully. 'I always locked the door and took the key with me,' he assured her.

'I'll stay right here,' Patsy promised. 'I don't want anyone to see me now, do I?'

'Do you want me to lock the door and take the key with me? Or shall I leave it in its hiding place under the stone outside?' he asked as he put on his donkey jacket and pulled on his cap.

'No, take the key with you in case anybody who knows where it's hidden comes looking for you and decides to let themselves in. I'll feed Liam and afterwards we'll both have a sleep,' she promised.

Sitting in the gloom Patsy felt nervous and on edge. There were so many strange noises that she kept looking over her shoulder. She wasn't sure if it was Samson as he munched away at his net of hay, or if it was a mouse, or rat, scuttling in one of the corners.

She knew Liam shouldn't be in such surroundings. Billy was right, she must move out as soon as possible. She'd thought her mam would have come looking for Billy before now to ask if she was all right, but it seemed she hadn't asked after her at all.

Billy had been a real brick and she didn't know what she would have done without his help, Patsy thought grimly. He'd cared for her and done far more to help her than she would have thought possible. Having to assist at Liam's birth must have been a terrible shock for him and she'd never be able to make up to him for the way he'd nursed her ever since.

He'd never had a steady girlfriend. Patsy suspected it was because of his feelings for her and that made her uneasy knowing she didn't feel the same way about him. He was good looking and a hard worker. He'd make some lucky girl a wonderful husband.

It was dark before Billy returned. She'd already lit the candle in the lantern, but it threw up such weird and grotesque shadows that she was starting to get jittery.

'I thought you might be hungry so I brought us some grub,' he said, tossing a newspaper-wrapped parcel on to the straw beside her as soon as he was inside the door.

Patsy's face lit up. 'Fish and chips!' She grinned up at him in delight.

They sat side by side sharing their impromptu supper. Billy had also brought some beer for himself and a bottle of sarsaparilla for her.

Patsy waited patiently for him to tell her how his trip to New Brighton had gone, but in the end she could stand the suspense no longer.

'It's bad news, isn't it?' she asked shrewdly.

He screwed his empty newspaper wrapper into a tight ball. 'Yeah! Well, it's not exactly good news.'

'Go on, tell me what Bruno said when you told him about the baby,' she said flatly.

'He didn't say anything. He wasn't there.'

Patsy stared in disbelief. 'What do you mean by that?' she asked in a bemused voice.

'He's left New Brighton. I asked around, but no one at the fairground seems to know where he's gone. One chap said back to Spain, another one said he'd gone to Blackpool.'

The colour drained from Patsy's face. 'You think

he's cleared off, don't you?' she asked in a strained voice.

Billy shrugged. 'I don't know.'

'He's seemed different lately,' Patsy went on in a reflective tone. 'Sort of offhand. I blamed it on the cold weather and with everything in New Brighton closed down it was so dreary.' She stopped and looked straight at Billy. 'Did they say if he'd gone on his own?'

Billy avoided her eyes. 'I've told you, no one seemed to have any details.'

'So what do I do now?' she asked in consternation. 'I suppose I'll have to stay on here,' she added dully.

'Unless you ask your mam if you can go back home. At least let me go and talk to her.'

'If you must,' she agreed reluctantly. 'Don't bother going to the house, she's bound to be in the Grafton at this time of night.'

Billy returned so speedily that Patsy knew he'd had no luck in finding her.

'Well?' she asked the minute he had closed the stable door behind him.

'She wasn't there.'

Patsy frowned. 'Perhaps it was too early for her. Maybe you should have gone to the house after all.'

Billy shook his head. 'Not much point. The barman said she's gone away. She told people that you'd moved out so she thought she'd take a holiday.'

'Did you check to see if it was true?'

Billy nodded. 'I went to the house, but there

was no one there and the curtains were closed.'

Patsy's green eyes were expressionless for a moment as she digested the news. 'I've nowhere else to go. What am I going to do, Billy?' she asked.

'You'll have to stay on here for the moment, I suppose.' He looked round the stable and shook his head disapprovingly. 'It's not suitable for a young baby though, is it? Or for you, when you have to use a bucket for a toilet and Samson's trough for water.'

'I've no choice,' she said sharply. 'I've hardly any money. You know me mam never gave me a proper wage, only a few shillings a week pocket money.'

Suddenly she was in floods of tears as the sheer hopelessness of her situation hit her like a hammer blow.

'Don't take on, Patsy. I'll look round tomorrow and see what other things I can get to make us more comfortable,' he promised.

Patsy's eyebrows shot up. 'Us? Oh, Billy, you can't stay here with me any longer. Your mam must be wondering why you've been here so long as it is. She isn't going to believe your story that Samson's not well for ever, you know.'

'I can't leave you and little Liam here on your own, now can I?' he blustered.

'And you can't go on living in a stable when you have a comfortable home to go to,' she insisted.

'It's not all that bad here. Anyway, it will only be for a couple of weeks, or so, until I can find somewhere better for you to live. There must be someone nearby who has rooms to rent. Leave it with me,' he told her confidently, 'I'll sort something out.' He pulled her into his arms and hugged her. 'You mustn't worry, Patsy, I'll see you through this. I'll take care of you, I promise.'

Her features softened. 'I know you will, Billy, and I really am grateful.' She kissed him warmly on the cheek. 'I've often wished I had a brother like you,' she told him affectionately.

'Thanks!' His lips rested on the top of her red curls. He couldn't meet her eyes. She might guess from the look on his face that her brother was the last thing he wanted to be. She meant so very much more to him than that, but now was probably not the right time to tell her.

When would there ever be a right time to tell her? he wondered. He spent most of his working day with Patsy, she was the first thing he thought about in the morning and the last thing he thought about at night when his head hit the pillow.

These last few days had been bittersweet. Something he would treasure for a long as he lived. He would happily marry her and take care of baby Liam, but he was afraid to offer to do so in case she thought he was putting her on the spot and taking advantage of the situation she was in.

He wanted her to tell him that she loved him before he asked her to marry him, but he wondered if that day would ever come. If it didn't, then perhaps he'd throw caution to the wind and pluck up the courage to ask her anyway.

Chapter Twenty-Two

Next day, left on her own, without even Samson for company, Patsy found that the hours dragged. She wished she hadn't agreed quite so readily that it was time Billy went back to work before he lost all the goodwill they'd taken so long to build up.

After she'd fed the baby and put him down to sleep in his makeshift cot Patsy took stock of her surroundings. The place was a shambles, she thought as she looked round the stable. It was not only gloomy, but it smelt to high heaven.

She made a start by brushing the floor and mucking out Samson's stall. Too late she remembered that Billy had not only locked the stable door but taken the key with him so the only thing she could do was to brush the dirty straw and droppings into a corner. At one end of the stable there was an archway, as though there had once been another door that was now closed off, so she brushed it all into there.

The place still looked cluttered so she tidied up all the baby's things and her own which seemed to be scattered everywhere. It was the first physical work she'd done since Liam was born and she was surprised at how exhausted she felt. She was so tired that when she sat down for a rest she fell asleep.

She was wakened by Liam crying from hunger. Still half asleep she fed him, changed him and put him back down to sleep.

She dragged the baby's cot as far away as possible from the recess where she'd piled the dirt, but the smell was still overpowering. The only window was a skylight in the roof and although this let in a fair amount of daylight it was so corroded that it was impossible to open.

She wished that she had told Billy to leave the key behind, but when she came to examine the lock on the stable door she wasn't even sure that it would open from the inside.

Patsy began to feel entombed. Her heart started to pound and she found herself gasping breathlessly. More than anything in the world she wanted to go outside and take a mouthful of fresh air.

She started pacing round and round the stable like a caged animal looking for some means of escape. She needed air. She wondered if perhaps some of the draughts they'd complained about over the past days meant that there was another door. They might even be coming from a window that had been bricked up to make the place more secure. That could be why it was always so gloomy.

Slowly she moved round the stable, holding her hand against the walls to try and locate where the draughts came from. The only place where there seemed to be air coming in was around the archway where she'd piled up the muck. Some of the mortar between the bricks appeared to be loose and crumbling, and a cold stream of air was coming in through the cracks.

She felt all round again but decided that it was probably her imagination playing tricks. Even so, if Billy didn't come back soon perhaps she would try and loosen some of the bricks, and see if it led into the street, she thought, sinking back on to the straw for a rest.

Patsy had no idea what time it was and how long it would be before Billy came back. She was feeling hungry herself and he'd promised her he would bring bread, milk and some cheese or a meat pie home with him. Since it must now be quite late in the day perhaps he'd bring fish and chips as well, she thought hopefully.

She strained her ears, listening for the clip-clop of Samson's huge feet on the cobbles outside, but all she heard was the occasional voice as people passing in the road called out a greeting to one another.

The gloom deepened so she lit the candle in the lantern. The flickering flame cast distorted shadows on the walls, which did little to cheer the place up and, as usual, sent shivers through her.

Restlessly Patsy began pacing up and down again. Surely Billy hadn't gone home and forgotten about her and the baby?

As her need to get out of the stable increased she felt more and more alarmed. Billy was the only one who knew they were there. Her mind filled with horror stories she'd heard on the docks about people being trapped in the holds of ships. When they were found days later they were dead.

Some of the dockers had taken a special delight in such gruesome yarns. One middle-aged man had told them about tunnels he'd played in as a youngster. Soldiers returning from the Napoleonic wars had built them under some mansion in Edge Hill and they ran for miles and miles. Some tunnels, he claimed, ran right into the centre of the city and had even been used when trains were first brought to Liverpool, because they were so well built. He said he'd been in them and although you could stand up and walk along in them they were full of rubbish and dead dogs and cats.

His words, 'They say there's an entrance to them through some old stable', kept reverberating through Patsy's head. Was this the old stable? she asked herself. Was that where the archway led? Could she get out if she managed to clear away the muck she'd piled up there?

She stared up at the skylight. It was now quite dark outside and since it was April that meant it must be eight o'clock at least. Billy had never been as late as this, not even when they were working together and had more work than they could get through. 'Even if we're not exhausted Samson is and he needs his food and rest,' he would always insist.

What on earth had happened to make him so late? A thousand possibilities jostled in her head but none of them made any real sense to her.

Liam was restless and she wondered if he was hungry again so she picked him up and undid the front of her blouse. He refused to feed. His body felt hot and damp, as though he was running a temperature, and his cry was thin and plaintive.

Patsy felt panic welling up inside her. She was locked in and only Billy knew she was there. Something drastic must have happened to delay him and make him this late. Now Liam seemed to be unwell and she had no idea what to do.

She walked up and down in the confined space trying to soothe the fractious baby and hoping he would go off to sleep again. All the time her mind was in turmoil. The tales of people being holed up for days and not being found until it was too late scared her.

She had to take some action, but she couldn't think what to do. It was no good banging on the door because the stable was separated from the roadway by the cobbled yard. No one walking by would hear her. She couldn't reach the skylight and even if she could she knew it wouldn't open.

Beads of perspiration trickled down her neck as her terror mounted. She must remain calm, she told herself. She was in a tight spot, but everything would be OK as long as she didn't give way to panic. There must be a way out. All she had to do was stay calm and think.

She concentrated her thoughts on the archway again. Supposing that docker had been right and this was the stable he had talked about. If the archway was an entrance to one of the tunnels then if she could move away enough of the bricks she'd be able to escape.

Filled with renewed optimism, she placed Liam down in his makeshift cot and covered him over. With the rake and shovel she'd used to clean out

Samson's stall she cleared away the dirty straw and muck. Then holding the lantern up high she tried to see the back of the recess more clearly.

Her heart thudded with excitement when she saw from its shape that the brick archway could have been a door that had been filled in. Using the edge of the shovel she banged at the mortar between the brickwork until she managed to dislodge some of the bricks and was able to ease a couple of them out.

She worked feverishly, struggling and banging, tearing at the bricks until her fingers were bleeding. When she held up the lantern again and peered into the gloom of the cavity she'd made she couldn't believe what she was seeing.

There was a tunnel! She peered more closely into the gloom: water was dripping from the top of it and the sides were green with slime but there was a tunnel. She could make an escape she hoped.

She pulled away more bricks to enlarge the opening and then cautiously stepped over the gaping hole into the abyss beyond.

The floor was damp and slippery, covered in green slime like the walls, but the tunnel seemed to be endless, vanishing into the distance. Patsy began walking along it, then stopped. Should she go on her own or should she take Liam with her? Which was the best thing to do?

On her own she could make faster progress, but was it safe to leave him behind in the stable on his own? He wasn't well. Supposing his fever got worse, or he cried so much he choked.

Yet if she took him with her what would Billy think if he came back and found them both missing?

Uncertainty undermined her confidence about what she was doing. Perhaps she ought to be patient and wait a little longer to see if Billy came back.

No, she told herself firmly, she wasn't going to wait. She couldn't stay in the stable a moment longer. When Billy returned he'd spot the hole in the wall and come along the tunnel after them. She'd take the baby with her, she resolved, as determinedly she struggled back through the opening. She couldn't leave the poor little mite there on his own.

Wrapping him securely in a blanket she cradled him in one arm so that she could carry the lantern in her free hand. Back in the tunnel she began walking, trying not to think about where it was leading, but to stay positive that it must be taking her into the city somewhere.

It seemed to go on for ever. She wanted to walk faster, but she was afraid of slipping on the damp greasy floor. If that happened and she broke a leg or knocked herself out, she thought pessimistically, it might be the end of her and Liam because no one, except Billy, would ever think of looking for them down there.

Tired and exhausted, Patsy finally had to stop and take a rest. Although Liam was a very tiny baby, because of her own weak state he seemed to grow heavier with every step she took. Crouched against one of the damp walls she brushed the tears from her face and wondered whether she should retrace her steps. Looking back through the gloom towards the stable, the distance seemed as endless as when she looked ahead so she decided to go on.

Soon her legs were aching even worse than they had been before she stopped. Slowly it dawned on her that it was because she was going uphill. What was more, the tunnel seemed to be loftier and there was more air all around her.

Jubilantly Patsy told herself that must mean the tunnel was about to come out at ground level. Filled with renewed hope she pressed on, straining her eyes, hoping to see a glimmer of daylight ahead. But, she reminded herself, it was probably night-time so even when she did reach the end of the tunnel there would still only be darkness.

Although the tunnel now had a high vaulted roof she found the going no easier. Her path was hampered by rubble of every description from ashes and clinkers from domestic firegrates to all sorts of other household junk that was rotting and stinking. As she tried to pick a way through it a scurrying in the shadows left by the lantern warned her there were rats and mice around.

Patsy pressed on determinedly. It was too far now for her to go back. Her arms ached from carrying Liam. He was still restless and he had started to cough. It was a harsh, dry little sound that ended in a whimper.

Poor little mite, she thought contritely. None of this was his fault. He hadn't asked to be born, or to be condemned to live in a stable. It had been her stupid concern about someone finding them there that had made Billy lock the door and take the key with him.

Where was Billy? she wondered, as she grappled her way through muck and rubbish. That was something she simply couldn't work out. He was always so reliable, so what on earth could have happened?

The last few hundred yards to freedom were the worst she had encountered. The muck that had been thrown down into the cavity was putrid. Decaying fruit and vegetables, as well as wet paper and cardboard that had disintegrated into soggy pulp, stuck to her feet and clothes.

When she eventually reached the roadway the fresh air was cold and damp. Patsy stood there for several minutes simply staring around, trying to work out where she was. It had to be somewhere in the city because of the noise and so many lights.

Discarding the lantern and tightening the shawl around Liam's little body she began making her way towards where she could see people and shops.

From somewhere close by she heard the familiar street cry, 'Echo! Evenin' Echo!' As she drew closer to the news-stand she saw the placard and the words sprang out at her.

ACCIDENT ON THE DOCKSIDE. HORSE DIES. MAN SERIOUSLY INJURED.

Patsy felt the blood drain to her feet. She swayed and would have fallen if she hadn't reached out and grabbed at the newspaper stand.

'Steady on, Missus, you nearly dropped your baby,' the news vendor told her as he grasped her by the arm. 'Want a paper, do you?'

Patsy shook her head. 'I've no money,' she mumbled. 'Can you tell me the name of the man who's been injured?'

'Think you know him do you, Missus?' His beady black eyes were curious.

'I'm not sure.'

'Nor is anyone else, luv,' he guffawed. 'Squashed flat he was by that great horse. I think they had to put the horse down, but they took the fella off to the Liverpool General. Look, there's a picture of it all on the front page.'

Patsy stared at the black-and-white picture and a lump came into her throat. There was no mistaking that the horse was Samson. He was lying on his side and the cart was overturned nearby.

So that meant the man involved, the man who'd been badly injured and taken to Liverpool General Hospital, must be Billy, she told herself numbly.

Chapter Twenty-Three

Tears streaming down her face, Liam held tightly in her arms, Patsy headed instinctively towards her home in Paradise Place.

As she trudged through the darkening streets she no longer worried about who saw her with the baby; there were other more important matters to be dealt with now. Her mind was filled with memories of Billy.

She recalled the days before he left school when he'd first worked for her dad cleaning out Samson's stable every Saturday morning. He'd been a sturdy lad in short trousers and a brown pullover that his mam had knitted for him. He had been so eager to please, and so fond of the horse, that in next to no time he was helping to feed and groom Samson every evening as well as before school in the morning. The minute he was old enough to leave school her dad had taken him on full time.

How proud Billy had been the first time her dad had let him handle the reins! His solemn face was transformed by a beaming smile that had made his light blue eyes shine as brilliantly as the sky on a cloudless summer day.

She loved it when Billy smiled, especially when he smiled at her. His smile was so warm and friendly, as if he really was pleased to see you, not a polite cold gesture like so many people gave you. Billy's smile not only lit up his eyes and his whole face, but it made you feel good. It was as if the world was suddenly a nicer place.

He was considerate of other people's feelings, too. She had never heard him say anything unkind about anyone. And he was always polite and helpful. Even the grumpiest of men down at the docks seemed pleased to see him and exchanged a comradely word with him. No matter how difficult to handle the load might be, or how heavy, Billy never grumbled. He simply got on with the job in hand whatever it might be and she knew this impressed the dockers, as well as the bosses they came into contact with when they were making deliveries.

He didn't talk a lot, but he watched and took an interest in all that was going on around him. He learned very quickly. She recalled her dad saying he only had to tell Billy once, or show him how to do something once, and after that he remembered.

Her dad had always been praising him. He would have been full of praise for the way the two of them had taken over the business and expanded it after he'd died, she thought proudly.

A shudder went through her. Her dad had died on the dock road and now the same thing had happened to Billy. Only Billy wasn't dead, she reminded herself. He was hurt, very badly hurt, but he wasn't dead. It was important that she remembered that. It was the one thing she had to hold on to now.

Patsy's steps took her home. The door was locked. She slipped her hand in the letterbox automatically searching for the piece of string with the key on it, but it seemed to be missing. Impatiently she banged on the door and called out through the letterbox, 'It's me, Mam. Let me in, I can't find the key.'

There was no answering call, but when she hammered again even harder on the door she heard footsteps coming down the hallway. The door swung open and a grey-haired woman wearing a bright red cotton apron over a grey dress stood there glaring at her angrily.

'Do you have to hammer the bloody door down, luv? I was out the back in the lavvy. What is it you want anyway?' Patsy stared back at the woman blankly. 'Who are you? What are you doing in me mam's house?'

'I'm not in your mam's house. This is my place.'

Patsy shook her head. 'You're wrong. Mrs Callaghan lives here! Maeve Callaghan. I'm her daughter, Patsy.'

'She might have lived here once, but she don't no longer,' the woman snapped. 'The last I heard of her she'd scarpered off to Blackpool.'

As she started to close the door Patsy put out a hand to stop her. 'Stop kidding me, Missus. I want me mam, she lives here and so do I if it comes to that.'

'Bugger off, there's no Callaghans living here. Go on!' The woman pushed hard at the door. 'Bugger off before I call the scuffers.'

Patsy watched perplexed as the door was

slammed in her face. She took a step back, staring up at the bedroom windows. When she saw the woman peering out from behind the front room curtains, as if to make sure she was going, she moved away.

Slowly it came back to her fuddled mind that Billy had told her he hadn't been able to find her mam when he'd gone to the Grafton. He'd said something about her going away, but not that she'd moved out of Paradise Place for good.

She wondered if she went back and explained all this to the woman who was living in their house now if it would help at all, but decided that it would probably be a waste of time. The woman probably wouldn't believe her.

She leaned against a lamppost wondering what to do next. Perhaps if she went along to the Grafton someone there might be able to tell her where her mam had gone. If she'd moved right away from Paradise Place, though, what good would that do? She had no money to go looking for her.

Liam squirmed uncomfortably in his cocoon of shawls and began to cry. He sounded far from well. He was probably ready for another feed, Patsy thought listlessly. A keen wind had sprung up and she shivered with cold. She'd have to find somewhere sheltered where she could sit and feed him.

He probably needed changing as well, but his clean nappy was back in the stable and she couldn't get in there because it was all locked up.

As she stood there shivering in the cold and

darkness she realised that there was only one place left where she could go and that was to Billy Grant's house.

Billy's mother answered the door. 'Patsy? What are you doing here?' she exclaimed, a startled look on her plump face as if she was seeing a ghost.

'Weren't you on the cart then when Billy had the accident?' she asked in surprise. 'The police came and said that Billy's in hospital, but then you must know that! My Joe's gone to the hospital. I thought it was him back, though he wouldn't be knocking, now would he. Oh, look, come on in and I'll make us both a cup of tea, you look in nearly as bad a state as I am,' she gabbled.

It wasn't until Patsy was in Mrs Grant's neat but overcrowded living room that she seemed to realise what Patsy was carrying in her arms.

Elaine Grant's motherly face registered shock and disquiet. 'This isn't yours, is it?' she asked coming closer and peeping inside the shawl. 'Is it a girl or a boy, luv?'

'It's a little boy. Liam.'

As Patsy peeled back the damp shawl so that Elaine could see him better, Liam gave a sharp dry cough and Elaine was immediately all concern.

'Poor little mite, it sounds to me as though he's got a touch of bronchitis. Have you taken him to the doctor?'

'No.' Patsy looked at her guiltily. 'No, not yet.'

Elaine looked anxious. 'The poor little soul is soaked right through, luv. Have you got a change of clothes we can put on him?'

Patsy shook her head dolefully.

'Here, give him to me, you look all in, Patsy. Sit down by the fire while I see to him and then I'll make a cup of tea for us both.'

Patsy watched in grateful silence as Elaine Grant stripped off Liam's soaking wet nappy and saturated clothes.

'How old is he, Patsy?' Elaine asked sharply as she wrapped the tiny body in a warm thick towel.

'Just over a week.'

Elaine was silent for a few seconds, her mind racing as she tried to sum up the situation.

'Stay there by the fire,' she said, handing the baby to Patsy, 'and I'll go and see what I can find to wrap him in while I wash and dry his clothes.'

She came back a few minutes later with some pieces of old sheet, a thick towel, and one of Joe's woollen vests.

'I'm sure we can make something out of these,' she said, taking a pair of scissors from the sideboard drawer and starting to cut up the sheet into squares.

'When I've done this I'll rub his little chest with some camphorated oil before I wrap him up. That'll help to soften his cough. I bet that's what your mam used to do for you when you were a bit chesty?'

'I can't find me mam,' Patsy said wearily. 'Do you know where she might be, Mrs Grant?'

Elaine Grant shook her head. 'I heard she'd gone away. There was a rumour going around that you'd left home and that she'd gone as well. It was a couple of weeks or more ago when I first heard it.'

Patsy nodded absently. 'I seem to remember

244

Billy said something like that.'

'You mean you haven't been home since . . . since you had the baby, luv?'

Patsy shook her head. 'Not until today. I was worried when it started to get dark and Billy hadn't come back.'

Elaine stared at her bemused. 'Has there been anything wrong with Samson over the last few weeks?' she asked in a bewildered voice. 'I thought Billy said he wasn't well, perhaps I misunderstood him.'

Patsy's face clouded. She wasn't sure exactly what Billy had told his mam to cover for the time he'd spent with her. She'd probably made a mistake coming to Elaine's but she felt so befuddled that she didn't know what else to do.

'Samson's dead, isn't he,' she said in an attempt to avoid Elaine's question. 'Do you know how the accident happened?'

'No, luv!' Elaine patted her shoulder. 'My Joe will be able to tell us when he gets home. He shouldn't be much longer now.'

'Will Billy be with him?'

'No, I shouldn't think so. He's been badly hurt, remember. They'll probably decide to keep him in hospital for a quite a while.'

'So what am I going to do? He's got the key,' Patsy exclaimed agitatedly. 'I can't get back into the stable without it and I can't go back down that long tunnel again, there's rats there!'

'Are you saying that you've been living there?' Elaine asked incredulously. 'Was your baby born there?'

Patsy nodded. 'Yes, just over a week ago.'

Elaine's mind raced as she wrapped the baby up in a makeshift shawl and handed him back to Patsy. She couldn't believe what she was hearing, she didn't even want to, yet she felt she had to know the facts.

'Patsy,' she asked very gently, 'who was with you when the baby was born, who helped you? Was it my Billy?'

Patsy nodded again, but avoided meeting Elaine's eyes and concentrated on suckling the baby.

Elaine thought back over what had been happening over the past two weeks, ever since Billy had told her that Samson wasn't well and that he had to stay on in the stable to keep an eye on him. She knew now that it hadn't been Samson at all, but Patsy and her baby that Billy had been looking after. She remembered all the food, the soups and stews that she had given him.

At the time it had struck her that his appetite was bigger than usual, but she'd said nothing because she'd seen how upset he was. Now she could understand why, as well as the reason for him needing almost twice the food he normally ate. And if there had only been him there when Patsy's baby was born then no wonder he'd been worried.

Why on earth didn't he come and fetch me if he couldn't find Patsy's mother? she thought angrily. Helping out at childbirth was a woman's job, certainly not something a young lad should be doing. No wonder he looked as though he had

the cares of the world on his shoulders: he probably wasn't even sure that he'd done everything
properly. Even if they hadn't sent for a doctor
when the baby was born then Patsy should have
seen one right away afterwards, but it didn't
sound as though she had.

Elaine looked across at the baby now sleeping
soundly in Patsy's arms. He was such a tiny little
scrap and if he'd had to start his life in nothing
better than a stable it was no wonder he had
bronchitis.

First thing tomorrow morning she'd get the
doctor in to have a look at him, she resolved. It
wouldn't do any harm and it would set her own
mind at rest to know that it wasn't Billy's fault
the child wasn't well.

Her mind went back to Billy and she longed
for Joe to come home from the hospital and let
her know he was going to be all right. Everything
seemed to be happening at once. First the accident
and now this.

She didn't understand why Patsy had been
living in the stable or what she meant about not
being able to get back in there because Billy had
taken the key with him. She sighed. It didn't really
matter, of course. She couldn't let her go back there
even if they could find a way of getting in.

'While we're waiting for my Joe to come home
I'll go and sort out where you and the baby can
sleep,' she told Patsy. 'You'd better have our
Janie's room for tonight and she can come down
here and sleep . . .'

'No . . . no, Mrs Grant. I can't do that. I can't

turn your Janie out of her bed,' Patsy protested.

'Gracious, why ever not? It won't hurt her to sleep on the sofa for one night!'

'No, please. I don't want to do that,' Patsy said awkwardly, colour rushing to her cheeks.

She and Janie had never got on very well when they'd been at school, but she didn't want to tell Mrs Grant that. Janie had always teased her about Billy and made fun of her for paying so much attention to Samson.

'It wouldn't be fair to disturb her. Janie has to get up and go to work in the morning,' she added lamely.

'Very well. Then you can have young Freddie's bed. He'll be glad of the excuse that he had to sleep on the sofa when he nods off in school tomorrow,' she smiled.

'I'm really sorry to put you out like this, Mrs Grant.'

'It's no trouble, no trouble at all,' Elaine Grant assured her. 'In fact,' she said suddenly, her face brightening, 'there's no need to disturb Freddie, you can have our Billy's bed. He won't be needing it if he's in hospital overnight, now will he? You sleep in our Billy's bed and we'll sort things out better tomorrow.'

Patsy looked apprehensive. 'Are you quite sure?'

'Of course I am. Anyway, it's what our Billy would want and it will put his mind at rest to know you and the baby are safe and sound,' she said firmly. 'While you finish feeding little Liam I'll go upstairs and empty one of the drawers in my chest-of-drawers and then I'll make up a bed for the baby in it. I'll put it right alongside your bed, Patsy, and then it will be easy for you to pick him up if he cries in the night.'

With Liam fed and comfortably settled, Elaine made a pot of tea and a plate of ham sandwiches for herself and Patsy as they waited for Joe to return with news of Billy.

Chapter Twenty-Four

Billy Grant had no idea where he was or even what his name was when he first regained consciousness. Hour after hour he stared at the white ceiling and the green walls, his handsome face expressionless.

For three days he lay cocooned in a blank world that was punctuated only by the routine of meal-times when he was fed liquids from a cup, and periodic visits by doctors who studied the medical charts clipped to the foot of his hospital bed. They then examined him and conferred with colleagues, with grave faces and much shaking of their heads.

Billy could hear the sound of their voices as they congregated around his bedside, but the words had no meaning for him.

Even the discomfort of having his right leg suspended high in the air by means of ropes and pulleys, or of having the many lacerations on his face and head dressed with antiseptic fluids and lotions, failed to penetrate his mind or concern him at all.

It was only on the third day, when he was subjected to the torture of having his broken ribs strapped up, that he regained a degree of consciousness. It was as if the hideous pain that was inflicted on him cleared some of the mists from his mind.

As he lay gasping in agony from the nurses' ministrations he started to question what they were doing to him. Where was he? What had happened to him? He couldn't remember, and he felt not only confused but apprehensive because from the nature of his injuries he knew it had been something serious.

The poker-faced nurses in their dark blue dresses, stiffly starched white aprons and crisp white caps were noncommittal. They admitted that he had been brought in by ambulance three days ago, but told him he must wait and talk to one of the doctors, as there was nothing else they could tell him.

He questioned the orderlies who washed him and shaved him and combed his thick brown hair, but they were too busy to tell him any details. When they brought him drinks of water or cups of tea and made a point of asking him how he was feeling, or made conversation about the weather, he didn't bother to answer them: it was all so unimportant.

Billy begged to see the doctor or anyone who could tell him the details of what had happened to him. He knew he must have been in an accident or he wouldn't have been brought into hospital, but where had it happened and what sort of accident had it been?

It was left to his father eventually to tell him the details.

Joe Grant hated the smell of disinfectant and

the sterile atmosphere of the hospital ward, but he refused to go home. He had been at Billy's bedside every day since the police had come to his house to tell him son was injured.

As soon as Billy regained consciousness and started asking questions Joe did his best to give him the answers, but in as circumspect a way as possible so as not to cause him any more trauma.

'Yes, lad, you were in an accident,' he said quietly. 'A pretty bad one at that.'

'Was I knocked down?'

'No, not exactly, not in the way you mean.'

'Then why are my ribs all bust and my leg broken?'

'That's because you were crushed, lad.' He hesitated, not wanting to distress his son, but Billy was not satisfied, he was determined to hear the whole story. He insisted on knowing where and when.

'It happened while you were leading Samson. He fell over on you,' Joe told him hesitantly.

'Samson did? What happened?' Billy looked alarmed. 'Is he all right?'

Joe shook his head. 'Samson's dead, I'm afraid.' He gripped Billy's hand. 'I'm sorry, lad, I know how fond you were of that horse.'

Billy took a deep breath and stared at his father in disbelief. 'How did it happen?' he asked weakly.

'The vet said that poor old Samson had some sort of heart attack. He keeled over without any warning. You'd just come back from the Wirral on the ferryboat with a very heavy load. You'd reached the top of the floating roadway, unhitched the spare horse that had helped to pull the cart up the slipway, and then it happened. You had hold of Samson's bridle and you were about to lead him on to the roadway when he buckled up. He collapsed and fell over sideways and landed on you. You were trapped underneath him and the cart.'

'And Samson was dead? Just like that?' Billy's voice was thick with disbelief.

'Dead as a doornail, lad. His heart gave out, so the police vet said. He wouldn't have felt a thing so there's no cause for you to take on.'

Billy ran his hand through his hair. 'Samson dead? I can't take it in,' he muttered.

'It was you that took the brunt of his fall. Squashed, you were,' Joe Grant went on. 'Tidy weight that old horse and to fall full on you like he did it's lucky you're still alive.'

Billy shook his head. 'I don't know about that, I feel half dead.'

'Well you would, lad. You've got three crushed ribs, a broken leg, lacerations to your face and head and you've been unconscious for almost three days.'

'Do you know when I'm going to get out of here?'

'Not for a while, I shouldn't think. Your ribs have got to knit together for a start and then there's your leg. It's broken in I don't know how many places so it will take some time.'

Billy became agitated. 'I've got to get back to work. Have you any idea what happened to the load I was carrying?'

'Nothing to worry about there. The dockers who were standing by waiting for you to bring the stuff alongside turned to and unloaded the cart. They took everything straight on to the ship. As for getting back to work, well you'd have a job to do that in your present state now, wouldn't you? What's more, the cart was smashed to smithereens and you have no horse so lie still and get yourself better.'

'You don't understand, Dad, I've got to work. Patsy needs money to live on.' A shadow passed over his face. 'Was Patsy hurt when Samson collapsed and the cart turned over?' He grabbed at Joe's hand. His voice sank to a strained whisper. 'Patsy wasn't killed, was she?' he asked hoarsely.

'Of course she wasn't,' Joe said firmly. 'She wasn't even with you!'

'She must have been, she always comes out with me,' Billy persisted.

'Well, she wasn't with you this time. You were on your own.'

Billy shook his head from side to side as if doubting what his father was telling him.

'Don't you worry your head about Patsy,' Joe said firmly. 'There's nothing at all wrong with her and she's well taken care of because she's moved into our place. Your mam's letting her sleep in your bed and that's where she'll stay until you come out of here. She's all right and so is the baby.'

'Baby? What baby?' Billy asked in a puzzled voice.

'Patsy's new baby, of course. Don't tell me you've forgotten about it?'

Billy rubbed his hand over his eyes as if to clear a mist from them and then pushed his fingers through his thick mat of hair. Slowly the blankness disappeared from his blue eyes and was replaced by a look of dawning enlightenment.

'Of course, the baby!' he muttered. 'Little Liam! Yes, you're right, I'd forgotten about him.' He grinned up at his father. 'It must have been some almighty bump I had on my head for me to forget about that!'

Joe Grant waited expectantly. Like his wife he was anxious to know if it was Billy's child, but Patsy had not said a word and because of her distressed state neither of them liked to question her. Janie had tried several times to draw her out, but Patsy had kept her own counsel.

The smile suddenly vanished from Billy's face. 'Where did you say Patsy was?'

'She's living with us. Sleeping in your bed for the moment,' his father repeated.

'How did she get out of the stable? I left her locked in and I took the key along with me. Did someone find it and let her out?'

'No, I don't think so.' Joe looked puzzled. 'They couldn't have done! When she turned up on our doorstep both Patsy and the little one were soaking wet and she told your mam she couldn't get into the stable to get dry clothes. Your mam had to cut up some sheets and towels and wrap the baby in one of my old woollen vests for warmth.'

'How did she get out of the stable, then?' Billy asked in bewilderment.

'She said something about a tunnel, but we didn't take too much notice at the time. Your mam thought that perhaps Patsy was rambling because she'd heard about your accident and was out her mind with worry.'

Billy looked perplexed. 'I don't understand how she could have heard about it if she was locked in the stable.'

'She told your mam that she'd seen it on a newspaper placard when she came out of the tunnel, but that didn't make much sense to us.'

Billy stared at Joe transfixed. 'She must have found those old tunnels, Dad.'

It was Joe's turn to look bemused. 'What bloody tunnels are you talking about, lad?'

'Some docker told us a tale about there being tunnels under the city. It seems they were dug out over a hundred years or more ago, just after the Napoleonic wars in fact. This fella said there was an entrance in a stable somewhere. It must have been our stable he was talking about and Patsy must have found it.'

Joe shook his head. 'You've lost me, lad. Anyway, the main thing is she's safe and well and so is the baby. He had a touch of bronchitis, but your mam knew how to deal with that. She rubbed his little chest with camphorated oil and he's as right as rain now. Bonny little fellow even though he's a bit on the thin side.'

Billy nodded but said nothing. His mind was racing. It was all coming back to him. Patsy's mother throwing her out because she was pregnant, his futile attempt to find Bruno, and Patsy

256

saying she'd have to move into the stable because she had nowhere else to stay.

He'd wanted her to come back to his home and let his mam help her, but she'd refused. She hadn't wanted anyone to know that she was pregnant. Then before they could decide what she ought to do she'd gone into labour.

He closed his eyes, wanting to shut out all memory of what had happened next. He'd felt so inept, so completely useless. Seeing Patsy in such terrible pain and distress and not knowing what to do had been so frightening. He'd done his best to help her, but had it been enough? If only she had let him fetch his mother, or Mrs Murphy, or a doctor. But he'd been afraid to provoke or vex her. Anyway, he couldn't have left her alone, not while she was in that state.

After the baby had been born she still wouldn't let him tell anyone. He'd done the best he could. He'd fitted the stable up with a Valor oil stove so that there was some heating and a Primus stove to warm up their food and to heat up water to bath the baby. It had been a rough and ready arrangement, but it was what she wanted.

Telling his mother that Samson was ill was the only way he could think of absenting himself from home so that he could stay with her. Now Samson was dead. It was almost like a punishment, he thought guiltily.

Samson wasn't a young horse and keeping him shut up for well over a week probably hadn't done him any good. Taking him out and expecting him to pull an extra-heavy load when he'd been idle for such a long spell had been too much for the poor beast. That's why his heart had given out so suddenly.

As he sat by Billy's bedside, Joe Grant questioned if he had done right to remind Billy of all this. He wondered why Billy had never told them about his feelings for Patsy or about the baby. For the baby to be born in such primitive conditions as a ramshackle old stable was unbelievable. There wasn't even any water or lighting there and certainly no heating. He and Patsy must have had a reason for carrying on like that and he wondered if Maeve Callaghan was against them marrying.

'Do you want Patsy to come in and see you tomorrow, lad?'

'Yeah,' Billy nodded, 'and me mam.'

'Right then I'll tell them. I wouldn't think they'd let the baby in so they probably won't be able to come together. If your mam comes in to see you tomorrow then she can mind the baby the day after while Patsy visits you.'

'Yeah, that'll do fine.'

'If Patsy comes on her own it will give the two of you a chance to make arrangements about what you want to do,' Joe added with heavy meaning.

Billy sighed. 'Yes, I suppose so. Neither of us have a job now if Samson's gone. Anyway,' he gave a mirthless grin, 'I'm not likely to be walking or able to do anything useful for quite a while, am I?'

'No, but there's still the baby to consider,' Joe reminded him.

'Right mess we're both in, aren't we,' Billy said grimly.

'There's no need for you to worry, lad,' Joe told him gruffly. 'Like I told you, Patsy has moved in with us and your mam'll keep an eye on her and the baby so you've nothing to worry about.'

'It's the future I'm worried about,' Billy told him. 'Where's Patsy and the baby going to live after I get out of hospital? They can't go back to living in the stable now, can they?'

'She'll have to stay with us then,' Joe told him.

'There isn't room! Not unless I move in with young Freddie and that wouldn't work because his room is so small he can hardly turn round in it.'

Joe didn't know what to say. He'd assumed that the baby was Billy's and that he and Patsy would get married as soon as Billy came out of hospital. From the way Billy was talking, though, that was the last thing he was planning. He didn't understand it. 'We'll manage somehow, lad, so don't you worry,' he muttered. 'You just get better and things will sort themselves out, you'll see.'

Seeing Billy lying there so helpless, his leg supported in a cradle, his head bandaged, his face a mass of cuts and grazes, tugged at Joe Grant's heart.

Billy was a chip off the old block. Perhaps it was because Billy was his first-born that he felt there was a stronger bond between them than he had with either of his other two children.

He'd looked just like Billy when he'd been in his twenties. He passed a hand over his bald head;

his hair had been as thick and brown as Billy's was when he'd first started going out with Elaine. A lot of water under the bridge since then, he reflected. He wondered if Billy would be as bald as he was in twenty years' time. He was certainly taking on his share of responsibilities!

He didn't understand what was going on between Billy and Patsy, nor could he work out why Maeve Callaghan hadn't taken care of her when the baby was born. The whole thing was a complete mystery to him.

When he'd asked Elaine why Patsy couldn't go and stay with her mother she'd said that Maeve Callaghan was gone, she'd left Paradise Place and a Mrs Blackwood was living in her house.

None of it made any sense as far as he was concerned, Joe thought, but he supposed the truth would come out in the end and all the pieces would fall into place. At the moment, all he wanted was for Billy to get better.

Chapter Twenty-Five

The night before Billy Grant came home from hospital, Patsy hardly slept a wink. She tossed and turned: so many conflicting thoughts were going through her mind. She wished she could get up and make herself a cup of tea or walk around, but she dare not do that because it might disturb everyone else.

The bed was comfortable, in fact from the very first night at the Grants' it had felt like the height of luxury to her. Yet she couldn't settle and it wasn't because Liam was restless.

He slept soundly. The poultice of brown paper, camphorated oil and grease that Elaine had put on his little chest that first night had made his breathing easier and after a couple of days he seemed to be quite recovered.

Elaine Grant had put a feather pillow in the drawer for him. The high sides protected Liam from any draught and he was covered over with a cut-down sheet and a white shawl so that he was both safe and snug.

Patsy tried to blame her sleeplessness on the strangeness of the situation she found herself in. Even now, after three months, she simply couldn't get used to being in Billy's home and sleeping in his bed.

Although she'd known Billy since even before they'd started school she had seldom been inside his home. Once or twice she had called for his younger sister Janie who'd been in her class at school.

Even then she had waited on the doorstep while whoever opened the door called out to Janie to let her know that Patsy was there. The only exception had been when Janie had hurt her ankle and couldn't go to school and she'd brought some homework that Janie was supposed to do. Janie had been lying on the sofa and Mrs Grant had asked Patsy if she'd like a biscuit and a glass of milk. She'd refused because the room had looked so spick and span and well polished that she'd been afraid she might make crumbs or spill the milk.

Now here she was, in the Grants' house, lying in Billy's bed with her own baby on the floor beside her. It all seemed so unreal and so different from when she'd been sleeping on a makeshift bed of straw in the stable.

She couldn't get over how loyal Billy had been and the way he had let his mother believe that he was staying at the stable all night because Samson wasn't well. She kept wondering what Elaine Grant had thought when she'd found out that it had been a lie. Yet she's never said anything about it the whole time I've been staying here, Patsy mused. In fact, none of them had asked any awkward questions about her and Billy, or about the baby.

From the moment she had arrived, Patsy felt

she owed it to Billy's mother to tell her that the baby wasn't his. Several times she'd been about to confide in Janie but she kept putting it off because she was afraid that if they knew the truth then Mrs Grant mightn't let her stay there and she had nowhere else to go.

It had been a shock to find that her mam had cleared off and that no one knew where she'd gone. When Billy had said that her mam had gone away she'd thought he meant that Maeve had cleared off with one of her fancy men. Patsy hadn't been too concerned because she'd thought that her mam would be back again the moment she was tired of him, or he'd had enough of her. She didn't for one moment think it meant that her mam had given up their house.

No doubt that was what she was planning to do when she kicked me out and threw all my things after me, Patsy reasoned.

She turned restlessly, her brain racing like a clockwork car. Why did other people's mams stay put and seem content with their lot? Her mam never had. All those horrible 'uncles' in the days when her dad was away at sea. All the rows between her mam and her dad when he'd decided to find a job ashore because she said she'd have no freedom if he did that.

For the first few weeks after her dad returned her mam had promised that from now on they'd look after each other and be really good friends.

And I really believed she meant it, Patsy thought sadly.

The business had been bringing them in a

comfortable living. Too comfortable, probably, she thought bitterly. There was always plenty of money available for her mam to spend in the Grafton. She'd started propping up the bar every night, and treating all and sundry to drinks, so she'd quickly made a whole host of new friends. It was probably one of these new fellas she'd gone off with. This time it must be serious if she's given up the house! Patsy thumped her pillow angrily.

Thinking about her mam and her new boyfriend didn't help her any, Patsy thought despairingly. She'd be better off thinking about her own future, especially now she'd got the baby to look after as well as herself.

Billy's mother seemed to think it would be months before Billy was going to be able to work again. And with Samson dead, their business venture was finished since neither of them had enough money to buy a new horse.

She finally fell asleep thinking about what sort of work she could do and dreamed that Bruno had come back and was so happy about the baby that he couldn't wait to take them both back to Spain.

Her dream was so real that when Liam's hungry cry wakened her she half expected to find Bruno there.

She put Liam back into his cot after she'd fed him, then snuggled back down into Billy's bed and pulled the covers up to her chin. She couldn't get back to sleep again, though, because all her doubts and worries had come rushing back.

She heard the day's routine start. First it was Joe Grant's heavy tread as he went downstairs and then the front door slamming behind him as he left the house. Next came the scuttle of Janie's feet on the stairs as she dashed up and down getting ready for work. Finally there was Freddie, who was now in his last few days at school, banging down the stairs calling out to ask what was for breakfast. Ten minutes later he slammed the front door behind him and Patsy heard the sound of his feet running down the street.

The tap on the bedroom door startled her. Today of all days, knowing that Billy was coming home from hospital, she should have got dressed straight after feeding Liam instead of settling down in bed again, she thought guiltily.

'I've brought you up a cuppa,' Elaine announced as she came into the room.

Patsy smiled gratefully. 'I . . . I was just about to get up,' she told her. 'I thought it was best for me to stay here as usual so as not to be in everyone's way while they were getting ready for work.'

'Quite right,' Elaine agreed as she bent over the makeshift cot and smiled down at Liam.

She was not only up and dressed, with a clean flowered apron covering her light blue cotton dress, but even her brown hair was neatly combed, Patsy noticed.

'There's no point in rushing,' Elaine went on as she picked Liam up. 'They won't be bringing Billy home until midday so we've got plenty of time to get things ready for him. He's going to see a great change in this little fella, isn't he?'

'Yes, three months has made a big difference,' Patsy agreed.

'He looked like a little skinned rabbit the night you turned up with him, the night of our Billy's accident,' Elaine went on.

Patsy nodded. She knew Elaine was waiting for her to say something more, perhaps tell her that Liam was Billy's baby. Despite her earlier resolution Patsy felt that now it was up to Billy to tell his mother whatever he thought fit so she remained quiet.

'Don't you think Billy would be happier to be back in his own bed rather than having to sleep downstairs on the couch?' she asked. 'I'm sure he'd be much more comfortable with all his own things around him.'

'No,' Elaine shook her head. 'It's better for Billy to be down there. If he's stuck away up here he'll feel like an invalid instead of being one of the family again.'

Patsy nodded. 'I suppose he would find it difficult to get up and down the stairs using crutches and with that metal calliper on his leg.'

'That's right, and don't forget the doctor said he mustn't bend his leg at all. Anyway, being downstairs will be handier for the nurse when she comes in twice a week to change the dressings.'

'How long does the doctor think the calliper will have to stay on?'

'Goodness only knows! When it does come off he's going to have to learn to walk again. The doctor said he'll probably always have problems with the leg and that he may have a permanent limp.'

'Well at least his ribs have healed and most of

the scars have gone from his face,' Patsy said brightly.

'Yeah! I suppose we should be grateful for small mercies,' Elaine Grant sighed. 'I've no doubt he'll be glad to get out of that hospital and be back home with us all, even if he's on crutches for months to come.'

The thought of Billy not being able to work for the foreseeable future worried Patsy a great deal. It meant that as well as providing for her and Liam, Joe and Elaine Grant would also have to keep Billy.

Joe Grant might earn good money, but it wouldn't stretch endlessly. He and Elaine had been very kind to let her stay there all this time. She couldn't expect them to let her go on living with them for ever, though, not unless she was able to contribute her fair share of the household expenses.

The trouble was that she had nothing to offer, Patsy thought unhappily. Although her mother had paid Billy a proper wage when he'd taken over the running of her dad's business she'd only ever given Patsy a few shillings a week pocket money.

'You don't need to worry,' her mam had said, 'I'll buy you all the new clothes you want as well as everything else. You won't go short of anything. As long as you've got some money in your pocket for the flicks that's all you need.'

Maeve never had bought her any new clothes, though. All the money that Billy handed over from the business her mam had kept for herself and spent it at the Grafton as fast as Billy earned it.

She hadn't even paid some of the bills. Several times they'd had a visit from the man who owned the stable pointing out that rent was well overdue and if they didn't pay up right away then they were out.

Now, if Billy was to be on crutches for months to come, even if they could get hold of another horse he wouldn't be able to manage to take it out on his own. Nor would he be able to cope with loading up the cart. And since she had the baby to look after she wouldn't be able to help him out on the cart either, not unless his mam would take care of Liam while they worked.

It hadn't seemed fair to worry Billy about such matters while he was so ill in hospital, but as soon as he was back at home, and settled in, Patsy knew she would have to discuss it with him and they'd have to try and work something out.

Perhaps the best thing they could do, Patsy thought sadly, would be to clear out whatever remained in the stable and call it a day. There might be a few bits and pieces that they could sell, like Samson's harness and tack and whatever remained of the feed and straw.

As for the immediate future, well once Billy was used to moving about perhaps he would be able to look after Liam for a couple of hours each day and she could go out to work. It would only be for a very short time because once Bruno came back, and she was able to tell him about the baby, then she hoped they would be married and off to Spain as soon as it could all be arranged.

It all seemed so very unsatisfactory and such a muddle that Patsy's mind was in turmoil. She wasn't at all sure how the Grants would feel about her and Liam staying on any longer. If, as she suspected, they were only making a home for her because they thought the baby was Billy's then once they knew the truth they might feel very different about having her there.

They had been kindness itself, Patsy thought gratefully. She'd never be able to repay Elaine for the way she had looked after Liam during those first couple of weeks when they'd first arrived on their doorstep. It had been Elaine who had nursed Liam back to health, found clothes for him and cared for them both. Apart from feeding him I was too ill to do very much for him, she thought.

Janie and Freddie had both been so good, too, helping to look after the baby so that she could go with Elaine to visit Billy in hospital.

Living with the Grants had been an eye-opener. It had shown her what a happy home life could be like. The more she witnessed the warmth and support they gave each other, the more she dreamed that one day she and Bruno would have a home life exactly like that.

Patsy constantly went over in her mind all the wonderful things Bruno had told her about his home in Spain. He said how friendly all the people were and that his family would love her. She could almost feel the warm sun and see the golden sands. She could visualise the people dancing, hear the music, and the happy laughter.

She dreamed of the day when Bruno would be

back in New Brighton and reunited with her and baby Liam. She could hardly wait for them to be together so that they could start making plans to go to his home in Spain as soon as the season ended.

She felt bitter. It was hard to understand why Bruno hadn't let her know that he was leaving New Brighton or told her where he was going. It wasn't as though they'd had a row. She knew he'd been frustrated because there was nowhere they could go in the cold weather so that they could be on their own. Perhaps she should have taken him home, but after what had happened on her sixteenth birthday how could she?

Perhaps Bruno had tried to get in touch with her and been unable to find her because she'd been living in the stable, she thought hopefully.

If he'd gone to her house after her mam had left he would have either found it empty or Mrs Blackwood living there and she wouldn't have been very helpful. She'd have said that me mam had gone and Bruno might think I'd gone with her.

Chapter Twenty-Six

Having Billy at home seemed to create problems no one had anticipated. For the first couple of days everyone was in a state of euphoria, dashing around waiting on him hand and foot. Once the novelty wore off, however, they all began to understand the full impact of what having an invalid to care for involved.

The bulk of the extra work fell on Elaine, but this was partly her own fault. When Patsy offered to help Billy to wash and dress each morning she was aghast.

'You can't do that!' she exclaimed in shocked tones. 'It wouldn't be right for you to see him without any clothes on when you're not married.'

Billy was not a good patient. Far from it. He was impatient, demanding and irritable. Because of his good looks and warm smile he had been a favourite with most of the nurses and as a result they had danced attendance on him more than was normal.

While he'd been in hospital he'd been longing to get home; now that he was at home he missed not only the nurses, but also the companionship of the other patients in the ward. 'Being in hospital was like being in a different world,' he told his mother and Patsy. 'There was always something new happening on the ward with people leaving or new patients being brought in.'

Even though he'd been confined to bed, and had been lying prone for most of the time, he hadn't been bored.

'There was so much going on I didn't have time to think,' he told them. 'Mealtimes, medicine rounds, bed-making and all the rest of it took up every hour of the day. All day long there were doctors or specialists coming into the ward to visit one or other of the patients. And each morning there was a tour of inspection by Matron and her sisters and nurses. Before she came round the place was full of cleaners and orderlies making sure everything was spick and span. Then the nurses would come round to check that all our beds were tidy. Everything had to be exactly right for Matron – even a creased bedcover would bring a stinging reprimand.'

Billy missed the muted noise and orderly bustle. His mother took him his breakfast and insisted that he should stay where he was.

'You rest that leg of yours and I'll come and give you a hand to wash and dress as soon as I've finished clearing up and done the shopping,' she would promise.

There was so much for her to do that often it was almost midday before she managed to find time to see to him.

Realising the pressure Elaine was under, Patsy did her best to help with tidying Billy's room and the rest of the house after she'd fed and bathed Liam.

The trouble was Liam always seemed to wake up when she was halfway through a cleaning job and the baby's crying irritated Billy. He only liked the baby when it was asleep or had just been fed and changed and was gurgling and contented.

Patsy tried hard to keep them both happy, but it was not always very successful. When the baby wasn't grizzling then Billy was complaining about something or other. A further problem was that Elaine, too, was becoming more and more tight-lipped and irritable.

In her case it was a combination of being over-worked and the fact that now Billy was at home, as well as Patsy and Liam living there, she was finding it difficult to stretch the weekly house-keeping money to cover all the food and other things that were needed.

'I was wondering about taking a part-time job now that I've started weaning Liam,' Patsy suggested tentatively. It was something that had been in her mind for quite a while, but she wasn't sure how Elaine would react to the idea.

Elaine sighed. 'It's a great thought, luv, but what about Liam? I'd look after him like a shot, but I've got me hands full as it is what with housework and shopping and looking after our Billy.'

'I thought that perhaps Billy could keep an eye on Liam,' she mused.

'Billy!' Elaine's eyes widened. 'How can Billy look after a young baby? He can't do much for himself let alone tend a baby.'

'Not right at this moment, perhaps,' Patsy conceded, 'but in a few weeks, when he's more used to getting about on his crutches. I thought he might enjoy it,' she said lamely.

'Well, you could ask him what he thinks about it, I suppose,' Elaine agreed reluctantly.

'Me carry a baby around, when I can't even balance on my bloody crutches?' he said bitterly. 'If I dropped him I wouldn't be able to pick him up!'

'Well I didn't mean right this moment,' Patsy said quickly. 'I meant later on, when you can balance or when you no longer have to use your crutches.'

'And when will that be?' he asked cynically.

'As soon as you stop feeling sorry for yourself and make yourself walk,' Patsy snapped, a look of exasperation on her face.

Billy stared at her in disbelief then for the first time since he'd come home from hospital he laughed.

'Still the same old slave driver, aren't you,' he guffawed. 'I'm not Samson so don't get the whip to me, just because I'm not moving quickly enough for you, luv.'

'I won't,' she promised, 'but I can't stand seeing you simply lying there accepting what's happened and not putting up a fight. One of us has got to work and help your mam with the housekeeping money.'

He looked at her blankly as though he didn't understand what she was talking about.

'I've been living here for months and I've not tipped up a penny piece,' Patsy pointed out. 'All I've done is take, take, and take. Food, things for

Liam and even clothes for me. Your mam's provided them all from the housekeeping money your dad hands over on a Friday night. It's not fair on either of them.'

Suddenly the old Billy was grinning back at her. The kind, considerate partner she'd known since she was a young girl. It was almost as though, because of his long stay in hospital, he'd forgotten about the need to earn money for food and home comforts. Now he was as anxious as she was to pay his way.

He ran a hand through his hair. 'No, you're right, but what can we do? You have the baby to look after and I'm pretty helpless no matter what you say.'

'We could clear out the stuff in the stable for a start,' she told him. 'The rent hasn't been paid and the owner is threatening to kick us out anyway. There's Samson's spare harness in there and there must also be straw and hay and perhaps some feed that we could sell.'

'How am I going to manage to sort that lot out when I'm on crutches?'

'I bet your dad would help if you asked him and Freddie would give a hand.'

'You're on, luv,' Billy grinned. 'We'll give it a go on Sunday.'

Elaine agreed to keep an eye on Liam while Patsy went to the stable with Billy, Joe and Freddie.

'Bloody hell, it stinks in here!' Joe exclaimed as they opened the door and the strong odour of horse manure that had been left untouched for about three months hit them. 'Have to clean this

275

lot up and air the place before the landlord sees it.'

'It's a stable, Dad, not a palace,' Billy told him.

'Bloody stinking one too. Look at the state of the place. Look at that bloody wall over there! It's falling apart!'

'I can explain that,' Patsy said quickly. 'I knocked that hole in it when I was trying to get out. That's the tunnel I was telling you about, the one I escaped through.'

Billy looked puzzled. 'Escaped? What are you on about?'

'The day you had your accident, Billy,' she reminded him, 'you'd left me locked in here and you'd taken the key with you, do you remember?'

Billy nodded. 'I'd forgotten all about that. You said something about the tunnel when I was in hospital. What's it got to do with this mess though?' he asked, indicating the crumbling wall.

'It's where I broke out,' she grinned. 'The tunnel is on the other side of it.'

'Can I go and look?' Freddie asked eagerly.

'Look yes, but don't try walking along the bloody thing. It might fall in on your head and one bugger on crutches is enough,' his father told him.

'No, it's safe enough structurally,' Patsy assured them. 'I walked miles through it, all the way into town, and it was fine apart from the dampness and slimy walls. Oh, and all the rubbish that had been tipped down into it, especially at the other end where it comes out behind the market. Masses of stinking fruit and vegetables and soggy card-board boxes,' she added with a shudder.

While Freddie and Joe explored the tunnel, Billy and Patsy took stock of what there was in the stable that might be saleable.

As they were finishing Elaine appeared with Liam in her arms, looking for Patsy.

'This baby needs a feed,' she announced, 'and the rest of you can pack up and come home because I've got a meal ready for you.'

While they tucked into generous helpings of scouse, they talked non-stop about the tunnel. Joe agreed that he and Freddie would walk the full length of it before Joe repaired the broken wall. He reluctantly admitted that he too had heard rumours about the tunnels that had been built by engineers returning from the Napoleonic wars.

'I always thought it was a load of bunkum,' he told them. 'Now I've got the chance to see for myself I'm going to do so.'

'And me as well, 'Freddie put in quickly, his boyish face full of excitement.

'It might be dangerous,' Elaine protested. 'If it's as old as you say then the roof could cave in at any moment.'

'I'm sure it's safe,' Patsy told her. 'The roof is sound and quite high so they won't have to crawl or anything. I walked upright the whole way and I'm as tall as Freddie.'

'Then Freddie and me will go and do it while you have a rest for an hour or so, Billy,' Joe said, pushing back his chair.

'Yes and then you and Patsy can go back and sort things out at the stable after she's fed Liam,'

Elaine said quickly when she saw that Billy was about to protest.

By the end of Sunday they had stacked up anything that they thought they could sell in the middle of the stable floor and cleaned the place up. Joe had even managed to fix the bricks back into the alcove wall.

The following week, with Joe's help, they found someone willing to buy the tack. When the man came to take it away he agreed to take the feed and hay as well as long as they agreed a knock-down price.

It seemed pointless to argue. They needed to get rid of it before the landlord turned them out and even the meagre sum they were being offered was better than nothing.

'Please take it,' Patsy insisted when they handed the money over to Elaine. 'You've done so much for me over the last months I know it's only a fraction of what I owe you. Apart from giving me somewhere to sleep and feeding me, everything I've got on you and Janie have given me. You've even cut up your sheets and towels and blankets for the baby, as well as buying him clothes.'

Cleaning out the stable seemed to clear the fog that had temporarily blurred Billy's mind and blotted out so much from the past.

'Have you heard from your mam?' he asked Patsy.

She shook her head. 'I don't know where she is. There's a Mrs Blackwood living in our house now.'

Billy frowned. 'Doesn't anyone know where your mam's gone?'

'No!' Patsy's face clouded. 'Mam doesn't even know that Liam's been born and he's over four months old now.'

'And what about Bruno?'

Patsy shook her head. 'I've not heard from him either.'

'So you haven't been over to New Brighton to tell him?'

Her mouth tightened. 'I thought of doing so hundreds of times, but I hadn't the money for the ferryboat and I couldn't bring myself to ask your mam for it. She'd want to know why I was gadding off to New Brighton, wouldn't she, and neither of us have ever said anything to her about Bruno. Anyway, I thought that he'd come looking for me before now.'

'It's probably best to leave things like that,' Billy admitted. 'Don't start rocking the boat, not when my mam's so taken with Liam.'

'She'll have to know one day, Billy! Supposing Bruno comes looking for me and finds strangers living where I used to and they tell him to try your house?'

'The season will be finished in another few weeks and he'll probably be off back to Spain so you may never see him again.'

Patsy shrugged, but her face softened as she looked down at the baby in her arms. 'I suppose he ought to know about Liam.'

'Then you'd better go over there and tell him!'

He fished in his pockets and held out some coins. 'Here, me dad gave me this when I was in hospital. He insisted I have a few bob in case I needed to buy a paper or soap or anything.'

Patsy looked at the money Billy was holding out and shook her head.

'Go on, take it,' he insisted. 'Go over and see Bruno and clear the air so that we all know where we stand one way or the other.'

Chapter Twenty-Seven

It took Patsy three days to pluck up the courage to go across to New Brighton and face Bruno Alvarez.

She hadn't been anywhere since Liam had been born, except when Elaine asked her to go to the nearby corner shop to buy groceries, and she found the thought of going that far on her own quite daunting.

She wished Billy was well enough to go with her, but he could still only walk very short distances on his crutches.

She could always ask Maureen Murphy, she supposed, but that would mean waiting until the weekend when Maureen wasn't at work and she wasn't sure if Maureen would come with her or not. They didn't have much to do with each other these days. They'd quarrelled the day she'd gone round to ask Mrs Murphy if she knew where her mam might have gone.

Mrs Murphy had told her that she had no idea at all. Maureen had insisted on taking a look at the baby and then she'd refused to believe it was Bruno's.

'It wouldn't have such light-coloured skin and fuzzy red hair if it was his,' she pronounced.

'Rubbish!' Patsy defended. 'Liam takes after my

side of the family. He looks like my dad. Anyway, he will probably change as he gets older. Babies often lose all their hair and the new lot is quite different to what they were born with.'

'And what about the colour of his eyes, then?'

'All babies' eyes are blue when they're born, everyone knows that!'

'His aren't!' Maureen exclaimed triumphantly. 'If you look closely they're a funny shade of green or hazel, I can't tell which.'

'They're blue,' Patsy insisted. It's the light in here, you can't see them properly.'

Maureen was not convinced. 'He's a lovely little thing, but he's not a bit like Bruno,' she'd insisted stubbornly.

Since then, on the few occasions when she'd seen Maureen in the street, Patsy had tried to avoid her. She'd often wondered herself why Liam had not the slightest trace of Bruno's Latin swarthiness and build, but she didn't want to listen to Maureen telling her so.

Each morning Patsy found some reason to put off her trip to New Brighton. One day it was because it was too wet, the next because it was too hot.

When Billy became increasingly irritable with the way she was prevaricating she finally forced herself to go. She dressed Liam in a white cotton romper suit that Elaine had bought for him and laid out her blue-and-white spotted voile dress that her dad had bought her. She hadn't worn it since Liam was born and she hoped she would be able to get into it.

Tears came to her eyes as she dressed. Her dad's birthday had been such a momentous night, she thought sadly. So many things had happened since then; things that she struggled daily to push to the back of her mind.

Much to her surprise Patsy found that she enjoyed the journey over to New Brighton. It was mid-morning so the trams were not very busy and no one was pushing or shoving. When she reached the Pier Head, though, it was a different story. The *Royal Iris* was at the landing stage and it was packed with day-trippers making the most of the last few days of late summer sunshine.

The Mersey was as calm as a millpond. Patsy managed to find a seat on deck and sat there in the warm sunshine, holding Liam in her arms, watching the boats moored alongside and the white gulls soaring and screeching around them.

As she gazed out over the blue-grey water to where New Brighton Tower rose high against a clear blue sky her heart began to pound at the thought of seeing Bruno again.

It was almost six months since she'd last seen him, before Liam had been born, even. It seemed a lifetime ago since they had strolled along the promenade and made love in the sandhills. She still felt bitter because he had never made any attempt to find her.

You don't know that for sure, she reminded herself. He'd known where she lived so he might have come looking for her and not been able to find her. After all, Billy had once gone across to New Brighton looking for him and not found him.

As the *Royal Iris* grated alongside the landing stage she joined the throng of people who were making their way on to the pier and along the promenade to the Tower Fairground.

She stood for a moment taking in the busy scene. The roundabouts, dodgem cars, and the variety of stalls selling everything from ice-cream and candyfloss to funny hats and trinkets were all busy. There were crowds at the hoop-la booths and at all the other sideshows; even a queue outside the fortune teller's tent.

She looked for the spot where the menagarie was normally housed, but couldn't see the huge green-and-white awning anywhere. In the end, because Liam was so heavy to carry around in such a crowded place, she asked one of the stall holders where it was.

'There's no menagerie here this year, luv,' he told her.

'No animals here at all? What about the lions and tigers?'

He shook his head. 'No, there's no circus this year.'

'Why is that? What's happened?'

The stall holder shrugged. 'Don't really know, luv. They never came back. I did hear the trainer had gone to Rhyl, or some other Welsh seaside place with the animals this year. Wanted a change, I suppose. Not such a bad idea really. Might try Margate or Southend myself next year. You get fed up with being in one place all the time, gorra try and see a bit of the world, haven't you?'

Patsy smiled and thanked him, but she still

wasn't satisfied so she crossed to another part of the fairground to see if she could find out anything more.

No matter whom she asked the answer was always the same. Bruno Alvarez had not been there that season. No one was quite sure where he was, but they didn't think he had gone back to Spain. Everyone seemed to know that he'd been at Blackpool during the winter. Some of them even told her that he had come back to New Brighton to put on a show over Christmas, but after that they had no idea where he'd gone.

Dispirited and disappointed, Patsy decided that since her trip had been a complete waste of time she might as well go straight back to Liverpool. The *Royal Iris* pulled away seconds before she reached the landing stage. Her heart sank as she stood there watching it sail into midstream and head for Liverpool. It would be another hour before there was another boat.

She was in no mood to walk along the crowded promenade. She wondered whether to wait for the next boat or take a bus to Seacombe and pick up the *Royal Daffodil* from there. The day had become oppressively hot and as she saw the dark clouds building over the Welsh mountains in the far distance she thought there might be a thunderstorm brewing up. If there was, then the sooner she was back in Liverpool the better.

She felt utterly drained. She'd been so tensed up about seeing Bruno again after all this time that now she felt bewildered and out of her depth. It was like having a door slammed in her face.

All the way back to Liverpool she wondered what she should tell Billy. He'd want to know how she got on, so how would he react when she told him the truth?

'I'm as disappointed as you are,' he scowled. 'I was hoping this trip would clear the air between you and Bruno for good and then the rest of us could get on with our lives.'

She stared at him nonplussed. She realised that getting rid of the stable had been a turning point for Billy. His apathy about life and the future had disappeared and understandably he wanted her to come to some decision about her future. The trouble was, she was pretty sure he meant *their* future.

She waited for Billy to speak out, to elaborate, but he said no more. There was an uneasy air of tension between them. She turned away quickly: from the look on his face Patsy was sure he was waiting for her to say she was going to forget all about Bruno now that she knew he was gone.

How could she do that when every fibre of her being cried out for the handsome Spaniard? He was not only the father of her child, he was her only love. How could she go into another man's arms when Bruno possessed her heart?

She was so fond of Billy that she couldn't bear to hurt him by telling him this. If only he *was* her brother! She'd wanted him to be that from the very first day he'd come to work for her dad, when she'd been little more than a child herself.

For the next few days Billy stayed morose and brooding, but he kept his own counsel about Bruno. Now that he realised that there was no longer a business waiting for him, even when he was well enough to pick up the reins again, he seemed anxious to start making plans.

He began to strive to walk further and further each day without crutches. Although it caused him considerable pain he insisted on trying to walk up the stairs and his look of triumph when he managed it brought a lump to Patsy's throat.

She had hated to see him so helpless. It was terrible that a man who was so well built and who had been so fit should be reduced to shambling around on crutches. Now, as each day he managed to walk a little bit further without them, she felt as pleased about his progress as he did.

'It's still going to be a long time before I'm fit enough to work again,' he said gloomily. 'No one will want to employ a cripple. What can I do? I can't lift anything and I can't walk very far or very fast. Even a job as a doorman is beyond me since they're expected to carry the guests' luggage up to their rooms.'

'You might manage to get a job as a night-watchman.'

'Not a chance! Once the burglars found out that I couldn't run after them they'd be breaking in every night of the week.'

Patsy chewed her lip thoughtfully. Perhaps this was the right time to suggest again that Billy should look after Liam and she should be the one to find a job.

'What sort of job were you thinking about?' he asked dubiously.

'I don't know really. Perhaps working in a shop

or something. Only part time,' she assured him quickly.

'And there's a lot of that sort of work around, is there?'

She shrugged. 'No, probably not. Perhaps I could get some work cleaning, then.'

'Charring? You? The girl who was a partner in her own business?'

'Well we haven't got a business now, have we,' she snapped. 'I don't want to go as a char, cleaning up other people's messes and I don't particularly want to work in a shop pandering to the whims of people who can afford to buy things that I can't, but what else is there for me to do? Tell me that, Billy Grant.'

'Wow! Temper, temper, Patsy Callaghan. It must be right what they say about red hair,' Billy laughed. 'Well, I'll tell you what you could do – you could become a nurse in a hospital.'

Patsy stared at him in disbelief. 'Are you mad, Billy? Do you know what I'd have to do to become a nurse?'

'Yes, you'd have to enrol for training. It's like an apprenticeship and it's hard work, but you're used to that so you'd manage.'

'So where would I go to train?'

'A hospital, of course. It takes about three years to become properly qualified and you'd have to live in the hospital.'

'You know all about this, do you?'

'Yes, I do,' he told her smugly. 'The nurses talked to me a lot, especially the night nurses when I couldn't sleep. They told me about how they had trained and all the rest of it.'

'And did they tell you what I'd do with a baby while I was training?'

Billy's face clouded. 'I'd forgotten about Liam.'

'Yes, well you may have managed to do so, but I can't.'

'Now he's weaned you could leave him with someone, couldn't you?' Billy asked mildly.

'That's what I was planning on doing when I said I'd get a job. I was planning to leave him with you! Only for a few hours each day, though,' she added swiftly.

'If you were training to be a nurse and earning some money then you could pay someone to look after Liam for you permanently.'

Patsy shook her head. 'I know it seems a good idea, Billy, but I couldn't bring myself to do that. Look at him!' She gazed down at the baby who was lying on a rug by her feet, kicking his legs and waving a rattle in the air. 'He's far too precious for me to hand over to anyone else to look after permanently.'

'Not if it was someone you knew really well, someone who'd loved him as much as you do,' he persisted.

She stared at him, puzzled. 'I don't follow. When I suggested that you should look after him for a few hours each day you didn't seem to like the idea.'

'No, not me! I'd be no good at looking after him. I mean my mam, of course! Liam would be perfectly safe with her so you'd have no worries about him at all.'

'I couldn't expect her to take on a young baby!' Patsy exclaimed, aghast. 'Think of all the work that's involved, Billy! Your mam's brought up one family. She probably can't wait for the day when I leave and she can have her home free of nappies airing on the fireguard and baby clothes all over the place.'

Chapter Twenty-Eight

Patsy kept toying with Billy's suggestion that she should train as a nurse. In many ways she liked the idea, because it would mean that she would be doing something worthwhile.

It would also make life easier for the Grants if she wasn't living there, she told herself. Now that Billy could manage to get up and down stairs he could have his bedroom back instead of having to sleep on the sofa.

The really big problem was Liam. Could she bear to leave him in someone else's care even if Elaine agreed to look after him?

He was now almost six months old and he was becoming aware of all that went on around him. He wasn't a robust child, but he was certainly very active and Patsy wondered if it would be asking too much of Elaine to have him all the time.

Liam reminded her so much of her own father with his light blue eyes and long thin build. He had her red curls, though, and freckles right across the bridge of his nose the same as she had. There seemed to be nothing at all of Bruno in either his colouring or features. Bruno's skin had been a warm olive brown that made his teeth look brilliantly white when he smiled. His eyes were as dark as chocolate under his heavy dark brows.

She wondered what Bruno would have thought of Liam if she'd been able to find him. There must be a reason why she hadn't heard a word from him in all this time. After all, he knew where she lived.

She pondered over all the advantages and drawbacks of having to leave Liam while she trained to be a nurse. Finally, she made her decision and plucked up the courage to mention the matter to Elaine.

'Billy has already asked me and I said I would,' Elaine smiled.

'It will be an awful lot of extra work for you to take on,' Patsy pointed out. 'Liam will be crawling any day now and once he starts toddling then you really will have your hands full.'

'I know all about that, luv! I've brought up three of my own, remember. Anyway,' she added, a wide smile on her plump face, 'if I can't look after my grandson then who else can?'

Patsy bit her lip. Her grandson? So Elaine still thought Liam was Billy's baby!

She opened her mouth to deny it then shut it again quickly, remembering Billy's warning that if they told Elaine that Bruno was Liam's father she certainly wouldn't want to look after him. She might even tell Patsy to get out right away and take her baby with her.

She wondered if Billy also still thought that the baby was his. Was that why he was trying to be so helpful and why he was suggesting that his mother would look after Liam for her?

But he couldn't be, she reasoned. She and Billy

had only ever made love once and she had been meeting Bruno every Sunday all through last summer. Anyway, Liam with his red hair wasn't a bit like Billy. He wasn't like Bruno either, she reminded herself.

The more she thought about becoming a nurse the more the idea appealed to her. She asked Billy if he knew the name of any of the nurses he'd talked to when he'd been in hospital so that she could go and ask them how she went about it.

'Go to the Labour Exchange and ask there,' he told her. 'They're sure to have all the details.'

Patsy followed his advice and a week later, full of nervous trepidation, she was on her way for an interview at Liverpool General Hospital.

When, two weeks later, a letter arrived telling her to report for her initial training, Patsy felt so nervous that she almost had second thoughts about what she was doing. Thinking about leaving Liam in Elaine's care was one thing; walking out of the house and leaving him there with her was another.

'After the first month of your training you'll be able to come home on your day off each week,' Billy reminded her.

'Maybe, but right now it's the first month I'm worried about. That's four whole weeks! How am I going to last that long without seeing Liam?'

'It will be over in no time at all,' he told her confidently.

'That's rubbish and you know it, Billy,' she told him angrily.

'No it's not and I do know what I'm talking

about. I was in hospital for months and it seemed like no time at all.'

'You hadn't left your baby behind though, had you?'

He didn't answer, but the look he gave her sent a *frisson* of fear through her and she felt herself colour up in embarrassment.

She tried to laugh it off. 'Well, you know what I mean, don't you!'

When he still remained silent Patsy said awkwardly, 'I'd better go and tell Elaine the news and see if she's still happy about our arrangement.'

The next two weeks were chaotic. Patsy spent every moment she could with Liam. Sometimes she felt like a drowning man clutching at the only thing that could save her life; at others like a protective lioness with her only cub. She couldn't bear to let Liam out of her sight or out of her arms.

'He'll still be here when you come home in a month's time,' Billy told her, when he saw Patsy sitting down nursing Liam instead of putting him into his cot to sleep.

'Yes, and by then he might be too big to want cuddling. Babies can change quite a lot in a month, you know.'

'Not him! He likes being cuddled too much, and I'll be cuddling him every day while you're away, and so will me mam and Janie and even young Freddie.'

Patsy buried her face in Liam's red curls. She didn't want Billy to see the tears in her eyes, not when they were all rallying round to help her.

The hospital was a grim and unfriendly red-brick building with five storeys of long narrow windows. She always thought that from the outside it resembled a prison as much as a hospital.

And that's what it is going to be for me for the next four weeks, Patsy thought miserably as she made her way inside. It was all very well Billy saying the time would fly by because she'd be so busy and there would be so many new people and new experiences, but already there was an ache in her heart.

By the end of the second day, Patsy really did feel like a prisoner. She'd been assigned a narrow, cell-like bedroom and issued with a uniform. The light blue dress was of stiff scratchy cotton and there was a heavily starched white apron to wear over it, as well as an equally crisply starched white cap to cover up her red curls.

There were so many rules that she was sure she would never remember half of them. Nurses must not behave in a frivolous manner; they must not wear jewellery, they must never eat while on the wards, they must never run no matter if it was an emergency.

Most important of all was the code about how they must address all those who were senior to them. Patsy could understand this and recognised that doctors wore white coats and that the matron was dressed in black with a snow white flowing head-dress. She found it difficult to work out what all the differently coloured uniforms and armbands worn by the nurses meant, though.

The six o'clock call in the morning didn't worry Patsy at all since she was used to getting up early. It was after breakfast, which was eaten in the enormous dining room along with about fifty other nurses, when she found she was going to spend most of the morning in a classroom, that was disconcerting.

She'd thought that being a nurse was looking after sick people, not having lessons as though she was still at school.

'How can we look after patients if we don't know anything about their illnesses or how to treat them?' one of her classmates commented in a withering tone.

'I thought we'd learn as we went along.'

'Well we will, but they teach us the basics first before they let us loose on the wards.'

In the afternoon, however, she was sent to a ward where she helped trained nurses and orderlies with bed-making, carrying in cups of tea and trays of food from the ward kitchen, and general tidying up.

After their last meal of the day in the staff dining room all probationers had to report back to the classroom for another two hours' study. When that ended they were allowed to collect a mug of hot cocoa from the dining room and then told to go straight to their rooms and that lights out would be in half an hour.

On her first night, as she lay there in the darkness, all the events of the day jostled in her mind. So many new experiences, so many rules and regulations. She remembered how difficult some of the patients had been, how sharply some of the older nurses had spoken to her, and all the countless things she was supposed to learn.

She'd thought looking after baby Liam had been difficult at times when he was peevish, but that had been easy compared to dealing with some of the women she'd encountered that afternoon. She knew they were sick, and probably in pain, but did they have to complain quite so much?

She fell asleep wondering if it would be any easier the next day when, according to the rota she'd been given, she would be on the men's ward.

Slowly a pattern of bed, study, nursing and then study again before bed began to emerge and the days blended one into the other.

Her longing to see Liam was always uppermost in her mind. She knew Elaine was capable and would take every care of him, but being separated from him was tearing Patsy apart. She longed to feel his little arms around her neck, his wet lips planted in a noisy kiss on her cheek. She missed the smell of him when he was warm from his bath, holding him in her arms and watching his eyelids droop as sleep claimed him.

She kept a piece of paper under her pillow with the days marked down on it and every night she crossed another one off.

By her third week at Liverpool General she was well into the routine and she particularly enjoyed carrying trays of food or drink to the patients. Now that she was feeling more confident she even exchanged chitchat with them and this made each day pass so much more quickly.

She was also being encouraged by the staff nurse to practise on the ward some of the things that she'd been taught in the classroom. It started with making beds, progressed to bedbaths and then to taking temperatures all under the eagle eye of the senior nurse or ward sister.

The day before her month's probation ended, Patsy went along to the Training School Office to ask for official permission to go home the following day.

Although permission was granted, Patsy had to listen to a lecture on behaviour. She must not go out into the street wearing her uniform or her cap, she was told, and when she returned she must not go into a ward while still wearing her outdoor clothes.

Patsy smiled to herself. Whatever made them think she would want to wear her uniform to go home in? Not having to put on the stiff uncomfortable dress and starched white apron would be wonderful.

Patsy was up long before the early morning bell sounded. She didn't stop to eat breakfast, but shot out the doors as soon as it was permissible for her to do so. On the tram all the way back to Paradise Place she was singing softly to herself, she felt so happy. A few more minutes and she would be holding Liam in her arms again.

When she burst into the house she found Billy nursing Liam, who'd been fed and dressed all ready to greet her. As she went to take him from Billy's arms, Liam drew back and his tiny face puckered up as if he was about to cry. Patsy felt mortified.

'He doesn't know me! He's forgotten me already!' Tears spilled down her cheeks as she looked from Elaine to Billy in distress.

'He'll be all right in a minute or two,' Billy assured her. 'A month is a long time for a little chap like him.'

'Come and sit down, luv. I've got some breakfast all ready for you. Sit down and eat that and let him get used to you being here,' Elaine added tactfully.

Patsy did as she was asked, but it almost choked her to swallow even the cup of tea Elaine poured out for her. She'd so looked forward to holding Liam. She'd expected him to hold out his little arms to her; instead he had drawn back as if she was a stranger.

Billy bounced the baby up and down on his knee, pointing to Patsy and talking to Liam softly. Within a few minutes the baby was gurgling noisily and went to Patsy quite happily.

She spent every moment of her time at home either nursing Liam, playing with him or sitting by his cot watching him sleep. Billy sensed that she wasn't at all sure that she'd be able to bring herself to go back to the hospital.

'The worst part is over now,' he reminded her. 'From now on you will have a day off every week.'

Patsy sighed. 'Even a week is a long time for Liam to remember who I am,' she pointed out.

Billy shook his head. 'He soon remembered you this time, now didn't he?'

'Yes, but if I'm always away, except for one day a week, he'll think your mother is his mam, not me.'

Billy looked taken aback. 'You're wrong, Patsy. My mother would never let him think that.'

'How can she stop him from thinking that?' she asked, tears spilling down her cheeks.

'There must be some way to prevent that happening,' Billy stated, anxious to put her mind at rest. 'I'll have a word with her and see if she can think of anything we can do.'

'Why don't you go into Jerome's, the photographers in Lord Street, and get a picture of yourself taken, Patsy?' Elaine suggested.

'Great idea,' Billy enthused. 'We can show it to Liam every morning when he wakes up and again every night before he's put to bed.'

'And we'll teach him to say "Mam" every time he sees it,' Elaine promised. 'That way you won't be a stranger to him. He'll know exactly who you are when you come home on your day off.'

Chapter Twenty-Nine

Gradually Patsy found herself settling into the long days of busy hospital routine and of being at home only one day each week. Billy made quite sure that there was no recurrence of the upsetting incident of little Liam not recognising her. As soon as Patsy brought home the framed photograph she'd had taken at Jerome's Studios it was placed in a prominent position on the mantelpiece.

Billy showed it to Liam last thing every night and first thing every morning. As Liam grew older, Billy taught him to point to the picture and say 'Mam' and encouraged him to kiss it each night before he went to bed.

Elaine was equally co-operative. She made sure right from the start that Liam called her 'Nana' so that there was no fear of confusion in the child's mind.

Although Patsy knew how lucky she was to have such a wonderful show of unity she still longed to spend more time with Liam. Each week, he seemed to have accomplished something new and she hadn't been there to see him doing it.

Liam had barely been crawling when she started training as a nurse yet in no time at all he had managed to pull himself up on to his feet. Then she found he was toddling around, grabbing at Elaine's skirt or Billy's leg or a piece of furniture to balance himself. A few weeks later when she came home he was toddling around unaided.

It was the same when he started to talk. She had been so proud the first time he had managed to say 'Mam' that she wanted the whole world to know. Yet, she felt heartbroken when on a subsequent visit he pointed to various familiar objects and called them all by their right name. She felt she had been cheated. She should have been the one there encouraging him to talk.

The only thing she could feel happy about, she thought, was that she was earning enough money to pay for everything he might need.

She gave Elaine the bulk of her wages. When Elaine protested, saying that she should be saving it towards the future, Patsy insisted that she still had a lot of paying back to do first before she started saving.

She knew Elaine appreciated what she was doing. Billy had still not found a job although he was now a great deal better and no longer needed crutches. In the house he simply held on to the furniture as he moved around. When he went out he used a walking stick. He moved very slowly and his limp was quite pronounced, but it was progress.

'Not many openings for a limp layabout,' he joked whenever Patsy asked him if he'd had any luck in finding a job.

'He does his share about the place, believe me,' Elaine would tell her. 'If our Billy found a job then

I'd have to find a playmate for Liam. The two of them get on like a house on fire, never out of each other's sight.'

As Elaine spoke Patsy was aware that she was looking at her speculatively and her heart pounded uneasily. For one moment she wondered whether she was going to start asking questions about the relationship between her and Billy.

She and Billy were still the best of friends, but that was all, and Patsy knew it puzzled Elaine and that she wanted to ask her about it, but so far she'd avoided her questions. Patsy knew that deep down she still thought of Liam as her grandson.

Patsy could never understand why Billy hadn't explained the situation to her himself. After all this time it was unlikely that Elaine would turn her and Liam out. She wondered if Billy was fondly harbouring the same idea as his mother did about Liam. If so, she was grateful that he had never tried to teach Liam to call him 'Dad'.

Some day Liam would have to be told the truth, but she still hoped that by then Bruno would have returned and would take his rightful place in their lives. Her feelings for him were still the same. She dreamed of him often, recalling every detail of his good looks, Mediterranean charm and fine physique.

Her feelings for Billy were on a different level. She would do anything she could to help him and she knew he would do the same for her. Their time spent working together when her father had been alive had been the happiest of her life. And her close affinity with Billy had remained when there was only the two of them running the business.

His accident had been a terrible blow to her as well as to him and his family. His mother's generosity was a debt she would never be able to repay. Even Joe, who was such a rough and ready character, had shown nothing but kindness to her, and Janie and Freddie had been as warm and loving as if they were her own brother and sister.

Patsy knew she had a great deal to be thankful for: without the help of the Grants she and Liam would have been in dire straits after her mam had disappeared.

Even her life at the hospital, strenuous though it could be, was enjoyable in a great many ways, Patsy thought. There was so much variety. Patients rarely stayed for more than a week or two. There were constantly fresh faces, different ailments to be dealt with, and varied treatments. As well as frequent changes of nursing staff and doctors, her own duties meant that she was often transferred to a different ward without any warning.

Whether she was nursing men, women or children, Patsy found she was learning something new all the time. Most important of all, she felt she was doing something worthwhile.

She had made a number of friends amongst the other nurses. She always took care, though, not to become too close to any of them because she didn't want details of her home life, especially information about Liam, to be known. The nursing authorities didn't look favourably on employing married women and certainly not those who had children to care for. As far as they were aware she was a single girl with no family ties.

Occasionally, on one of her days off, Patsy was tempted to go over to New Brighton and see if there was any news of Bruno, but something always stopped her. Usually it was her longing to spend every minute she could with Liam.

She told herself that next summer she'd definitely take Liam there. Bruno and the animals would be back by then, she felt sure, and she could imagine how excited Liam would be when he saw the ferocious lions and the tigers being trained. She wondered what Bruno would say when he saw Liam for the first time and she went hot all over as she imagined the astonished pride on his face.

She never did make the journey. In fact, when Billy suggested taking Liam on the ferryboat for a day trip she vetoed the idea. Common sense told her that Bruno knew where she lived if he wanted to see her again. Since he'd never done so it was much better, she decided, to keep her dreams and illusions rather than have them shattered.

Patsy never managed to find out where her mother had gone either. She had not heard a word from her mam since the day she had turned her out with her belongings stuffed inside an old canvas sack. No one in Paradise Place ever mentioned her name. It was as if Maeve Callaghan had never existed.

Patsy often asked herself how long her present settled and relatively happy state could last. Liam was now three years old and very active. He wanted to be doing something, or going somewhere with Billy, every minute of the day. When Billy was not around he pestered Elaine to take him out. He loved going to the shops, but most of all he liked to visit St John's Market, which was noisy and packed with a medley of stalls.

Each time she saw him Patsy was aware that he seemed to be growing more and more like her dad. Liam had her red curly hair, but his eyes were a pale hazel shade, and looked huge in his small pointed face. He had pale skin and the sprinkling of freckles over the bridge of his nose matched hers exactly.

He would never be a very robust child, but he was wiry and full of energy. His curiosity about everything going on around him was tremendous and even Billy sometimes tired of his constant barrage of questions.

On her day at home she always tried to take Liam out somewhere so as to give Elaine a chance to have some time on her own. She knew it was the only real rest she got from him, except at the weekends when either Joe or Freddie would take him to the park.

Janie loved him dearly, but now that she had a regular boyfriend the amount of time she wanted to spend with Liam was limited. Once Freddie left school and become an assistant in an iron-mongers he had to work all day on a Saturday, so Sunday was the only time he had for Liam.

Patsy's bubble of contentment burst suddenly a week after Liam's fourth birthday.

When she was told to report immediately to Matron's office she tried to think of anything she might have done wrong or any rule she might have contravened.

The news she was given was far worse than any chastisement for a minor infringement of rules.

'I have received a request from a Mrs Grant asking if you can be allowed home immediately,' Matron told her. She stared hard at Patsy from over the top of her gold-rimmed glasses. 'Who is this Mrs Grant?'

'She's . . . she's the lady I live with,' Patsy told her.

'A relation?'

'No, not exactly. I have lived with her ever since I was a child, though,' she mumbled.

'So do you know why she should need you at home so urgently?'

Patsy shook her head. Her mind was racing. She was sure something awful must have happened for Elaine to send for her. She wondered if Billy had met with another accident. She prayed it was nothing to do with Liam. He had seemed well enough when she'd been home three days ago. If he'd a bad cold, or even fallen over, Elaine would have dealt with it like she always did without sending for her to come home. Unless Elaine was ill? If she couldn't look after Liam then Billy would be able to see to him.

'So you have no idea why she has sent for you?'

Matron persisted, cutting into the thoughts that were jumbling around in Patsy's head.

'No, Ma'am. No idea at all.'

Matron frowned and studied the duty rota lying on her desk. 'It is very inconvenient for you to expect time off without due notice, Nurse Callaghan. You may take two hours off in the middle of your shift, but I rely on you to report back for work on time.'

Reluctantly, Patsy went back to the ward, but her mind was not on her work. She couldn't settle. She felt certain that Elaine asking for her to come home had something to do with Liam.

Because she was not concentrating on what she was doing, Patsy made several silly mistakes. When she apologised to Sister Pringle who was in charge of the ward, and explained about the message, Sister Pringle decided that it might be better if she went home right away before she made some serious error.

'It's two o'clock now, so I'll expect you back on duty at five o'clock, remember.'

Patsy wasted no time. She dashed up to her room, tore off her apron and cap and stuffed them in her locker. She knew it was against hospital rules to go out in uniform, but she didn't stop to change out of her blue dress. She just fastened her topcoat over it and hoped no one would notice.

All the way back to Paradise Place, Patsy kept telling herself that she mustn't panic. In her heart though she knew that Elaine would not have sent for her unless it was something very serious.

'Thank God you've managed to get away,'

Elaine greeted her the moment she entered the house. She looked hollow-eyed with worry.

'It's little Liam, isn't it?' Patsy asked.

Elaine nodded. 'We're not sure what's wrong with him, luv. He's had a bit of a cough and this morning he brought up some blood so I sent for the doctor . . .'

'Blood! How is he now?' Patsy demanded anxiously, looking round the room, expecting to see Billy sitting there nursing him.

'He's in hospital, luv. Billy's staying there with him. I wanted to be here to tell you myself or I wouldn't have left his bedside, either.'

'Can I go and see him?'

'Of course. Do you want to go right away or would you like a cup of tea first?'

'Right away. I only have a couple of hours off and then I'm due back on duty.'

Elaine looked shocked. 'Must you go back so soon? I thought you would want to be with Liam.'

'I do want to be with him more than anything in the world,' Patsy answered sharply, 'but this is all the time I can get off.'

When she saw Liam lying listlessly in the hospital bed, every vestige of colour drained from his cheeks, all thought of getting back to her own hospital on time went from Patsy's mind.

'I'm not leaving until I've seen a doctor and found out exactly what's wrong with him,' she insisted.

'There won't be a doctor on the ward again until tomorrow morning,' the sister in charge warned her.

'Wouldn't it be best if you went back and explained the situation and then asked if you could have more time off?' Billy suggested. 'I'll stay here with Liam until you manage to get back, even if it takes you until tomorrow.'

Patsy shook her head. 'I really don't know, Billy. No one there knows about Liam, I never said anything about him when I applied to become a nurse because I knew they wouldn't take me on if they knew I had a young child. And I've never mentioned him to anyone since.'

'Billy is right, though, luv. You should ask for time off. It's the best thing you can do,' Elaine urged.

Patsy felt in a complete daze as she went back to the Liverpool General. She knew she was going to be late, but it didn't seem to matter since she intended leaving again right away.

Nevertheless, she put her starched white apron and cap back on, deciding it would create a better impression than if she went straight on to the ward in outdoor clothes, which was strictly forbidden.

As she pinned her cap into place on her unruly curls, she couldn't put the sight of Liam lying there so wan and listless out of her mind. It had all happened so quickly. Only a few days ago, when she'd last been home, he had been running around so full of life that it didn't seem possible that he could be so ill.

Sister Pringle tapped her watch irritably when Patsy appeared on the ward and could hardly control her anger when Patsy told her that she needed more time off. 'Really, Nurse Callaghan, this is most inconvenient,' she said sharply. 'You'd better go and ask the duty sister and see what she has to say. She's the one who has overall responsibility for all the nurses at the hospital.'

'It's not up to me, you'll have to ask Matron,' the duty sister snapped after Patsy had explained the situation. 'Wait here and I'll go and find out if she will see you.'

Patsy thought the duty sister was never going to come back, but when she did it was to tell her that Matron would see her as soon as she was free.

'Go and take a seat in the corridor outside Matron's office and wait until you are called,' she told her. 'You'd better go and put a clean apron on first, that one looks rather creased,' she remarked, looking Patsy up and down critically.

It was almost an hour before Matron summoned her into her room and it seemed like eternity to Patsy. Several times she was on the point of walking out of the hospital and rushing back to Liam's bedside. When she was finally called into Matron's office she felt numb with anxiety.

She knew she was telling her story badly, but she was so worried about Liam that her brain refused to function properly.

'This is all very irregular, Nurse Callaghan,' Matron told her. She gave her a steely glare and drummed on the desk with her pen. 'Have you taken your annual holiday yet?' she barked.

Patsy shook her head.

'Very well, then I think the best thing you can

do is to take it now,' she pronounced. 'In your absence I will consider your situation very carefully and let you have my decision as to whether we wish to retain you as a nurse here or not.'

Chapter Thirty

Every day Patsy visited Liam at the Liverpool Children's Hospital and stayed by his bedside for as long as the hospital staff would permit her to do so. She watched anxiously as different doctors were brought in to examine him and carry out various tests, but no one would say what was the matter with him.

The diagnosis when it finally came was a tremendous blow both to Patsy and to the Grants. Liam, they were told, had tuberculosis.

Once the hospital had decided on the nature of his illness Liam was taken off the danger list and all special visiting privileges were withdrawn. To their dismay they found they were only allowed to see him for one hour each day and only two people were allowed at his bedside at any one time.

Patsy knew this was standard hospital practice, but she still couldn't reconcile herself to it. She wanted to be with him all the time, night and day. She wanted to be the one to feed him, amuse him, hold his hand or stroke his forehead when he wasn't feeling well.

'This child needs rest, not constant attention and stimulation,' the ward sister told Patsy briskly when she begged to be allowed to stay a little longer.

Billy and Elaine were also upset by the curtailment of the visiting hours. Realising that Patsy wanted to stay with him for the whole of the hour, when they were allowed into the ward they were forced to take it in turns to be at his bedside.

They all tried their best to appear bright and cheerful when they visited Liam. But although they assured him that he would soon be back home again, they were filled with a sense of unease as he seemed to grow paler and thinner and weaker each time they saw him.

Elaine was beside herself with distress. In her eyes, having tuberculosis was as bad as having the plague. She refused to believe that there was any cure and she was suspicious and critical of everything the hospital was doing for Liam.

'I can't think how this has happened,' she said over and over again as they left the hospital and made their way back to Paradise Place. 'I've taken the greatest care of him, Patsy. He's never been allowed out without a coat, his feet have always been kept dry . . .'

'You make him sound like a horse, not a little child,' Billy snapped. He felt terrible that such a thing should have happened while Liam was entrusted to their care. Having to walk away and leave him lying there in hospital made his senses spin and he became tense and angry at the slightest thing.

'I know you've looked after Liam,' Patsy told Elaine, putting her arms round the plump motherly figure and hugging her. 'No one could have cared for him better.'

Elaine was inconsolable though and nothing Patsy said seemed to make any difference. Every night after they returned from the hospital they would sit drinking tea and going over and over the situation. It was as if talking out loud about the child helped to ease the concern they were all feeling.

Deep in her heart Patsy felt it was her fault. She should never have left him to be brought up by someone else, no matter how kind and considerate they might be. Liam was her responsibility and she should have been there looking out for him.

'Might be the bloody bad start he had in life,' Joe Grant said. His bony face was drawn and grey with worry.

'Joe!' Elaine frowned and shook her head, signalling him to be silent.

'It's all right,' Patsy said dully. 'I've been wondering the same thing. An old stable wasn't the ideal place for a newborn baby.'

'It was probably something I didn't do right when he was born,' Billy muttered.

Patsy grabbed hold of his hand and squeezed it. 'You were wonderful, Billy, no one could have done any better.'

'Perhaps we ought to tell the doctors about the hardships he suffered at birth,' Elaine said worriedly. 'They did ask if he'd had any health problems, or whether there were any unusual circumstances, or if he had been in contact with anyone who had TB.'

Patsy shrugged. 'Tell them if you like. But I'm quite sure that Billy did everything right at the time and that where Liam was born has nothing at all to do with him being ill now.'

'Well, he hasn't been in touch with anyone who has TB. None of us have,' Elaine pointed out.

'Gerraway! You don't know who the hell you're rubbing shoulders with when you take him to the shops or down the bloody market,' Joe told her.

'I take him to the swings in the park and he sometimes plays around with the other kids who are there. Any one of them could have TB,' Billy added.

'Then there's that bloody hospital where you work, Patsy. You come straight home from there and the first thing you do when you get in the bloody house is pick Liam up and kiss him,' Joe pointed out.

Patsy shook her head. 'I don't think there is any chance of me bringing germs home. I always change out of my uniform before I leave the hospital. I have to, it's one of the rules.'

'It's no good us sitting around blaming each other,' Billy said quietly. 'What we've got to do now is decide what steps we're going to take to get him better.'

'Not much bloody choice, is there,' Joe said irritably. 'They say he's got to go into an isolation hospital so that's that! It's out of our hands once they cart him off to one of those places.'

Elaine sighed. 'They haven't told us which hospital it will be yet. I hope they don't send him too far away because it will be so difficult to visit him if they do.'

'They probably won't allow much visiting,'

Patsy warned. 'The treatment is very tiring for the patient, especially for one as small as he is, so they'll want him to be kept as quiet as possible.'

'Oh, I suppose you know all about that. So what is the treatment then? Come on, give us the griff,' Joe demanded.'

'It depends on how bad he is. I looked it all up in the medical books. In some cases they collapse the lungs to give them a chance to heal.'

'What, both the buggers?' Joe looked aghast. 'How do you bloody well breathe if they does that?'

'Not both lungs at once! They do it one at a time, that's why the treatment takes such a long time.'

Billy frowned. 'How do they collapse a lung, Patsy?'

'They pump air into the chest cavity and surround the lung with it. The air gradually seeps out so they repeat it every week or ten days and gradually the lung repairs itself.'

'Would they do that to a tiny little mite like Liam?' Elaine asked.

'I'm not sure. We'll have to wait and see.'

'First things first,' Billy told them. 'Let's find out where Liam is being sent.'

It was another two days before they were informed where he was to be treated and when they were told all of them were shocked.

'Wallasey Isolation Hospital! That's the other side of the bloody Mersey,' Joe ranted. 'That could mean a journey of well over an hour each sodding way!'

'All that way and we'll only be able to stay half

an hour!' Elaine agreed, shaking her head sadly.

'And we can only visit on a Wednesday or Sunday afternoon,' Billy added, reading from the sheet of instruction they'd been handed.

'It says only two visitors at a time,' Elaine reminded them.

When her leave was over Patsy reported back for duty at Liverpool General, but her mind was not really on her work. She wanted to be with Liam. To be at his bedside, to comfort him when he cried, to try and explain the procedures to him when they began his treatment so that he wouldn't be frightened.

He was little more than a toddler; he'd been well loved and cosseted all his life. He was the centre of a warm, loving family, even if they weren't strictly blood relations, and now he was going to have to face this ordeal on his own.

For all his rough and ready ways Joe loved him dearly and Janie and Freddie treated him as they would a little brother. Janie was forever bringing home toys and colouring books for him. Freddie always bought him some sweets or a bar of chocolate when he got his pay packet on a Friday night and sometimes played a game of some kind with him.

Elaine was like a second mother to Liam. She'd fed him, clothed him, played with him, taught him to talk and how to behave. She's done more for him than I have, Patsy thought guiltily.

Was this her punishment for not being a real mother to Liam? Was God punishing her for her sins? She'd never even had Liam christened, but that wasn't because she didn't believe in God, but because she couldn't face Father O'Brian. He'd want to know why she'd neglected her faith and lecture her about falling from a state of Grace.

Going to Mass had been the last thing on Patsy's mind after her dad had died. It had been Billy, not God, who'd come to her aid and made her see sense. It had been sheer hard work, not prayers, that had helped her to pull through and get back on her feet.

If God was all-seeing, as he was supposed to be, then he must know all about that. Anyway, she reminded herself, Jesus had been born in a stable, the same as Liam, so surely he would understand the plight she'd been in.

The Grants weren't Catholics, in fact they didn't seem to go to any sort of church, so how could she expect them to take Liam to Mass every Sunday when she was working?

Even now, with Liam's life in the balance, she didn't feel that prayers would do any good. The right diagnosis, the skill of the doctor who was in charge of his treatment, and the care and ministrations of the nurses looking after him were what would pull him through.

She only wished she could be one of those nurses. The moment the thought came into her head, Patsy wondered if it was at all possible. She said nothing to anyone, but the idea haunted her and went over and over in her mind so often that she decided she would make some enquiries.

She started her quest by finding out as much as she possibly could about the hospital where

Liam had been sent. When she had all the details, and was completely sure about what she intended to do, she told Billy that she was going to find out if she could work as a nurse at the isolation hospital.

His face lit up. 'That's a wonderful idea, Patsy,' he enthused. 'Poor kid, he'll think we've all deserted him. When you're his age, seeing someone for half an hour twice a week is no good. Anyway, waiting from Wednesday to the following Sunday is far too long.'

'Well don't say anything to your mam yet,' she cautioned. 'It may not come off. I've got to find out first if they want any nurses there.'

'It's worth a try. What are you going to do – go over to the hospital and ask?'

'I don't know, I haven't thought that far,' she admitted.

'I'll come over with you, if you like.'

'Thanks, Billy. You might have to wait around for a long time though. The matron, or whoever takes on new staff, mightn't even see me. I might have to go back again another day.'

'That's all right by me. I don't mind waiting. I'm good at it, I've had plenty of practice of hanging around doing nothing,' he added with a wry smile.

Patsy's eyes filled with tears. 'Oh, Billy. I feel awful saddling you and your mam and family with all this trouble.'

'Hey, that will do!' Gently he brushed her tears away then wrapped his arms round her, holding her so close that she could feel the heat of his body.

'No more crying, luv. Right?'

She buried her face against the comforting warmth of his broad shoulder. 'I'm listening and I would like you to come with me. I promise not to break down and cry if they turn me down and send me packing.'

'I wouldn't think they'd do that, not when they know you're a fully trained nurse. You never know, you might be able to arrange for a transfer from the Liverpool General to the Wallasey Isolation Hospital without any trouble at all.'

'Always the optimist, aren't you, Billy?' Patsy said with a smile. 'I don't know where I would be without you!' She kissed his cheek before gently pulling away from him.

'Why don't you start making some enquiries at the isolation hospital when you go over on your first visit there to see Liam next Wednesday?'

'You'll come as well?'

'I've already said so, haven't I? Yes, of course I'll come with you.'

Travelling across on the ferryboat brought back bittersweet memories for both of them. Patsy clutched Billy's hand tightly as they reached the spot on the floating roadway where he had met with his accident.

She was glad they were going to Seacombe and not New Brighton and would be getting a bus from there into the centre of Wallasey where the hospital was.

When they reached mid-river she was unable to resist studying the New Brighton coastline and picking out the familiar landmarks. As she surveyed the huge Tower Building she couldn't help wondering if there was still a circus in the fairground that surrounded it.

She was shaking with nerves by the time they arrived at the hospital.

'Come on, let's visit Liam first and then we'll deal with the other matter afterwards,' Billy told her.

Liam was in a long narrow ward with ground-to-ceiling glass doors that opened on to a stretch of green grass. Although there was quite a keen breeze the doors were wide open.

'He'll catch his death of cold in this place,' Billy commented as he turned up his jacket collar.

'Fresh air is all part of the treatment,' Patsy assured him.

'What, even in winter?'

'So I understand. We'll have to bring him in a woolly hat and some gloves when it gets colder.'

Billy shot her a sideways glance to see if she was smiling and then frowned heavily when he saw she was quite serious.

Liam was so pleased to see them that it brought a lump into Patsy's throat. She made a pretence of putting some of the things she had brought for him into the locker by his bedside so that he wouldn't see the tears in her eyes.

Patsy's heart sank as she looked at his thin little legs and arms. He had always been on the skinny side, but now they were like matchsticks. She found herself wondering why she had never suspected that something was wrong with him when he didn't fill out. He'd been a very small baby, but with all the food Elaine gave him he should have been quite tubby when he reached the toddler stage.

Patsy sighed. She'd always told herself that he was going to be tall and lean like her dad, but she should have known that those characteristics wouldn't have developed until he was entering manhood.

It was no good dwelling on the past, she thought, swallowing back her tears. If she'd made mistakes then she must try and rectify them.

It made her all the more determined to work at the hospital he was in. As a nurse, even if it wasn't on his ward, she would be able to find a way to monitor his progress first hand and to be there to comfort and reassure him while he was undergoing treatment.

Chapter Thirty-One

Patsy found it much easier to transfer from one hospital to the other than she had thought possible.

Not everyone liked the idea of nursing TB patients because of the fear of catching the disease, or infecting someone in their own family, so the isolation hospital was always ready to consider suitable applicants.

A further point that made the transition easy was the fact that the matron at Liverpool General Hospital was not very pleased with the way Nurse Callaghan had been acting over the last few months and was quite relieved to see her go. First of all there had been the summons for Nurse Callaghan to go home in the middle of the day because of a family crisis, followed almost immediately by the necessity of taking her leave early.

According to Sister Pringle, when eventually Nurse Callaghan did return to duty she seemed to have her mind on other things and her work on the ward had suffered because of this. It was only the inconvenience of being short-staffed that had stopped Matron dismissing her right away.

Patsy settled in quickly at the new hospital. She was not working on the children's ward, but hoped that perhaps she would be transferred in the near future. But she managed to see Liam most days, even though sometimes it was from a distance.

She had told no one in the hospital that she was his mother, but being under the same roof as him was comforting even when she wasn't able to sit with him or even speak to him.

Patsy tried to be as discreet as possible, but she suspected that the nurses on the children's ward wondered why she was always pausing by the door. On the first two or three occasions she had explained that she was new to the hospital and had lost her way, but she knew she couldn't go on making such an excuse for ever.

The truth emerged the night after Liam underwent his first major treatment. She had slipped along to his ward late in the evening, at a time when she knew the night staff would have completed their rounds and would be in the staff room, to check if he was all right.

Her heart ached as she saw him lying there awake, and in obvious distress. Before she could help herself she was kneeling at his bedside, stroking his damp hair back from his brow and murmuring words of comfort.

When she tried to leave he clung on to her, sobbing so loudly that the duty nurse came hurrying in to see what was wrong. When she found Patsy at Liam's bedside she demanded to know what was going on. She listened in obvious disbelief as Patsy explained she was Liam's mother. She then insisted that Patsy must leave the ward and said she would have to report the incident to Sister.

Patsy didn't sleep a wink that night. She knew she had broken hospital rules and that there would be trouble the next day. It was no surprise at all when around mid-morning the staff nurse on the ward where she was working told her to report immediately to Matron.

Outside the door to Matron's office, Patsy smoothed down her starched white apron, straightened her white cap and took a deep breath to steady her nerves before she knocked. As she waited nervously for the summons to enter, Patsy braced herself for an onslaught.

She had gone over and over in her mind what she should say and had decided that the truth would carry more weight than any excuses. She was sure that once Matron knew that Liam was her child she would understand her fears and anxiety and why she was constantly hovering near his bedside.

She was quite wrong. Matron was completely unsympathetic.

'You have been trained to look after people who are sick, Nurse Callaghan, not your relations,' she said icily. 'What you have been doing not only transgresses the trust I have placed in you, but is highly unprofessional.'

'Liam is my son, I am terribly concerned about him,' Patsy responded heatedly. 'He is not yet five years old and this is the first time he has been away from his home. I'm not interfering in his treatment in any way.'

'That will do, Nurse Callaghan! I do not consider these to be mitigating circumstances and

I will not enter into any further discussion of the matter. Do you understand?' she added sternly.

Patsy tried to bite back the angry retort that rose to her lips but the words gushed out like a jet of scalding hot water.

'You can't do this, you can't stop me seeing him!' she raged. 'He needs me at his bedside, he needs my reassurance.'

'Nurse Callaghan!' Matron's face was red with anger. 'How dare you dispute my judgement!'

'Liam is a desperately sick little boy and he needs to know that his mother is there near him,' Patsy repeated stubbornly.

'Why should one child receive different treatment from all the others? Have you stopped and considered what it is doing to the other patients to see one small boy getting preferential treatment?'

Too choked to answer, Patsy looked down at her shoes.

'I'm waiting for your answer, Nurse Callaghan,' Matron snapped.

Patsy knew she was defeated. 'I'm sorry, Matron. I won't do it again,' she said meekly.

'You most certainly won't, Nurse Callaghan,' Matron said frostily. 'You are dismissed. I want you off the hospital premises within the hour. Do you understand?'

The colour drained from Patsy's face. 'You can't mean that,' she gasped.

Matron gave her a withering look. 'You should have thought about the consequences before you behaved in such an unprofessional way. Kindly close the door as you leave.'

Patsy went straight from Matron's office to the ward where Liam was. Without asking anyone's permission she walked over to his bed and gave him a big hug.

'Look, luv, I won't be able to see you again until visiting day,' she told him.

He looked crestfallen. 'You said you'd come and kiss me good-night every night while I was in here,' he reminded her.

'I know, pet, but things have changed. I'm not working at this hospital any more. I'll be in to see you on Wednesday though. Who shall I bring with me?'

'Nana said she'd come, and Billy was going to come as well,' he pouted.

'Well so they can.'

'If they come then you won't come.'

'We'll all come,' she promised. 'Billy can pop in for a few minutes and then he'll wait outside while Nana comes in to see you and I'll be here the whole time. How about that?'

Liam's pallid face brightened. 'And will you all bring me something?'

'You'll have to wait and see, won't you,' Patsy smiled, as she hugged and kissed him again.

'Nurse Callaghan, what are you doing here? Matron said you were not to be allowed on this ward except at normal visiting times so will you please leave immediately.'

'I've got to go now, Liam,' Patsy told him, tears trickling down her cheeks. 'I'll see you on Wednesday, I promise.'

When she left the isolation hospital she couldn't bring herself to go back to Paradise Place. How was she to explain to Elaine and Billy what a mess she had made of things?

She walked slowly up Mill Lane to Liscard Road and walked round for almost half an hour staring unseeingly into the shop windows. What was she going to do now? She was out of work at a time when they needed as much money as possible for Liam. When he came out of hospital he would need plenty of nourishing food to build up his strength and she could hardly ask to go back to Liverpool General.

Her feeling of gloom deepened. Perhaps Liam never would come out of hospital. So few children recovered, because they hadn't the stamina to fight the disease or stand up to the long, arduous treatment.

The thought that he might die filled her with even deeper fear. He'd never even met his father! Bruno didn't even know he existed.

She had to do something about that and there was no better time than the present, she decided. She was in Wallasey so she was only a bus ride away from New Brighton. She'd go to the fairground again and this time she would definitely find out what had happened to Bruno. Someone there must know.

The fairground was thronged with people and everything seemed to have changed from when she had last been there. There were far more swings and roundabouts and a great many new sideshows, but there was still no circus.

'Bruno Alvarez? Yes, I remember him,' one of the stall holders told her. 'Tall, dark-haired chap, came from Spain or one of those Mediterranean places. He used to train the lions and big cats. Is that the fellow?'

'Yes,' Patsy agreed eagerly. 'That sounds like Bruno. Can you tell me where I can find him?'

The man pushed his hat back and scratched his head. 'No, not really. He left a few years back, took his animals with him and hasn't been back since.'

'You must know where he went?'

The man scratched his head again. 'Can't say I do, really. There were rumours that he'd gone to Blackpool and then someone said Rhyl and someone else said Morecambe. There's any number of seaside places up and down the coast so he could be at any of them.'

'Thanks.'

'Hold on,' the man said as Patsy turned away. 'There was something that happened the day before he left that might interest you.'

'Go on.'

'Some woman, quite a bit older than him, came here looking for him. She was quite a looker and she had lovely hair. Reddish blonde it was. Bruno seemed a bit surprised to see her, but she grabbed hold of him and began hugging and kissing him and a couple of minutes later he had his arm round her waist and they went off towards his van.'

'Is that all?'

'Well yes. Except that next morning Bruno packed up all his belongings and he and the woman and the animals took off. Like I said, no one's seen or heard of them since.'

'Thanks!' It wasn't what she'd wanted to hear. From the man's description there was very little doubt in her mind who the woman had been.

Patsy felt numb as she left the fairground, wandered out on to the promenade and made her way across to the pier. Leaning on the railings she stared out unseeingly across the choppy waters of the Mersey.

The disappearance of her mother from their house in Paradise Place, and of Bruno from the fairground, had happened about the same time. Linked to what she had just been told the pieces fitted together like a jigsaw. I should have known from the way mam carried on with Bruno when she met him on my sixteenth birthday that she was involved, Patsy thought bitterly.

She had tried to forget about finding them in bed together the next morning. Or the way Bruno had seemed to change towards her immediately afterwards.

She knew now why her mam had given up the house.

Yet, when Mam found out that I was pregnant I told her that it was Bruno's baby, she thought angrily. Even though she knew that she still went away with him. She abandoned me and pinched my boyfriend, knowing I was going to need help from both of them. If it hadn't been for Billy and his family looking after me I would have had no one.

Patsy thought of the countless times he had taken her in his arms and comforted her, and the look in his eyes whenever he'd done so. Above all she remembered his tenderness on the one and only occasion when they'd made love. The more she thought about the way Billy had behaved, his kindness, his steadfastness throughout all her troubles, the more incredible it seemed that he still felt the same way about her.

Billy really must love me a great deal, she thought with astonishment. His feelings for her had withstood the countless difficulties they'd gone through together.

She'd taken him so much for granted. She hadn't treated him anywhere near as well as she should have done. It was something she would always regret, but it wasn't too late to do something about it.

The time had come to admit to him and to herself just how much she cared for him, to openly acknowledge that she loved him.

Filled with a mixture of relief, joy and hope for the future she headed for the nearest bus that would take her back to Seacombe ferry. It would make her journey longer, but she didn't want to catch a boat from New Brighton: the crossing would bring back too many sad memories.

Anyway, there was no immediate hurry. As far as Billy and Elaine knew, she was at work so they wouldn't be expecting her. The longer the journey took, the more time she had to decide what she was going to tell them about losing her job.

The only good thing that she could see coming out of all this was that she would be able to visit Liam regularly every Wednesday and Sunday.

Chapter Thirty-Two

Patsy was so immersed in her misery as she stood leaning on the rail of the ferryboat as it pulled alongside at Liverpool that she didn't notice the young man in grey flannels, brown tweed jacket and brown cap patiently waiting on the slipway.

The gangplank was lowered and she was making her way on to the floating roadway when she was startled by him limping towards her. He grasped her by the arm.

'Where the hell have you been, Patsy? I've met every boat from New Brighton and Seacombe for the past two hours. I thought I must have missed you. I even rushed back to Paradise Place and left messages with everyone I could find to tell you to get back to the hospital as quickly as you could. Then I came back here to the Pier Head to check if you were on any of the boats as they arrived.'

'Billy! What are you doing here? How did you know I was on the way home?'

'We had a policeman call at the house to say they'd had a phone message from the Wallasey Hospital, that's why I'm here. We've been at our wits' end trying to find you.'

Patsy turned a brick red, her green eyes flaming. 'They had no right to do that! My quarrel with the matron was nothing at all to do with you. Why send the police, anyway? What I did wasn't criminal!'

'I don't know what the devil you're on about,' Billy frowned. 'The police came with a message about Liam. They said we ought to go over there right away. When me mam and me got there we couldn't find you and we were told that you had left the hospital.'

'What's happened to him?' she asked anxiously.

'He's much worse. They want us to be with him. Come on.' He turned her round and hurried her back on to the boat she'd just arrived on, which was already preparing to cast off again for a return journey to Seacombe.

Patsy felt numb and then guilty as she listened to Billy's account of what he and Elaine had been told when they reached the hospital.

'They said there had been some sort of disturbance on the ward this morning and that as a result Liam was very upset. It seems he cried so much that it brought on a severe bout of coughing that wouldn't stop. In the end he was coughing up so much blood that they had to take emergency measures.'

'Oh my God!' The colour drained from Patsy's face.

Bill looked puzzled. 'Mam thought you were there at the hospital with him and that you'd been the one to send for us.' He frowned. 'You should have been there. Where were you?'

Patsy ignored his question. 'Liam is going to be all right, isn't he?' she asked anxiously.

'I'm sure he is.' Billy put an arm round her shoulder and hugged her close to him. 'Don't worry, they're doing everything they can for him,' he said confidently, planting a reassuring kiss on the top of her red curls.

Patsy flinched and pulled away. 'I should have been there. He needs me.' She sniffed and dabbed at her eyes. 'Oh, Billy, why does everything always go wrong for me?'

'Don't worry, me mam's there with him,' he reminded her. 'She'll do all she can to comfort him.'

'That's not the point. I'm the one who should be there, I'm his mother,' Patsy insisted angrily. 'What if they told him I was coming to see him and he's been expecting me? He won't understand why I'm not there and he'll be breaking his little heart.'

'Well, there's nothing you can do about it now, Patsy. Neither of us can turn the clock back. What on earth made you leave the hospital in the middle of the morning, anyway? You still haven't told me.'

'I was ordered to leave. I broke the rules. I was caught cuddling Liam when I shouldn't have been anywhere near the ward he's in. I was sent to Matron and when I tried to explain that Liam was my child she dismissed me on the spot and told me to be off the premises within an hour. She said I'd been trained to nurse the sick, not my own family,' she added bitterly.

'What a right cow!' Billy exclaimed indignantly. 'Liam is sick and if he's in hospital then he's a patient, isn't he! And she made you leave right away?'

'I was supposed to, but I went back to say goodbye to Liam. I couldn't disappear without trying to explain to him why I wouldn't be seeing him again until Wednesday afternoon.'

'Do you think that's what upset him?'

'I suppose so, but I had no choice, Billy. Sister Beasley who's in charge of that ward insisted I leave immediately. She ranted on and on, saying that I had no right to be there. I know she was only doing what she was told to do,' she added quickly as she saw the anger in Billy's eyes.

'Be that as it may, she could have let you have a few minutes to explain things to him.'

Patsy looked embarrassed. 'I suppose it was my fault for breaking the rules. Liam was awfully upset, though, when I left, poor little luv. That's probably why he was crying so much.'

Billy shook his head in disbelief. He still didn't agree with the treatment that had been meted out to Patsy.

'If you left the hospital before midday why has it taken you three hours to get home?' he asked, frowning.

Patsy shot a sideways glance at Billy, wondering how he'd react if she told him the truth.

'Well?'

'I went to New Brighton to see if I could find any trace of Bruno,' she muttered. 'I thought that since Liam was so ill Bruno ought to know about him. I thought he might even want to come and see Liam.'

Billy's face darkened and his jaw tightened, but he said nothing.

'I didn't find him,' Patsy went on. 'I did manage to get some news about what had happened to him, though.'

'Go on!'

Patsy shook her head. 'I don't want to talk about it.'

'Well I do,' Billy said grimly. 'Now you've told me this much you might as well tell me the rest.'

'He's gone, no one is quite sure where, but . . . he went off with a woman who was older than him. From the description I was given there's no doubt in my mind who it was.'

Billy stared at her, astounded. 'Surely you don't mean . . .'

'Yes, I mean my mam,' she admitted dully. 'I'm not really surprised. In fact, I think I've suspected something like that all along, but I couldn't bring myself to admit it.'

Billy gave a soundless whistle. 'Well, she certainly paid plenty of attention to Bruno the night you brought him over to meet her,' he admitted.

'He stayed the night. I told you that,' Patsy said bitterly. 'He was supposed to be sleeping on the sofa, but I found them in bed together next morning. That must have been the start of it.'

'So that's why she cleared out of the house without a word to anyone!'

Patsy nodded. 'They both did a disappearing act at about the same time.'

Billy placed an arm around Patsy's shoulder. 'That's the end of it then, luv. No more nonsense or dreams about going to live in Spain. The best

337

thing you can do is put all that out of your head and make the most of what you've got here.'

'I know,' Patsy sniffed. 'I've been an idiot, haven't I, Billy?'

'We all have our dreams, Patsy. That's what keeps us going most of the time,' he said stiffly.

She looked up at him questioningly. His face was impassive, but there was such grim sadness registered there that it made her feel guilty about the way she'd treated him over the years.

'You know, Billy, you're really the only true friend I've ever had,' she said thoughtfully. She slipped her hand into his and squeezed it, aware that she would be needing all the warmth and friendship he could offer over the next few days.

When this was all over and Liam was safe and well, she'd do her best to make up to Billy for the way she'd treated him in the past, she resolved. He'd been through so much, especially since his accident, yet he rarely grumbled or complained and he put her and Liam's needs first all the time.

When they arrived at the hospital they were not allowed to go straight to Liam's bedside, but were kept waiting in the reception area. Patsy fretted over the delay and wondered if it was because of what had happened between her and Sister Beasley earlier in the day.

She paced up and down, ignoring Billy's advice to try and be patient for a little longer. She couldn't sit still knowing that Liam was lying so desperately ill somewhere in the building. She wanted to be with him, to do whatever she could to alleviate his pain and misery.

When finally they were told to go to Matron's office instead of to the ward, Patsy felt ready to explode with indignation and frustration. She stalked down the corridor, her head high, anger flaring in her green eyes. Inwardly she was trembling, fear in her heart in case Matron was going to exert her power and not allow her to see Liam after all.

When they entered Matron's office she was surprised to see Elaine was already there. Billy had told her that his mam was with Liam, that he had left her at the bedside.

Patsy's fear escalated. Did this mean that Liam was worse and that he wasn't being allowed visitors at all? Or did it mean they had found it necessary to operate on him and Matron had undertaken personally to explain all this to them?

Patsy looked from Elaine to Matron and back again. Elaine's face was white and drawn, her eyes red-rimmed as though she had been crying copiously. The moment she saw Patsy she burst into choking sobs.

Patsy reached out to take her hand, but Elaine pushed her away. 'Why couldn't you have been here?' she said hoarsely. 'You should have been the one with poor little Liam, not me.'

Stunned by the anger in Elaine's voice, Patsy drew back and looked questioningly at Matron.

Matron, her face expressionless, looked first at Patsy and then at Billy. 'I'm afraid Liam is dead,' she told them crisply.

'Dead?' Patsy shook her head in disbelief. 'He was perfectly all right when I left here this morning,' she said accusingly. 'He was a very sick child, but he wasn't about to die.'

'Liam was very upset, Miss Callaghan, by whatever it was you had said to him when you left. He started crying, which resulted in a severe bout of coughing. In spite of all Sister Beasley and the rest of my staff could do his condition deteriorated rapidly. We sent for you immediately,' she added stiffly.

'He brought up so much blood, Patsy, it was really terrible,' Elaine shuddered. 'There was blood everywhere! His nightclothes and his bedding were soaked in it. I've never seen so much blood in my life.'

Patsy shook her head in disbelief. 'No, it can't be true!' She looked round her wildly. 'Where is he? I want to see my baby!'

'Please calm down, Miss Callaghan. You will be allowed to see him before you leave,' Matron told her coldly.

'It's all your fault that this happened!' Patsy flared up accusingly.

Matron didn't deign to answer. She stretched out a hand and pressed a buzzer on her desk. 'Someone is coming to take you along right now,' she told Patsy calmly. She turned to Elaine. 'Do you wish to see the body again?'

Elaine shook her head; she was trembling so much she couldn't speak.

'Then someone will take you back to reception and you can wait there until the rest of your family have seen the child's body and are ready to leave,' she said dismissively.

Patsy stumbled from the room too numb to make any reply. The words 'see the body' echoed over and over in her head. She couldn't believe that those cold, impersonal words meant Liam. When she'd left the hospital at mid-morning he'd been alive and expressing his love for her with hugs and kisses. She could still feel his warm little body in her arms as she'd held him close.

Now she would never see him again. Never be able to kiss and cuddle him or tell him how much she loved him and how precious he was to her, she thought, distraught, as she and Billy were taken into a small side ward where he was lying. She gazed down at him through a haze of tears. He was so still and white, and his face was so serene, that he looked almost like a china doll.

As Patsy bent to pick him up Sister Beasley placed a restraining hand on her arm and stopped her.

'You may kiss him goodbye, but you know you must not move him,' she reminded her gravely.

Patsy shook her hand away. 'He's still mine, even if you have killed him,' she said bitterly.

'Kiss him goodbye, Patsy, that's all you can do now,' Billy whispered, putting a comforting arm around her shoulders. He leaned forward and placed his own lips against the child's icy brow and then pulled back and waited until Patsy had done the same.

Silently she turned away and Billy led her from the room, back to where Elaine was waiting for them.

Chapter Thirty-Three

Patsy tried desperately to block out all memories of Liam's death and funeral from her mind, but it was impossible. Throughout the day, as well as the moment she closed her eyes at night, she saw again the tiny white coffin with its gleaming brass handles being carried on the shoulders of Billy and Joe Grant to its final resting place.

She had been so distraught over Liam's death that she'd left Billy and his family to arrange the funeral. She couldn't face Father O'Brian knowing how greatly she had sinned. She hadn't been to Mass or even inside his church since Liam was born so she felt it would be hypocritical to ask him to officiate at her child's funeral.

Billy and Joe had done everything and because they weren't Catholics themselves they had gone along with Elaine's suggestion that Liam should be buried in the same plot as her own mother and father. Patsy hadn't argued. She'd felt so numb with pain that she couldn't focus her thoughts to make any decisions. Afterwards she'd felt both sad and guilty because she knew Liam should have been laid to rest alongside her own dad.

It had been a very quiet funeral. Apart from the Grants, no one else attended. Maureen and Megan Murphy and their mother refused to come. They denounced what was happening as blasphemous and told Patsy that Father O'Brian would be horrified when he found out and probably excommunicate her.

The threat of damnation did nothing to ease the bitter sting of Liam's death. As the tiny white coffin was lowered into the ground she had stood there shrinking back into the past, knowing she would never be able to forget that she had been the cause of the upset that had brought about Liam's death. Even worse, she should have been there to hold and comfort him in his final hour, not Elaine.

If she hadn't sneaked in to talk to him none of this might have happened. Liam might still be alive, she told herself over and over again. He would probably still be seriously ill and needing treatment for tuberculosis. It might have taken years of careful nursing before he was completely well, but he would still have been alive.

Afterwards, she lost all track of time, she was so consumed by guilt.

It also troubled her that she had been culpable of negligence when he'd been born because of her own pig-headedness. This, as much as anything else, had probably contributed to the fact that he had always been underweight and small for his age.

If only Liam had been born at home or in a hospital with a midwife, where he would have had the right sort of attention. For him to have been born in a stable with only Billy there to help her had been asking for trouble.

One of the first things she had been taught when she began her training to be a nurse was the need for scrupulous cleanliness. Billy hadn't even been able to wash his hands before he helped to deliver Liam. There had been no fresh water available and not even a clean sheet to wrap the baby in.

If Liam had been taken from the stable into normal surroundings right away he might have stood a better chance. His earliest days, when he was most vulnerable to infection, had been spent lying in a makeshift cot with only a Valor oil stove for heating and with Samson standing in a corner breathing the same air as him.

She kept the guilt and misgivings to herself, constantly mulling them over, knowing she was the one who must shoulder the blame. To talk about them to Billy or Elaine would be to heap recriminations on them and that would be unjust. Billy would feel he should have done more when Liam had been born. Elaine might think that she hadn't looked after Liam as well as she might have done while he was in her care.

Patsy didn't want either of them to think that these things were true. The blame, and she felt there was plenty of it, lay on her shoulders. She was the one who was at fault, not them. All the Grants, even Joe, had done their utmost for Liam, certainly far more than her own mam had done.

Thinking about her mam made Patsy's blood boil and resentment rise up inside her. How could her mother have been so callous as to turn her out into the street when she found out she was pregnant? Even after all this time it seemed unbelievably harsh.

Patsy still found it hard to accept that her own mam should connive to steal Bruno away from her, especially after she'd told her that Bruno was the father of the baby she was carrying. I'd even told her that Bruno was going to marry me and that when the season ended we were going back to his home in Spain together, she thought bitterly.

She was glad her mam had left Paradise Place and hoped she would never have to face her again.

Perhaps she had done the right thing, Patsy reflected. Paradise Place had not brought either of them any great happiness or contentment. Maybe I should do the same, she thought wryly. Leave Paradise Place and all its bittersweet memories behind and go somewhere where I'm not known and start afresh.

She was a trained nurse so surely she would find it easy enough to find work somewhere away from Liverpool and make a completely new life for herself?

There was only one thing which made her hesitate to take such a radical step and that was leaving Billy behind. He had been so good to her, so caring, the greatest friend she'd had throughout all her troubles. Now, when he had problems of his own it seemed heartless to walk away and leave him.

Since his accident he had not found any kind of permanent work. He was still young and good looking, but his damaged leg was a tremendous handicap. He would always have a limp and when he was tired or not feeling very well the limp became much more pronounced.

Patsy walked round for days in a complete daze trying to decide about her future. She longed to discuss it, to talk her ideas through with someone, but she didn't feel there was anyone she could confide in.

Elaine was as heartbroken as she was. Patsy knew she'd have loved to have been able to openly claim Liam as her grandson. Several times she had pointed out that he had a tiny birthmark at the base of his spine and that Billy had one in exactly the same place, as though that might prove he was Billy's child.

Elaine's grieving took the form of cleaning the house from top to bottom and washing everything in sight. She seemed to resent anyone at all being in the house so Patsy had taken to wandering round the town, staring unseeingly into shop windows.

She missed Samson. She'd found him a wonderful source of comfort when she had problems. She had always talked to him while she groomed him and his companionable snorts, or friendly head butts, had so often inspired the resolution of any uncertainties she had.

She knew Billy was grieving over Liam yet neither of them could talk about it to each other. It had become a taboo subject. After the funeral Billy went his way and she went hers. It was almost as if they were deliberately avoiding each other. The only time they were in the same room together was at mealtimes and more often than not Billy was absent from these. Elaine would cover his dinner over with a plate and leave it in the oven to keep warm so that he could have it whenever he came home.

Patsy had no idea where he went; nor did anyone else. He looked so haggard and had lost so much weight that she felt concerned about his health.

Joe still dropped into the Grafton on his way home, and very often he and Billy met up in there and came home together.

The fact that Billy seemed to be going for a beer regularly worried Patsy because he never had been much of a drinker. In moderation having a beer didn't matter, but Patsy was concerned in case drinking was becoming his way of coping with his grief.

Janie and Freddie were upset by what had happened. They had both been very fond of Liam too. They were young and leading full and busy lives, though, so the bonds between them and Liam were nowhere near as strong or as binding.

Patsy felt that perhaps if they all talked about Liam more, instead of shying away from even mentioning his name, then she and Billy as well as Elaine and Joe would come to terms with their loss much better.

Perhaps she was the one who must act first, Patsy thought. She wondered if she went to Liam's graveside and spent some time there whether she would find peace. She hadn't been near his grave since the day of the funeral because it was in the graveyard of a Protestant church, which she'd been brought up to think of as a place she mustn't go.

Now, as she made her way there, and walked between the long rows of gravestones to the spot where Liam had been buried, she thought how stupid it was to have let such a trivial reason prevent her from coming before.

When she reached the newly formed grave she was surprised to see that a little headstone had been erected and that the ground around the grave had been carefully tended.

Even on this point, I've failed him, she thought bitterly as she knelt down beside the mound of freshly raked earth. Someone else has done what I should have been doing and they've cared for him in death more than I have.

The tears which seemed to have dried up since the day of the funeral flowed down her cheeks. She made no attempt to stop them, for they brought such a wonderful feeling of relief.

As she placed on the grave the carousel her father had bought for her when she'd been only a child herself she told herself that this was to be her final farewell both to Liam and to everything that had ever happened before in her life.

It was time to move on, perhaps to leave Paradise Place for ever.

Chapter Thirty-Four

Patsy was still kneeling at the side of Liam's grave, tears trickling unchecked down her cheeks, when Billy found her.

'I've been looking for you. I thought I might find you here,' he said gently, crouching down beside her and placing his arm around her shoulders.

Patsy half turned and buried her face against his shoulder. 'I sometimes think you must be my guardian angel,' she sobbed. 'You're always around when I need you most.'

He held her in silence for a few moments, until her sobs quietened. Then very gently he pulled away and dabbed at her eyes with his handkerchief.

'Come on, let's take a little walk, shall we? It's sometimes easier to talk when you are on the move. There's a great deal I want to say to you, Patsy.'

Stiffly she rose to her feet, her eyes still on the tiny grave.

'Where did I go wrong, Billy?' she pleaded, looking up into his face.

'I don't think you went wrong, it was the way things happened,' he said gently.

She shook her head. 'It's more than that. Things

don't simply happen. You do things that make them come about and if you make the wrong decision, go down the wrong path, then that's when things start to go wrong.'

He looked at her despairingly, shaking his head in protest.

'You couldn't have done anything any different, Patsy,' he told her gravely. 'It wasn't your fault that your dad had an accident, it wasn't even his. The weather that day was treacherous and as a result there was a mishap.'

'And your accident? That was my fault now, wasn't it?' she asked sadly.

'No, of course it wasn't. How could it be your fault that poor old Samson had a heart attack? If anything, it was mine for overloading the cart.'

'You wouldn't have done that if I'd been there. You were working on your own and struggling to save time by trying to carry two loads in one journey.'

Billy shook his head. 'I don't think that was the problem at all. You might just as well say that the relief horse I hitched on to help Samson up the slipway didn't pull as well as he should and that Samson had to take the full brunt of the load and that was what did his heart in.'

Patsy sighed. 'Yes, Samson wasn't at his peak, was he?' she said thoughtfully. 'And that *was* my fault,' she added stubbornly. 'He hadn't been exercised or taken out of the stable for a week and he was used to going out every day except Sunday.'

'Think that if you like,' Billy said, 'but it's a load of nonsense. He was getting on in years. He had to die some time, we all do. It was just bad luck that he fell over sideways and I was trapped underneath.'

'If I'd been on the run with you that day, as I usually was, then I would have been the one leading him, not you,' Patsy pointed out.

Billy gave a forced laugh. 'Yes, you might have been! So think yourself lucky that it wasn't you!'

'Don't you understand, I can't think like that?' Patsy fumed. 'I feel guilty because in a way it was my fault. If I'd been there you wouldn't have been injured.'

Billy shrugged his shoulders dismissively. 'Well, that's the luck of the draw now, isn't it. Call it Fate or what you will, it's something we have no control over so there's no point in worrying about it.'

'I can't help worrying because as a result of what happened you're lame in one leg and you've been out of work ever since.'

'I earn a crust now and again,' he joked. 'Anyway, in the last few years you've stumped up more than your fair share towards the house-keeping, Patsy. All the money handed over to my mam goes into the same pot, you know.'

'You, your mam and your entire family have been so good to me, Billy, that I'll never be able to repay you all. The way you helped to look after little Liam was wonderful.'

Billy's face clouded. 'My mam is taking it pretty hard not having Liam around, you know. She doesn't say very much about it, but I know it's cut her to the quick. Having a baby in the house to look after gave her a new lease of life.'

'I don't think she'd have been able to cope with him though if you hadn't been there to help keep an eye on him,' Patsy said thoughtfully. 'Once he started walking he was quite a handful, wasn't he?'

'That's true enough,' Billy smiled. 'He could move like greased lightning. I'm going to miss him as well. I'll have to find another way of filling in my time now.'

'So have you any plans about what you are going to do in the future, Billy? Is it worth trying to start up the haulage business again?'

He shrugged. 'I don't know. Times are changing so rapidly that there's not much point in buying another horse. That sort of transport is finished. Whenever I go down to the docks it seems to me that more and more of the haulage firms are using lorries.'

'I suppose you could get a job driving one of those?' Patsy said tentatively.

'No!' Billy said firmly. 'I have thought about it, but I can't face up to learning to drive a lorry. I don't think I'd make a very good job of it with my gammy leg.'

'You don't know until you give it a try.'

He grinned dismissively. 'That's enough about me, what about you? Are you going to carry on nursing?'

'I don't know. Some days when I remember how much I enjoyed working at the Liverpool General I can't wait to be back nursing. Then, when I think about Liam dying, I never want to go inside a hospital ever again. I think I'd be much better off packing it all in and doing something completely different.'

'I can understand you having doubts,' Billy agreed, 'only it seems a pity to throw away all that training, doesn't it?'

'I don't know, Billy.' Patsy's voice wobbled and tears once more began to trickle down her cheeks. 'If only I didn't feel so guilty about Liam it would be easier to make my mind up, perhaps. I keep wondering if I should leave Paradise Place, go right away from Liverpool like my mother's done, and start afresh. If I did that then I might manage to shake off all the bad luck I seem to be having.'

'You haven't really had all that much bad luck,' Billy protested.

She looked sceptical. 'I haven't?'

'No more than most people,' he muttered.

'How can you say that? Unless, of course, you agree that all the bad things that have happened to me are my own fault.'

'No, I'm not saying that, but it's too late to change anything that's happened. Life's too short to worry about the past. You're young and healthy so think of the future.'

'At the moment I can only think about the past,' Patsy said ruefully. 'Every minute of the day and night I blame myself for Liam's death.'

Billy looked angry. A muscle twitched at the side of his face. 'That's absolutely ridiculous!' he fumed.

She shook her head emphatically. 'No, it's not. If Liam hadn't been born in a stable, if I hadn't

353

refused to let you fetch a doctor, if I had done something about moving him into a proper house instead of insisting upon hiding out in the stable after he was born . . .'

'Hey, stop it!' Billy exclaimed in alarm. 'You did what you thought was right at the time, remember! We both did. Bear in mind that I went along with your decisions. If you think for one minute that you are responsible for what happened to Liam then I'm just as guilty and I refuse to accept that.'

'Oh, Billy!' Patsy stopped walking and turned towards him imploringly, a haunted look in her green eyes. 'What would I do without you?'

'Hey! Steady on, you know I'm always around if you want a friendly shoulder to lean on.'

'I want more than that,' she whispered contritely.

'What do you mean?'

'Oh, Billy! I've been such a fool. All the heartache I must have caused you because I've always refused to recognise my feelings for you.' She held up a hand as he made to speak. 'Let me finish,' she begged softly. 'I want you to know that I do love you very, very deeply. I think I always have, but I wouldn't admit it even to myself. I was infatuated by Bruno, but I know now that was all it was. He was larger than life with his foreign charm and glamorous uniform and job. I was just a fling for him, but pride wouldn't let me admit that. What I feel for you, Billy, is something quite different. It's a deep, tender feeling that grows stronger every day.'

Billy drew her into his arms, burying his face in her bright red curls. 'What would we do without each other, Patsy?' He sighed. 'You didn't really mean it when you said you were thinking of leaving Paradise Place, did you?'

'I certainly have thought about it a number of times,' she admitted. 'Some day, I suppose, I might find the courage to move away from Paradise Place and all its harowing memories, but I'm not sure I'd have the guts to do it on my own. Would you come with me?'

Billy's eyes were thoughtful as they held hers in a long, steady gaze. 'I think you should remember, Patsy, that Paradise Place has made both of us what we are and we belong here,' he told her solemnly.

'Maybe, but what sort of a life is it going to provide us with in the future?' she asked bleakly.

He looked at her earnestly. 'If you promise to stick around then I'll tell you about the plan I've been mulling over,' he offered.

Her face brightened. 'Go on! I'll tell you if I'll stay when I hear what your plan is, so it had better be something special.'

He pushed back his cap and ran his hand over his thick hair. 'I don't really know how to start,' he admitted.

'I'm waiting! It had better be good. And don't forget, I haven't made that promise yet,' she said teasingly.

'Right!' He hesitated as if searching for the right words. 'Well, I'm thinking of opening a shop in Paradise Place. The sort of place that sells all sorts of household item. Everything from coal and fire-wood to pots and pans, from cutlery to ladders and paint, even tools like hammers and saws . . .'

'You mean a hardware shop and chandlers combined?' Patsy interrupted.

'Yeah! Something like that. A place where local people can buy anything and everything they might need for their home. What do you think of the idea?'

'The idea's great. Do you think you'd be able to manage to run it on your own?'

Billy ran his hand through his hair again. 'That might be a problem. I'd probably need someone to help me,' he admitted.

Patsy nodded. 'It would need to be someone that you know you can work side by side with,' she said with a knowing smirk.

'You think so? Well, do you know anyone at all who might be suitable for the job?' he asked, trying not to smile.

'I do, but only if it was a proper partnership you were offering. It would have to be legally binding, not simply a handshake.'

He looked at her, bewildered, then his eyes blazed with anticipation. 'Do you mean what I think you mean?' he asked cautiously.

'Depends what you think that is.'

'That you're interested not only in the business proposition, but that you're willing to marry me?'

Patsy gave an emphatic nod. 'If it can be arranged?'

He grabbed hold of her, smiling, hugging her enthusiastically. 'Oh, Patsy! My darling Patsy. You have no idea how often I've wanted to ask you to marry me. I've loved you ever since the first day

I came to work for your dad. I watched you grow up, more beautiful every day and I vowed that one day, when you were old enough, I would ask you to marry me.'

'So why didn't you?' she said wistfully.

'I was afraid to ask in case you refused me.'

'I suppose there was a time when I might have done so,' she admitted, 'but that was in the distant past.'

'So what changed your mind? Has it anything to do with the fact that you know Bruno will never come back?' he asked in a grim voice.

She shook her head. 'No, it's because at long last I have grown up. I have always realised that you are the most wonderful person I've ever known,' she added with a warm smile.

He held her face between his hands and kissed her tenderly. 'My sweet, precious Patsy. You are all I've ever wanted and now that I know that wish has come true I'm the happiest man alive.'

'So we can both make our fresh start right here in Paradise Place,' she smiled. 'We know we can work well together so you can open your shop and we'll work in it side by side.'

'Oh, Patsy, you've made me so happy. It's more than I dared to dream about!'

'It will be a joint venture,' she agreed softly.

'And a success because of my wonderful, beautiful partner,' Billy told her.

Patsy sighed. It would be a fresh start for both of them, but especially for her, she thought contentedly.

As they went to tell Elaine and Joe Grant of

their plans, Patsy felt an almost unbearable excitement about their hopes.

Yet, even though she and Billy were to be married and some day, in the not too distant future, there would be another baby, she would never forget baby Liam or stop grieving for him, she thought wistfully. Liam would always have a very special corner in her heart.

If you enjoyed *Patsy of Paradise Place* why not try Rosie Harris's gripping new novel . . .

ONE STEP FORWARD

Ever since she was eight years old, Katie Roberts has dreamed of getting away from the Cardiff slums where she lives.

When she is only a girl, her handsome but wicked father, Lewis, is imprisoned for theft leaving Katie and her mother homeless and penniless. Life is hard for Katie – not only because of their poverty but also because of the stigma of her father's shame.

When Lewis is released years later, it seems that life must improve. But to Katie's horror, it becomes worse than she has ever known it. When she and her father are left alone together, Katie seeks happiness and love elsewhere but, as she struggles to make a new life for herself, there is difficulty and danger at every turn . . .

Read on for an extract . . .

Chapter One

Eight-year-old Katie Roberts struggled to her feet and wiped away the tears streaming from her big grey eyes with the back of her hand. She would remember September 1926, and starting school in Tiger Bay, for the rest of her life.

Her long fair hair was caked with mud and there was a cut on one cheek of her heart-shaped face. Her white pinny was stained with grass and mud, her blue cotton dress was torn and there were angry red patches on her arms where the other three children had seized hold of her and forced her face down onto the ground.

Around her mouth were cuts and grazes where one of the boys had forced a handful of grass, flower heads and mud between her lips.

'Don't cry, you're all right now!'

Although her lip was bleeding she tried to smile as she looked gratefully at Aled Phillips, the gangly older boy who had rescued her from her tormentors.

Inwardly she was shaking with fear. Ever since she and her mother had come to live in Tiger Bay a month ago her whole life had changed and most of the time she felt lost and forlorn.

She thought back with deep longing to the time when her entire universe had been her home in

Catherine Street, where she and her mam and dad had lived with her nana, Sian Roberts.

In those halcyon days, life had revolved around Katie's needs, her likes and dislikes. Nana Roberts had always been petting her, asking her what she wanted to do, or what she would like to eat. She had cared for her, cuddled her, taken her out to the park or to the shops, read stories to her and sung her to sleep at night for as long as Katie could remember.

There had never been any loud voices or harsh words when she'd lived in Catherine Street, not until the day the police had come and taken her father away.

That was when everything had started to change.

They claimed that Lewis Roberts had been stealing but Nana Roberts declared that was nonsense. Why should he steal when he had everything he wanted?

Sometimes Katie found it hard to remember exactly what he looked like. At other times she could see him clearly, as if he was standing right beside her; a handsome, stocky-built man with grey eyes and a square chin, a glass of beer in one hand and a cigarette in the other.

When she'd been very small he used to carry her on his wide shoulders all the way from Catherine Street to Roath Park. She remembered how she used to cling onto his shock of black hair, scared she was going to fall off because he walked so fast.

She hadn't seen him since the two policemen

came hammering on the front door, but Nana Roberts told her he'd been sent to prison and wouldn't be coming home again for ages and ages.

Her mam had cried for days, bringing out huge blotchy red lumps on her face. She kept saying she really hated him for the disgrace he'd brought down on their heads, and that she would never be able to show her face outside again.

Nana Roberts had tut-tutted a lot as if she was going over and over everything in her head. Sometimes her lined face had looked so sad that Katie had cried as well. Not harsh, ugly, choking sobs like her mam made, but snuffly mewing sounds just to show how much she cared.

She'd expected Nana Roberts to pick her up and cuddle her and feed her sweets to make everything better, but she'd simply ignored her. Then, a few weeks after her dada had been taken away, Nana Roberts had gone upstairs and shut herself in her bedroom.

Hours later, when her mother told her to go and tell nana to come down and have a cup of tea she'd found her sprawled on the bed, her face a funny grey colour. She'd tried to waken her, but even though she'd shaken her arm and tugged at her black skirt, Nana Roberts had gone on sleeping.

Katie knew something was wrong so she'd gone back downstairs and tried to tell her mam, but Rachael had been too immersed in her own grief to take any notice. It was almost dark before Katie managed to get her mam to go upstairs to see what was wrong with Nana Roberts. And by then it was too late.

Her mam started screaming, rushed down the stairs and banged on the front door of the house next door, gabbling so hysterically that Stan Parsons couldn't make head or tail of what she was saying. He'd called out to his wife, Mona, and the pair of them went upstairs to Nana Roberts's bedroom to find out for themselves what had happened.

Katie watched in terrified silence as Mona held the hand mirror to Nana Roberts's mouth and then shook her head sadly when nothing happened. Not a single blur appeared on the shining surface, only a reflection of Nana Roberts's small round face with her eyes tight shut and her grey hair drawn back into a tight bun on top of her head.

Stan Parsons went for an ambulance, but when it arrived the men didn't even bother to carry Nana Roberts downstairs and put her into it.

'She's dead, mun! Looks like a heart attack. Been gone for hours, I'd say. Left it a bit late, like, to send for us, didn't you?'

Katie's mam had looked bewildered. 'I . . . I didn't know there was anything wrong,' she whispered.

'Not been having a barney, the two of you, then?'

Her mam had shaken her head. 'No, nothing like that. She did have something of an upset a couple of weeks back, mind.'

'Oh yes?' The ambulance man looked at her questioningly.

'Bit of bad news, like, about her son,' Rachael said evasively. 'Upset her a lot, there's no doubt about that.'

364

'Better send for your doctor,' the ambulance man advised. 'No point in us taking the old lady to hospital when she's been dead for hours now, is there?'

That was when everything seemed to get really bad. There were people coming and going to the house for several days after that, Katie remembered.

The doctor had come right away with his black bag, and a stethoscope dangling around his neck like a necklace. He hurried upstairs with her mam and they'd shut the door, so she could only sit on the stairs and wait and wonder what was going on.

A little while later Father Patrick came, rosary beads in hand and an elaborate stole draped over his black vestments. She and her mam followed him upstairs and they'd all spent a long time in Nana Roberts's room saying prayers, mostly *Our Father* and *Hail Mary* over and over again.

The next day, two men in black brought a shiny wooden box and stood it on the big table in the best room. Her mam said it was a coffin and that they were going to put Nana Roberts in it so that she could go on sleeping peacefully for as long as she liked.

Later in the week, a horse wearing black feathers on its head and pulling a long carriage with glass sides stopped outside the house. Her mam said it was the hearse and that it had come to take Nana Roberts, and all the flowers that friends and neighbours had brought along, to the church for Nana Roberts's funeral.

Katie didn't like that part at all. Even though it was a warm summer day she'd had to wear a black dress, shiny black shoes and long white socks, and her long fair hair had been tied back with a black ribbon.

Her mam had been wearing black as well. With her shining fair hair and slim figure she'd looked lovely, even though her face had been sad and there were tears in her eyes. They'd sat in the front pew in church, which was full of Nana's friends and people who lived nearby. Father Patrick said special prayers and lots of things about Nana Roberts that she didn't understand.

Then they'd all gone along to the cemetery and Father Patrick had said more prayers as the men who were carrying her nana's coffin lowered it down into a big hole.

Her mam had thrown some earth down onto the coffin and she'd been told to do the same. She had shaken her head and hidden behind her mam. She didn't want to throw dirt down onto it because she knew Nana Roberts wouldn't have liked that one little bit! She felt angry that her mam had done it, even though Father Patrick had done the same.

Nana Roberts always liked things to be spick and span. She hated dust, cobwebs and dirt of any kind. She liked everywhere to be scrubbed spotless and polished until you could see your face in it. She always put old newspapers down on the floors when it was raining so that no dirt was walked indoors.

Katie hadn't wanted to come away and leave Nana Roberts there. She'd be so lonely all on her own, she reasoned. Anyway, how were they going to manage without her? She was always in charge of everything at home. She was the one who laid down the law and made all the rules. It was Nana Roberts, not her mam, who did all the cooking and the baking. It was Nana Roberts she turned to when she wanted something, so she knew she was going to miss her something terrible.

They'd left all the lovely flowers and wreaths behind in the cemetery. Her mam said that after the men had filled in the grave they'd pile them all on top of it. Her mam promised they'd both come back the next day and make sure they were arranged properly.

Katie had thought that meant things would go back to normal after they'd made sure the flowers were all in the right place. She knew the house would seem empty without Nana Roberts bustling around with her duster and polish, but she thought that perhaps her mam would do all those sort of things instead.

It hadn't been like that at all. Next morning her mam had said they had to start packing. At first she'd been quite excited because she thought they were going on holiday. She remembered when Nana Roberts had taken her to Swansea and they'd stayed in a boarding house for a whole week. It had been wonderful! She'd been able to play on the sand, building sandcastles with her bucket and spade, and she had gone paddling in the sea until the water came right up over her knees.

It wasn't going to be like that at all this time.

She couldn't believe it when her mam said they were packing because they were leaving Catherine Street and never coming back.

'Where are we going, then?'

'I'm not sure yet, cariad. We have to find somewhere cheaper to live. This was Nana Roberts's house, see, and now the landlord wants us out.'

'Why?'

'Someone else is coming to live here.'

Katie felt bewildered. 'Why don't we want to live here anymore?' she asked.

Her mam hugged her. 'We do, cariad, but we can't afford the rent. Your poor mam hasn't any money. Nana Roberts was the one who paid all the bills, even before your dada went to prison. Now we've got no money coming in at all, not even money to buy food. That's why we'll have to move out of this lovely house and find a cheap room somewhere. I'm going to have to get a job, cariad.'

As she piled all her clothes, dolls and toys into one of Nana Roberts's big suitcases, Katie pursed her little rosebud mouth and frowned. It didn't make any sense at all to her. Why did they have to move? If her mam was going to go out to work then why couldn't they pay rent like Nana Roberts had done and stay where they were?

She tried to ask her mam about this, but Rachael was too worried to listen, let alone give her an answer.

'You go and pack your dolls. I'll explain everything to you later, I've far too much to do now,' she said rather crossly. 'There's a man coming here later on this morning to tell me how much he will give me for Nana Roberts's furniture and I want to make sure everything is ready for him.'

'I've already done that!' Katie told her. She sat on the windowsill and watched as her mother emptied out all Nana Roberts's clothes from the big mahogany chest of drawers and from the cupboards and drawers in the matching dressing table.

'Can I look at Nana's jewels?' she asked plaintively.

'Yes, if you want to. Make sure you don't drop any of them on the floor, though, or put them down anywhere and forget them. I'm taking those to the pawnbroker later on to see what he will give me for them.'

Katie picked up the handsome walnut box with its elaborate gold leaf decoration that had been Nana Roberts's pride and joy, and scrambled up onto the bed with it. Carefully she turned the little gold key. As she opened back the lid, displaying the assortment of rings, brooches and necklaces inside, she looked at her mam accusingly. 'Are you going to sell all of Nana Roberts's jewels?' she frowned.

Rachael pushed her straggling blonde hair back behind her ears and her hazel eyes were clouded with unhappiness as she nodded. 'Yes, cariad,' she sighed. 'We'll need every penny to get by on for the next few weeks until I find some work, so I'm afraid they'll have to go.'

'Every single one of them?' Katie persisted.

Rachael nodded, then hesitated. 'Well, perhaps

you could keep just one piece. You decide which one you like the best.'

'They're all lovely!'

'I know that, but we need the money. No more arguing. If you can't decide which piece you want then I shall sell them all.'

While her mother polished the furniture to make sure it was looking its very best, Katie spread out all the pieces of jewellery and looked at each one of them very carefully, trying to make up her mind which one she liked the most.

She was still sitting on the windowsill doing this when the man who was to buy the furniture arrived. She felt the tears in her eyes as she saw the horse and cart with two men on it stop outside. A rough looking man in brown cord trousers, brown tweed jacket and wearing a greasy brown cap, jumped down and walked to their door.

He knocked so loudly that Rachael almost jumped out of her skin. Then she smoothed back her untidy hair, straightened her apron and went to open the door.

Jake Adcock was a burly man with small sharp eyes and a heavy moustache, which he kept stroking as if it helped him to think. He pawed over the furniture, sniffing and stroking his moustache, and pushing his cap back on his head as if he couldn't make up his mind whether to buy the pieces or not.

Rachael followed him from room to room, nervously rolling the edge of her apron between her fingers. She kept opening her mouth to speak, then closing it again and chewing on her lower lip as if afraid she might say something to upset him or put him off the deal.

'Look yer, missus, it's a load of terribly old stuff you got here,' Jake Adcock told her. 'Worn out most of it! Not sure if I want to take it off your hands or not.'

'It's been very well looked after,' Rachael told him timidly. 'And it was top quality when my mother-in-law bought it.'

He pushed his cap back and scratched his head. 'That was a long time ago though, wasn't it, missus?'

Rachael nodded but didn't answer.

'Tell yer what, I'll give you twenty pounds for the lot, and I won't charge yer anything for taking it all away. How's that?'

Rachael looked shocked. Her thin downturned mouth quivered and she looked so worried that Katie jumped down off the windowsill and went over and clung to her arm.

Rachael looked down at her and then hugged her close.

'I was expecting a lot more than that,' she told Jake Adcock in a strained voice. 'It's all me and my little girl will have to live on until I can find work.'

Jake Adcock pulled at the ends of his droopy moustache. 'I'm being generous, missus, but if yer want to try someone else then it's up to you.'

Rachael felt undecided about what to do. She knew he was cheating her. She was sure that if Lewis had been there he would have managed to get twice that amount for his mother's belongings.

Katie sidled away and went back to the

windowsill. She didn't like this man one little bit and she certainly didn't like the horrible things he was saying about Nana Roberts's furniture.

Jake Adcock's eyes followed her as she began picking up the rings and brooches she'd been looking at and putting them back into the jewellery box.

"Course, if you've got anything else yer want to sell, missus, then I might be able to do yer a better deal.'

Rachael shook her head. 'That is everything she left. Except her clothes.'

'I suppose I could give yer a few bob for those,' he said reluctantly, 'though if they're anything like the furniture they'll only be good for the rag and bone man. Isn't there any jewellery? Rings, and bits and bobs of that sort?'

Katie tried to push the rings and brooches she was sorting through under her skirt out of sight, but he'd already seen them and his eyes were glistening greedily.

'There's a few pieces, but I didn't think you'd be interested in things of that sort. I . . . was going to keep them, or perhaps sell them later on.'

Jake Adcock shrugged. 'It's up to you, missus, but if it's now yer wanting money then I'd do yer a better deal than old Manny the pawnbroker, mind. Right twisting old tyke he is and no mistake. Shall I take a look and see what you've got to offer?'

Rachael shivered. She felt so completely out of control. She needed money now, enough to pay for a room for the two of them and keep them in food for at least a couple of weeks until she could find herself a job.

'Yes, I suppose you could look at them,' she agreed cautiously. She took a deep breath and looked Adcock straight in the eye. 'They're good pieces, all of them, mind. I won't be selling unless you make me a decent offer.'

Adcock placed his hand on his wide barrel chest. 'Cross my heart, missus, I'll be as generous as a man can be.'

'Katie, bring that box of nana's things over here,' Rachael told her.

'Yes, Mam.' Katie hesitated for a moment then scrabbled all the pieces she'd been looking at together and pushed them into the box higgledy-piggledy. She didn't stop to lay each one in its own little velvet nest because she didn't want them to look nice, she didn't want this horrible man to take them away.

Jake Adcock's eyes gleamed avariciously as he sorted through the contents of the jewellery box, but when he looked up his face was dour and he was pulling at the ends of his moustache as if he wasn't sure what to do.

'Another fiver for the clothes and bedding and another fiver for this lot, how about that?'

'No!' cried Katie. 'They're worth tons more than that! They're worth a fortune! My nana called them her Crown Jewels.'

Jake Adcock scowled at Katie, frightening her so much that she felt tears stinging her eyes.

'Mrs Roberts always did say they were all valuable pieces,' Rachael agreed.

'Duw anwyl! Yer a hard woman to deal with,' Jake Adcock muttered. 'Tell you what, missus. Seeing as how I'm kind-hearted and can see you're in a spot of trouble, I'll make my offer up to fifty pounds. That's my final offer, mind. Fifty pounds and that includes everything in the house!' He gave a deep belly laugh. 'No wonder they call me generous Jake. Fool to myself, I am.'

'Very well then.' Rachael made her voice casual.

Fifty pounds! It seemed like a fortune and far more than she had expected. With fifty pounds she'd not only be able to pay a month's rent in advance on a cheap furnished room, but she'd have enough left over to feed them for three or four weeks as well. By then she would have found a job and they'd have no worries.

Katie watched wide-eyed as the man called out to the lad he'd left outside holding the horse and the two of them began moving the furniture out and piling it on the cart.

He left the jewellery box until last and he tucked this under his arm after he'd counted out a pile of dirty notes and handed them to Rachael.

'Right, that's it then. Good luck to yer, missus.' He doffed his cap and made for the door before Rachael could even count her money.

Katie looked around the bare rooms. Every step she took echoed and she wondered where they would be sleeping that night now that all the beds and blankets had gone. There wasn't even a kettle left on the hob or a cup in the kitchen cupboards. Jake Adcock had stripped the house bare.

'Come on, Katie,' Rachael held out Katie's coat for her to put on. 'We'd best be going.'

'Yes, Mam.' Katie fastened up her coat then stooped down and opened up one of the suitcases.

'Come on, girl, what do you think you are doing? If we go now, before the rent man comes, that will be one less thing to pay out for and he'll never find us once we've left Catherine Street.'

'I want to put these in my suitcase, Mam,' she giggled, as she fished a ring and two brooches out of her knicker leg, 'they're scratching my botty.'

'Katie! Where did those come from, they're out of Nana Roberts's jewellery box!' Rachael exclaimed in shocked tones.

'You said I could keep whichever one I liked best. And I liked all of these.'

Rachael regarded her severely for a minute then she burst out laughing.

'Fair-dos', I suppose,' she said as she shrugged on her coat and pulled her blue cloche hat well down on her ears. 'What Jake Adcock didn't see and doesn't know about he'll never miss, will he!'

**Order further Rosie Harris titles
from your local bookshop, or have them delivered
direct to your door by Bookpost**

☐	**The Cobbler's Kids**	0099481774	£5.99
☐	**At Sixes & Sevens**	0099463237	£5.99
☐	**Winnie of the**		
	Waterfront	0099460394	£5.99
☐	**Pins & Needles**	0099460386	£5.99
☐	**Looking for Love**	0099460378	£5.99
☐	**One Step Forward**	0099436264	£6.99
☐	**Patsy of**		
	Paradise Place	0099436248	£6.99
☐	**Turn of the Tide**	0099421291	£6.99

Free post and packing
Overseas customers allow £2 per paperback
Phone: 01624 677237

Post: Random House Books
c/o Bookpost, PO Box 29, Douglas, Isle of Man IM99 1BQ

Fax: 01624 670923

email: bookshop@enterprise.net

Cheques (payable to Bookpost) and credit cards accepted

Prices and availability subject to change without notice.
Allow 28 days for delivery.
When placing your order, please state if you do not wish to receive any
additional information.

www.randomhouse.co.uk/arrowbooks

a r r o w   b o o k s